CW00647008

LARK RISING

VIOLET FENN

First published by Harker House Publishing 2023

Copyright © 2023 by Violet Fenn

All rights reserved. No part of this book may be reproduced in any form or by any electronic or mechanical means, including information storage and retrieval systems, without written permission from the author, except for the use of brief quotations in a book review. It is illegal to copy this book, post it to a website, or distribute it by any other means without permission.

This novel is entirely a work of fiction. The names, characters and incidents portrayed in it are the work of the author's imagination. Any resemblance to actual persons, living or dead, events or localities is entirely coincidental.

Violet Fenn asserts the moral right to be identified as the author of this work.

Cover design by GetCovers.

"Hell is empty, and all the devils are here."

The Tempest, William Shakespeare

Map Of Revenant Territories

1.Liverpool 2.London 3.Shrewsbury
4.Chester 5.Hereford

THE BASTARD'S BACK

W*ake up.*
　　　"No." I wasn't asleep anyway, and the voice knew that.
　　Wake up wake up wake up wake up WAKE UP!
"Fucking hell!" I shrieked, sitting bolt upright in the bed, "can't a woman get any peace and quiet round here?"

The city never sleeps. And neither do you. A pause. *And neither does the vampire downstairs, clearly.* The flat was in darkness, but steady banging came from the floor below, as if someone was slowly and methodically hitting their head against the wall in frustration. The flat beneath mine was occupied by the most tormented vampire in history, and sometimes I regretted letting her move in. Seriously, Louis de Pointe du Lac has nothing on Rachel and her wailing. But she'd helped save my (after)life and one good turn deserves another. I had a brief daydream about taking Eadric Silverton up on his offer of the apartment down in the Albert Dock. I'd actually got as far as going to look at it, purely to humour Aunt Kitty. Kitty might have been dead this last sixty years, but she still appreciates a good view. And there was no getting away from the fact that the apartment was incredible. But I wasn't going to leave Harrington Street and everyone knew it. I don't have much hands-on input in the coffee shop downstairs anymore, but

1

that's because my best friend Izzy has proved herself more than capable of looking after it without my help. Also Izzy's a living, breathing human, and apparently customers prefer that to being served by someone who occasionally forgets it isn't normal to pass someone their coffee before they've even finished asking for it.

It would certainly be more suited to someone with your power and status, said the city in my head.

It's not actually the city itself, you understand—it's more the spirit of those who've made Liverpool what it is today. And what Liverpool mostly is today is a fucking weird mash-up of both human and supernatural inhabitants, the human side of which is, for the most part, happily oblivious of the others' existence. Either way, there's a voice in my head and sometimes that voice is really fucking annoying.

"I didn't have you down as a snob," I said aloud, but there was no answer. Giving in to the inevitable, I climbed out from under the duvet, toppling Grimm onto the floor as I did so. The banging had stopped, which was a relief. I don't really get headaches these days, but the noise had been going on for long enough that my teeth were clenched and I could feel tightness behind my eyes. "Your reactions are sometimes very slow, for a cat," I said to Grimm. He arched one furry eyebrow and stalked out of the room, presumably to get himself a midnight snack. Grimm mostly sorts his own meals out these days, which suits me just fine. But when I walked into the living room, he was sitting on the windowsill and Kitty was next to him. They were both looking down onto the street and had serious expressions on their faces. "What are you two looking at?"

"Billy's talking to someone," said Kitty, without turning round. "And he doesn't look happy about it." Anyone walking past the pile of old blankets and sleeping bags that's permanently installed in the empty doorway opposite Flora's would suppose Billy was just another of the endless rough sleepers that call the city centre their home. It's certainly what I'd assumed for the first couple of years I'd owned Flora's. But then I'd died and everything got extremely strange and the upshot is that I'm still here, but now I know Billy is actually a ghost. Like I said—Liverpool is *weird*. I walked over to the window and peered out into the darkness. Billy was standing in front of his blanket nest, gesturing at someone in the middle of the street. The second person had his hands in his pockets and a casual posture, his pomaded quiff glinting under the streetlights.

"It's Alan," I said. At that moment, both men looked up towards the building. I ducked quickly.

"What are you doing?" asked Kitty. Banging started up again from the floor below.

"Hiding from Alan," I said, "obviously. He'll be hoping to see Rachel, but she's clearly not in a good mood and I can't deal with any more madness right now." I crawled away from the window before getting back onto my feet. "I'm going to see Eadric, won't be long. If Rachel kicks off again, bang the floor."

"What do you need to see Eadric about at this time of night?"

"Stuff," I said, then relented. "Just boring stuff." Kitty looked unconvinced. "Honestly. Bella needs some maintenance and I've promised to sit with her while the work's being done." I shrugged. "She gets nervous when people start welding around her feet." Bella's the Liver Bird that faces onto the river and, although she's generally better tempered than her brother Bertie, she sometimes needs a bit of emotional support. I figured it was much like taking a kid to the dentist and holding their hand whilst they had a filling done. "I just want to know when it's scheduled, cos I'm working in Flora's a bit this week. And it's not as if Eadric will be in bed."

"Izzy's allowing you back behind the counter?" asked Kitty. "I thought she said never again, after that incident with the bread knife and the delivery man?"

"He shouldn't have snuck up on me like that," I said. "Anyway, I only nicked his ear. And I said sorry."

"Didn't Izzy have to find a new supplier of coffee beans after that?"

"It was time for a change, anyway," I said. "Anyway, I'm off out. Mind you behave yourselves." My deceased aunt and my very-much-alive cat watched me go out through the kitchen door, before turning back to the window. I bounced my way down the fire escape at speed, and was past the pair of bickering ghosts before either of them could drag me into their ridiculous argument. And it *was* ridiculous—I knew that without even having to get involved. Alan had a crush on Rachel, and Billy didn't approve. There wasn't any jealousy on Billy's part, he just didn't think Rachel should be getting into relationships with ghosts until she'd got used to being a vampire. I'd tried telling him that Rachel seemed quite keen on Alan in return and maybe Billy should drop the dad act a bit, but it hadn't made any difference.

We're basically just one big happy, argumentative family—it's just that most of us are dead.

As I approached the Liver Building, I could see from Bertie's clock that it had just gone two in the morning. I gave him a wave and he creaked a small nod in response, before going back to staring out over the city. Because it was dark and quiet, I didn't bother with the official entrance and instead just went the direct route, scaling the side of the building like a red-headed bug. When I reached the windows of the Silvertons' rooms, I tapped the window. "Have you forgotten how doors work?" asked Nikolaus Silverton, as I dropped in over the stone windowsill. Nik was wearing an embroidered silk dressing gown and his bare feet poked out from under what appeared to be satin pyjamas.

"All you need is marabou slippers," I said, ignoring him, "and that outfit would be perfect."

"Who says I don't have any?" he replied. I was about to snark back when the door from Eadric's office opened and the man himself stalked into the room. Now, Nik Silverton is undeniably handsome, if you like your men on the foppish side. But Eadric is something else entirely. Tall and lithe, with distinctively sharp features and wavy chestnut hair, he looks like he plays guitar in an indie band in between writing poetry and painting masterpieces. What Eadric *actually* is, is a notoriously powerful leader of the undead realms who celebrates his one thousandth birthday sometime this century. I suggested a party, but apparently he can't remember the actual date on account of how that sort of thing becomes less important once you've been around a few hundred years. Right now, he had a look on his face that suggested he wasn't in the mood for jokes.

"I've just had Laithlind on the phone," he said, tension visible on his face. "He had information he felt we needed. I should call Elizabeth." He was already pulling his phone out of the pocket of his immaculately tailored trousers.

"Whoah," said Nik, putting a hand up, "want to tell *us* what's going on first? Before you speak to Elizabeth? And I thought you were never going to speak to Ivo again?" Ivo Laithlind is even older than Eadric, and they were friends for centuries—until we discovered Ivo had been shagging Eadric's wife. Anyway, I'd chopped her head off (long story) by the time the secret came out and Ivo had wisely done a bunk. But then he'd come back and I'd saved his (after)life and Eadric clearly thought I shouldn't have bothered, so we'd all agreed to just not talk about him. And I certainly didn't mention the not-so-pure thoughts I occasionally had about Ivo. Things like that are best kept between a girl and her closed bedroom door. Eadric looked at each of us in turn—me in my scruffy nightclothes with a definite case of bed-head, and Nik looking worried yet immaculate next to me—and appeared to be wondering just how he'd ended up with such a hopeless pair of sidekicks.

"It's happening," he said, "after all these centuries. After everything we've done to secure our place in the human world. We've had suspicions for a while, of course. We had discussed it before...well. Before." He shook his head. "But now it's confirmed."

"What's confirmed?" I asked. I was feeling nervous myself now. Eadric looked me in the eye and seemed to consider his words for a long time before he eventually spoke.

"The bastard's back."

POP GOES THE WEASEL

William of Normandy was born in 1027, the product of a relationship between Robert I, Duke of Normandy and a woman called Herleva. Herleva was either a concubine, or the daughter of a local burgher whom Robert loved but could not marry because of their differing social statuses. It depends which history you read—and both versions are pretty bloody sexist, if you ask me. Either way, Robert was fond enough of his illegitimate son to make him heir to the Duchy of Normandy. Which landed young William in the hot seat at the age of eight, after his father died whilst on pilgrimage to Jerusalem. Being an eight-year-old duke would mean a life of frolicsome luxury these days; a thousand years ago, things were a bit more hair-raising. Before William had hit his teens, he'd gone through at least three legal guardians, each one replacing the previous who'd been killed during attempts on the boy's life. One was actually murdered in William's own bedroom, whilst the youthful duke slept nearby. It's alleged that he occasionally had to be hidden in the houses of local peasants, such was the determination to overthrow Normandy's prepubescent ruler. So it's perhaps no surprise that, having somehow survived adolescence, young William grew up to be quite the determined soldier. When Edward the Confessor—who should have perhaps confessed to being pretty rubbish at political organisation—died in 1066, it transpired he'd promised the English throne to both William *and* Harold Godwinson. This left the country in one hell of an ecumenical mess, which William solved by invading England and sticking Harold in the eye with an arrow. You can see the storyboard version of the whole sorry saga on the Bayeux Tapestry.

William—better known to most as William the Conqueror—is the reason Eadric Silverton and Ivo Laithlind have been tied together in a co-dependent (and now resentful) friendship this past thousand years. Having failed to keep control of his own lands in the west of the country, the then-still-alive Eadric had no option but to join William's invading forces. He doesn't like to talk about it, but seems to have cracked on with the slaying and conquering for a while (which is probably why he doesn't like to talk about it; go figure). He belatedly discovered his moral limits when William took it upon himself to destroy what should have been Ivo's final resting place in Derbyshire. During the melee, Eadric somehow realised that the primary target of the attack was maybe not quite as dead as he should have been. Which was impressive, given Ivo had been in the mound for a couple hundred years by that point. Eadric helped the walking, talking Yorkshire zombie escape, and they'd been friends ever since. I can only assume that Eadric himself was mortally injured later on and somehow caught a severe case of the undeads from his bestie, cos the pair of them have been bouncing around Britain ever since. Or at least, Ivo has—he seems to enjoy travelling and meeting people, even if he does occasionally threaten said people with death if they don't do as they're told. Eadric goes pretty much nowhere. Okay, so he's been coaxed out of his ivory tower (actually the cast-concrete clock tower of the Liver Building) a few times since I arrived on the immortal scene, but it's a rare occurrence. And according to anyone who knows him, he certainly didn't go anywhere before I was around to bully him into it. Not that he's out of touch—he seems to know what's going on without anyone telling him. I suspect Bella's got better hearing than she lets on and likes a good gossip. It's more that Eadric prefers the 'iron fist in a velvet glove' approach. He stays in his tower and everyone in his undead realm more or less behaves themselves for fear of what he might do if he gets angry. I've seen Eadric get angry and was very disappointed that he didn't turn green and burst out of his trousers, but you can't have everything in this life. Ivo's territory is a bit more unsettled, although my personal theory is that it's Ivo himself doing most of the unsettling. Ivo is, shall we say, *charismatic*. In fact, I sometimes think I'd quite like to bounce around on his charisma and see for myself whether he deserves his reputation as a legendary swordsman, if you know what I'm saying. But that would only lead to trouble and confusion, and we've all had enough of that lately. "I thought he was dead?" I said. Eadric looked at me blankly. "William, I mean," I went on. "I thought he was dead and gone? Got old and fat and everyone hated him and they squished his corpse into the grave until it popped with a stinky squelch. That sort of gone. What?" Nik was looking at me with an expression of polite disgust on his face. "Learned it at school," I said. "Vikings, Domesday Book, miss a bit, Henry the stupid bloody Eighth, miss a bit more, Industrial Revolutions, world wars. All the essential facts for the modern schoolchild."

"You did a history degree," Nik pointed out. "I'd have thought you'd know a bit more than the basic facts."

"Stuck with the Victorians," I said. "Them and the Industrial Revolutions were enough to be going on with. Did you know there were actually three? Industrial Revolutions, I mean. And that's just the old ones—don't even *start* me on the technological versions."

"Have you *quite* finished?" said Eadric.

I narrowed my eyes at him. "For now," I said. "But you really should know the basics of British history, Eadric Silverton. Considering you were involved in half of it."

"Lilith," said Eadric, "I am going to have to ask you, politely, to shut the fuck up." Both Nik and I gaped at him. I'd never heard Eadric swear before. A tiny bit of me was quite proud to have been the one to force it from him.

"Consider it shut," I said, making a zipping motion across my mouth. Nik rolled his eyes, but I could see he was trying not to laugh.

"We knew William wasn't dead, but neither was he active in the netherworld." said Eadric. "The assumption was that he'd simply gone to ground, having decided to live out eternity in the peace and quiet of the countryside. But then things began to happen that made both

Laithlind and myself consider that perhaps our old foe wasn't resting quite as peacefully as one would have liked." He gazed out of the window across the flat, dark waters of the Mersey. "I suspect he's been plotting a comeback for quite some time."

"Since around 1087, at a guess." I said, and then, "Sorry," when I saw Eadric's expression.

"We can't risk all-out war, Lilith," said Eadric. "As we all know, revenants are stronger than humans and the collateral damage that could be caused by fighting between territories would be bad news for all of us. Our existence would no longer be secret." The strength thing is undoubtedly true—at least, for most of us. I can run faster than any Olympic sprinter, and I've seen Nik throw books into the Mersey with such force that they've bounced off the surface like skimming stones and been found by dog walkers over on New Brighton beach. There are exceptions, though. I'm pretty sure my friend Heggie is also undead— I've never dared ask him, it just seems rude somehow—but he doesn't seem to have any powers other than a personal odour stronger than the most rancid fox shit. That, and an absolutely bottomless pit of adora- tion for Mapp, who runs the bookshop up on Renshaw Street. The two men are pretty much inseparable, although I've never been entirely sure what their relationship really is. Aunt Kitty says I should stop wondering and let them be. But then Aunt Kitty is a ghost who has a 'friends with benefits' thing going on with a man who left her for dead sixty years ago, so I generally take her relationship advice with a very large pinch of salt. "Are you still with us?" Eadric's voice broke into my meandering thoughts. "Lilith?"

"Uh huh," I said. "Dead guy come back, big scary. What are we doing about Bella's feet?"

Eadric stared at me. "Did you hear anything of what I actually said?"

"Yes," I replied, "I did. Politics, territory, blah blah. I told you, I'm having nothing to do with any of it."

It's doubtful you'll have any choice in the matter.

"Don't you start!" I closed my eyes tightly. Then I opened them again slowly and looked at Eadric. "That was to the city," I said, "not you. Sometimes it can be a mardy little scrote that doesn't know when to keep its stupid communal mouth shut."

Charmed, we're sure.

I opened my mouth in the hope of coming up with something snappy, but Eadric beat me to it. "Lilith," he said, in the sort of voice usually reserved for very small children or the easily confused, "the fact that this entire city chooses to communicate with you, and you alone, suggests to me you need to be involved in its politics. Whether you like it or not."

Told you.

Fucksake. Politics is dangerous. And boring. Dangerously boring. I hate you all—

"Are you having a conversation in your head again?" asked Eadric.

"What makes you think that?"

"You've got that blank look on your face. The one you get when you're having a mental argument. And your mouth's moving, but there's no sound coming out."

"We can't all hold conversations with our mouths shut," I said, giving him a sour look. "This city is going to drive me quite literally mad if it carries on."

Ha, it said inside my head, **as if anyone would even notice.**

"Also," I went on, "it is *very* rude." I was sure I heard a tiny snigger right at the back of my mind.

"That's as maybe," said Eadric patiently, "but clearly you are important to it."

"God only knows why," said Nik under his breath. I scowled at him, and he flashed a bright smile in return. I love Nik—I really, really do—but sometimes he is incredibly irritating. These days he's basically like an annoying sibling—the sort who knows exactly how to wind you up, but would fight to the death for you if it came to the crunch. Although Nik's weapon of choice would probably be one of the endless trashy romance books he's always reading, so maybe not so much help after all.

"What does it matter if," I hesitated, because even after months of immortality, talking about a legendary king as if he was just a normal person we all knew still seemed odd somehow, "William takes over? He controlled the entire country when he was alive. Why not give it to him after death? He can't do a worse job than the real life government. And all you lot who are supposedly in charge of your *territories* just spend most of your time moaning about it. Why not retire?" Eadric raised an eyebrow, but silently let me continue. "Move to the country! Take up chicken-keeping or something. Bella could fly over for a little holiday now and then."

"Do you have *any* idea how ridiculous you are at times?" said Eadric. He was squinting at me as if not entirely sure I was real.

"Yeah," I said, "I do. Izzy tells me so on the reg."

"Isobel is a wiser woman than you," said Eadric. "Perhaps *she* would be better suited to the role you so clearly disdain."

"Izzy is human," I pointed out, "and before you *dare* to suggest it, the chances are that if she did happen to die, she would *literally* die." I stopped for a second to listen to the murmuring in my head. "And the city says it wouldn't work with Izzy. It's me or nothing."

"Sometimes," said Eadric, "nothing seems by far the easier option. As for your question," I'd almost forgotten I'd even *asked* a question and had to drag myself back in the conversation, "letting the Bastard take over would be disastrous. For everyone."

"We're in the twenty-first century," I said, "and illegitimacy is now the norm, rather than the exception. Isn't it about time you stopped calling him a bastard?"

"I don't care about William's parentage," said Eadric with a thin smile. "I'm referring to his behaviour. William was a nasty piece of work a thousand years ago, and I very much doubt the intervening millennium has lessened that any."

"Where's he been all this time?" asked Nik. "How has no one spotted him before now?"

"As I said," replied Eadric, "there have been rumours for a long time. A *very* long time. But they were mostly unfounded—until a few months ago."

"When Lil died," Nik said, nodding his head towards me.

"Yes," said Eadric, "around the time Lilith joined us. Strange, don't you think?"

"I'm not discussing this again," I said stubbornly. Sure, plenty of people dream of power and glory and eternity and all that bullshit. But all I've ever wanted, even since I woke up dead, is to be left alone to run Flora's. Not that I get much of a look-in these days, but even sitting in the staff kitchen doing paperwork and supervising from a distance is better than having to face life in the underworld.

"Lil," said Nik, "you died and then everything kicked off. *Everything*. It had been quiet for decades, but now there are vampires and mermaids and gods only know what else wandering round the place."

"Not mermaids," I said. "Asrai. Big difference." Daisy is our local asrai and most people do call her a mermaid—even me, half the time—but she doesn't have a fish's tail and is all the creepier for it. Asrai are a kind of water nymph, that people assume are like those depicted in those wishy-washy romantic paintings so beloved of the Pre-Raphaelites. In reality, they look like weirdly elongated humans, with pale skin and webbed fingers and toes. Daisy's the only one I know personally, but I've seen enough distantly bobbing heads in the Mersey to be pretty sure she's got plenty of friends out there. I hadn't seen her for a week or so, but someone over the Birkenhead side had reported seeing someone in the water a few days earlier, only for the person to swim off at super-human speed when they realised they'd been spotted, so I wasn't too worried. And Eadric was enjoying the break from having live fish dumped on his carpet. What can I say, Daisy's generous with her catch. And she's an excellent climber.

"What*everrrrr*," said Nik, narrowing his eyes at me. Sometimes Nikolaus Silverton is brattier than an extra from *Interview With The Vampire*. He's also one of the most famous poets in history, but he makes a show of it being a big secret. I like to pretend I still haven't guessed, just to wind him up. "You died," he went on, "and woke up as a revenant. Then they all started coming back. The rest of *them*." He pulled a face.

"Stop being such a snob," I told him. "Eternity isn't an exclusive club, Nik. We don't gatekeep here."

"We bloody well should," said Nik.

"Can we get back to the matter at hand?" asked Eadric. "Regardless of how the current situation came to be, one of the most dangerous men in all history is back on the scene. And he isn't going to be happy with settling down in the countryside and just meeting up on the holidays."

"How do you know?" I asked. Eadric and Nik both looked at me blankly. "How do you know what he wants?" I repeated. "He can hardly bounce back into society and claim to be rightful heir to the throne, can he? The current King's only just got his bum in the chair, and he waited *decades*. He isn't going to hand it over to a reanimated corpse, however powerful the dead guy thinks he is."

"He won't be after the actual throne, Lilith," said Eadric. "He'll want power over the undead ones. All of them."

"How many are there?" It suddenly occurred to me I didn't actually know. I'd had it explained to me once or twice, but in all honesty I wasn't listening. Eadric's territory is where I live, so I know it well enough. Ivo controls everything to the right of us, across to the north-east coast. And Elizabeth holds Middlesex, which fans out from London and covers everything from the east coast inwards as far as Southampton.

"Seven of us, not including those over the water." Eadric meant Ireland. I suspected there was a *lot* going on in Ireland, but for the sake of a peaceful life, I mostly avoided asking about it. "Plus the wild territory, of course." He meant the relatively small patch of no-man's-land between Elizabeth and Ivo, the boundary of which also runs for a short distance along Eadric's line. It causes no end of bickering, mostly from Ivo. He thinks he should have it, but geographically it should probably go to Elizabeth. Who either doesn't want it, can't be arsed to think about it, or leaves it there just to fuck with Ivo's head, I've yet to figure out which.

"So he'll be in the wild territory," I said.

Eadric shook his head. "No," he said, "Elizabeth thinks he's below us at the moment. Somewhere near Bristol. He's probably working his way up."

"Who runs Bristol?" I asked. Eadric stepped over to where an enormous map hung on the wall in a plain frame. I hadn't noticed it before. Reluctantly, I walked over to join Eadric. The map was old enough to not have any of the usual county boundaries marked. It was also almost certainly authentic. I'd once had to go through the files in Eadric's office in order to find some leases he'd 'conveniently' lost (I found them and proved he did indeed own the building Izzy lives in and then guilted him a bit, which is how she now lives rent-free because coping with undead shenanigans on the daily deserves *some* perks) and had been amazed by just how much ancient paperwork was in there. That man could produce the Mappa Mundi from his desk drawer, and it wouldn't be the most surprising thing that had happened to me over the past few months. "It's bigger than that," he said, pointing at the map. "Starts here," he touched the glass lightly just below Birmingham, "and forms the other side of Elizabeth's boundary line, all the way down to Southampton."

"And across Wales," I said, "underneath us?"

"Precisely," said Eadric.

I belatedly noticed what looked like pencil markings on the map, barely visible under artificial light. "These are the boundary lines?" Eadric nodded. I peered closely at the divisions marked across the country. Divisions that living people had no idea even existed. "Why does ours have this weird junction with Ivo?" I asked, running my finger along our lower boundary line. It curved upwards around Birmingham and would have bent neatly round to Manchester, if it wasn't for a sudden left-hand turn just west of Leicester. Ivo's territory pushed out into ours to take Derby, before curving back onto the more logical track.

"He was originally buried there," said Eadric, "so it seemed only fair to let him keep the area."

"And you think William is somewhere down here?" I pointed to the sizeable chunk of south Wales that carried on down through Somerset to the English Channel. "Why would he go there?"

"William still has a lot of friends in Herefordshire," said Eadric. "Some of whom will be more than happy to see him back. But I don't think he does want the entire country—at least, not yet." He peered thoughtfully at the map. "No," he said, "he's too clever for that. He'll want to establish the absolute facts before making a move. Which will almost certainly involve coming here."

"Why?"

Eadric turned to me and smiled thinly. "To meet you, I suspect," he said. "You're developing quite the name for yourself, Lilith. Carrying on like a human instead of a revenant, but taking time out to chop people's heads off if they get in your way." I grimaced. Chopping off heads had never sounded like a fun pastime. And now I'd had to do it—more than once—I knew that for a fact. "So yes, I think he'll come here."

"Who's up there?" I said, pointing to the area above Ivo on the map. It began on his northern boundary just below Middlesborough and took the entire width of the country, all the way up to the Scottish border. No one ever seemed to talk about Scotland, which I found interesting. It seemed to me that Wales was fair game, but Scotland was maybe a bit too '*here be monsters*' for the Silvertons' liking. Perhaps Welsh dragons were simply less aggressive. Maybe I should get Daisy to unearth some of the more unusual creatures around the Powys area, see how they liked that for a game of fishy soldiers.

"Well now," said Eadric, "there's the thing. That should probably be William's territory, by rights. But as you can see, its only border is with Laithlind. And he isn't going to want to have his would-be murderer living next door."

"Ivo was long dead by the time William and his boys arrived," I pointed out.

"Yes," said Eadric patiently, "but as we both know, he wasn't *entirely* dead. Just..." he trailed off.

"Just what?" I frowned. "Waiting for a princess to appear and kiss him so he woke up? This is getting into fairytale territory, for heaven's sake."

"And you don't think revenants and vampires and," Eadric gestured at the window that looked out over the Mersey, "*mermaids* are the stuff of fairytales?" He looked impatient. "We *are* the fairytales, Lilith. Nightmares come to life. The dead walking the earth. All the things that humans like to make into stories and films and scare themselves with, safe in the knowledge that none of it's real. But it *is* real, isn't it? We're real and right here in the present day trying to deal with it all." He sighed.

"You look tired," I said helpfully. "Maybe you need a holiday." Eadric rolled his eyes, but didn't bother saying anything. "So," I went on, "what was so important about Ivo that William went to such an effort to destroy his grave? Did he suspect something even then?"

"Laithlind was a legend in his own lifetime," said Eadric, "and the legend grew even further after his death. He'd arranged in advance that he should be buried in a ceremonial mound and declared that no invasion of Britain would be successful whilst he still lay in his grave on this island. He was believed to be the country's protector, long after he was dead and gone. The stories had faded by the time William got to these shores, but he wasn't going to take chances. Not even with fairytales." He gave a hollow little laugh. "So orders were given to destroy Laithlind's burial mound, and for his bones to be scattered."

"But you saved him."

"I did."

"Why?" I was genuinely curious.

"Because I'd already let my people down by taking sides with the Bastard," said Eadric, "even though I'd had no choice in the matter. So when I reached Laithlind's tomb and found him sitting there waiting, I—"

"Hang on," I interrupted, "you broke into the tomb of someone who'd been dead a good couple of centuries," Eadric nodded, "only to find him happily sitting there awaiting your arrival?"

"Well," said Eadric, "I wouldn't have described him as happy. Determined and angry, would be more like it. He'd woken up in a tomb knowing it could only mean an invasion was happening, but with no idea how much time had passed. I broke through the entrance and there he was, sitting with his arms folded. Just...waiting."

"So you got him out." Eadric nodded. "What did ol' Bill think of that, then?"

"I wouldn't know," said Eadric, a faint smile crinkling at the corners of his eyes. "We made a run for it before anyone had realised what had happened."

"Didn't work though," I said, "did it?"

"What didn't work?"

"Ivo's protection," I said. "William took over, and you two went on the run."

"Indeed," said Eadric. "But things are different now. Which is why I plan to do things properly."

"Scaredy-cat," I said. Nik made a choking noise, but said nothing.

Eadric merely raised an eyebrow. "I'm not scared, Lilith," he said. "I'm *careful*. It's a technique you could do with learning." I huffed at that, but he ignored me. "Not only is William a latecomer to a country that is now well-settled in all meanings of the word, it is also a very different country to the one he left all those centuries ago. Regardless of how long he's been lurking in the background, it is a very long time since Normandy had genuine power." He sat down at his desk and looked at me over steepled fingers. "We will treat William as a favoured guest," he went on, "but nothing more." I wondered, for the millionth time, at how such a beautiful and clever man had managed to become so sensible. And, well...*dull*.

"Just give him the top portion and leave him to fester up there," I said. "Problem solved."

"He won't fester forever, Lilith," said Eadric patiently. "Have you listened to *anything* I've said?" I made gestures implying that I was, as always, all ears. "He'll settle for a while, then he'll start encroaching."

"But that's Ivo's problem," I pointed out, "not ours."

"You think he'll stop at taking Ivo's land?" Eadric frowned. "If he even manages it, of course. Regardless, our problems are rather more immediate. William will need to travel through this territory in order to get to the north. It's a reasonable request, and one I can't refuse."

"Why?"

"Why what?" Eadric looked confused.

"Why can't you refuse? Tell him to bugger off and be done with, for heaven's sake!"

Nik snorted. "She's got a point," he said. "You *could* just refuse. No one else would let him through if you said no. Although," he looked pensive, "you'd have to have strong words with Chester."

"I can't refuse," Eadric said doggedly. "It wouldn't be correct."

"Fucksake," I sighed. "You're such a wet bloody lettuce, Eadric Silverton! Isn't Billy Bollocks capable of getting on a plane? That's what Elizabeth did last time she visited." She'd hired a private jet, mind, but a plane was a plane. "If she could cope, then I reckon ol' Billy boy can do the same."

"I wish you wouldn't use such awful names for people," said Eadric. "And William's still old-fashioned in some ways. He doesn't trust technology. From what I hear, the fastest thing he's likely to travel in is a train."

"How do you know he isn't already here?" I said. "What if he gets himself a hire car and just zips up the M6? He could be in Cumbria before anyone knew what he was doing."

"We'd know," said Eadric flatly. "We'd all know."

"Fucking hell," I said, "does no one have any oomph around here?" I pointed vaguely in the direction of south Wales on the map. "Leave the argumentative bugger in Bristol," I said. "If you don't let him through, then he can't cause trouble elsewhere."

"You don't understand—"started Eadric, but I was ahead of him.

"No," I said, "I don't. I don't understand why you're flailing around, fretting about undead politics and being polite to people who clearly don't deserve it. 'No' is a sentence in itself, Eadric! Tell them you're staying out of it entirely, if you really want to make a polite excuse. But don't be moaning at me about the dangers of letting someone come through this territory if you're not prepared to stop them yourself."

"Ooh," said Nik, "she's finally getting into it!"

"I'm getting into nothing," I said, glaring at him. "I'm just sick of listening to you all mithering, but doing nothing. Tell him no. End of argument. Now," I looked at both of them in turn, "who's going to be brave enough to clip Bella's claws?"

Is A Doughnut Too Much To Ask?

D awn was breaking by the time I left the Silvertons ruminating over future plans up in their tower. In deference to those commuters already out on the streets, I took the official route back down to ground level. The small elevator creaked its way downwards as I fumbled for the key that hung around my neck. It opened the door to Bella's tower as well as the one onto street level and when Eadric first gave it to me, it had been on a heavy silver chain, which I'd managed to snap within days. Izzy had produced a length of leather string and after threading the key onto it, had tied it round my neck with a tight knot. "This will stretch, rather than break," she'd said optimistically. And it had indeed stayed attached to me ever since. Unfortunately, Izzy had made it rather shorter than was entirely comfortable and I now had to bend at a weird angle in order to open the locks. The elevator clattered to a halt, and I pulled the old-fashioned ironwork door open in order to step out into the plant room with its endless pipes and cables. After a brief fight with the keys, I managed to lock myself safely out of the building. I pulled my spine straight with a satisfying crunch before skipping up the steps and round onto St Nicholas Place. The sight of a woman with strikingly pale hair walking along the Strand gave me a jolt until I remembered that Mab—aka the one person who would very much like to see me dead, mostly because I'd been forced to kill her mother a few months earlier—hadn't popped up on anyone's radar for a long while. That knowledge doesn't stop me from being nervous around blonde women, though. As I walked back to Harrington Street, I wondered what this William might look like. My memory had been getting sharper over the last few months and now had an unfortunate tendency to throw random recollections into my mind at inopportune moments. Usually really embarrassing ones, like the time I was convinced Dave Grohl was standing next to me at the bar in Lanigans. I'd tried to chat casually to him about music, only for Izzy to drag me away. When I complained, she pointed out Dave Grohl wasn't known for drinking in Liverpool city centre and anyway, she was pretty sure he didn't have a receding hairline. That sort of thing. Unfortunately, my memory hadn't yet got up to speed on remembering things I might actually find useful. I had vague recollections from school history lessons of William being a dark-haired bloke with a beard, but that would describe a vast amount of men of that era. I thought maybe I'd read somewhere that he was quite tall. How tall was 'quite' tall, though? Five-ten? Six-eight? It depended on the average height of the rest of the population at the time, I figured. "You in?" I asked. The woman coming out of the budget hotel on Castle Street just ahead of me looked at me in confusion.

"I'm just leaving," she said. "Do I know you?"

"Sorry, sorry," I floundered, "I'm on the phone." I pointed at my ear to imply a hands-free earpiece, but she didn't look convinced. She was still watching me as I turned onto the lower section of Harrington Street. *You in?* I asked again, silently this time.

We're always in, said the city.

Yeah, I muttered to myself, *that's what I'm afraid of.*

Don't worry, Lilith, it said. **We're not overly interested in the mundanities of your daily life.**

Yeah, you keep saying that. Sometimes I think you protest a bit too much. Anyway, my life isn't mundane! How very dare—

Did you want something? Or are you just bored and looking for company?

Quite frankly, I said, *I'd quite like the* opportunity *to be bored and looking for company. But as you're here, what do you know about William the Conqueror?*

Aah**,* said the city, ***the Bastard. I decided not to bother arguing about the potential offensiveness of derogatory terms with an unseen force that somehow lived inside my head. For one thing, the name had clearly stuck for good reason, and for another, I wasn't yet sure just how powerful the city might be. It was probably safest to keep it onside, at least for now. ***We're not going to hurt you, Lilith. We're on your side. How many times do we have to explain that?***

See? This is why I lose my shit all the time—I can't even have a quiet moan inside my own bloody head without you popping up like a psychic smart-arse.

We seem to recall it was you who called for our attention?

Hhhnnnngfth. I huffed my way up Harrington Street and crossed the road to the northern section, where Flora's sits halfway up on the right. Billy's spot in the doorway opposite was mercifully empty, so I sat at the bottom of my fire escape and glared out onto the street.

So you want to know about the Bastard.

Yes. On account of how he's always just been 'that bloke from the history books' but now he's suddenly a real person in my real life and how the fuck do I hold a conversation with someone who died a thousand years ago and won't even know what a text message is?

Eadric's just as old, yet he knows how to communicate.

Yeah, but Eadric's been here—I gestured impatiently around my head at the world in general—*all the time. He's had no option but to get used to it.*

Why do you think William has reappeared? A pause. ***If not because of you, then why?***

I considered this for a long minute. *I don't know*, I said eventually. *I just can't see how all of this could have been caused by me arriving on the scene. I know I keep going on about it, but I really am just a normal person.* The city coughed somewhere in the back of my head. *I am, though! I don't have famous or powerful ancestors and my parents aren't secretly wizards. Nothing like that. So there's no reason I should be the catalyst.*

And yet here we are.

I sighed heavily. There is something very satisfying about a good dramatic sigh, even when you don't have an audience to witness it. After a difficult few weeks early in my afterlife, when I couldn't get the hang of breathing without either choking or accidentally sucking the life—literally—out of nearby humans, I've *almost* got the hang of it. I don't even *need* to breathe, revenants being powered by something more basic than that. Mapp says it's all the untapped potential from when we were alive—everything we might have done as humans, but didn't get chance. So all the mental and physical energy we'd have used over a human life-time is still within us, like a battery. And because our physical selves are all but frozen—seriously, my pulse beats around once an hour, at the most—it takes the equivalent of many human lifetimes to use it up. And we can top up whenever we like anyway, just by breathing in the energy that emanates from living humans. It's a bit like filling your car with fuel, or putting your phone on charge. Feeling a bit tired? Go sit on Mathew Street for an hour or so and suck up some of the life-juice that's swirling around you like a living, breathing punchbowl. Just be careful not to take too much from individual people, because you risk leaving them with the weirdest hangover they've had in their lives, along with a horrible suspicion they might have lost a few hours somewhere along the line. And it can go *very* wrong, if you're unlucky, or if you just don't quite know what you're doing. Which is what happened to me just after I'd died, when I accidentally offed a would-be rapist by literally sucking the life out of him. He tasted bitter and left an unpleasant aftertaste. On the upside, I'd had a sudden surge of energy bigger than that time I washed down four ProPlus with a can of Red Bull whilst trying to get my university thesis in on time.

Mapp thinks the power was rising anyway, I said eventually, *and I just triggered something.*

Making you the catalyst.

Maybe. I don't know. It's all too bloody complicated. And now I'm supposed to just deal with an ancient king turning up?

Apparently so. You will undoubtedly manage it with your usual verve and wit.

You're being sarcastic again, aren't you? No answer. *If you're going to live rent-free in my head, the least you could do is—*

"Mornin', Red," called a voice from down the street. Billy was walking up from North John Street, his usual bundle of assorted bedding wedged underneath one arm. "Thought it could do with a rinse through," he said, indicating the old blankets and sleeping bags with which he made his daily nest. I had a careful sniff in his direction.

"Been at the Lenor?"

Billy grinned. "Piotr said he'd do me a service wash." Piotr was the owner of a small laundromat just around the corner. "Did my clothes as well." He held up a reusable shopping bag as proof.

"My my," I said, "aren't we coming up in the world? Next thing you know, you'll be wanting a flat and a job."

"I wouldn't go that far," he said, dropping his bags into the doorway opposite Flora's. "I'd feel claustrophobic with a roof over my head, I reckon."

"Can ghosts get claustrophobia?" I asked. "I'd have thought you could just disappear and pop up elsewhere if things started getting cramped."

"That's as maybe," Billy grinned, "but I'd still have to do the laundry."

It was too early, but I decided to go into Flora's and start work, rather than having to deal with the vampire upstairs. The thudding noise had stopped now, but in the silence of the unopened cafe, I was sure I could hear voices from the upper floors. There are three flats above Flora's, with me at the top and Rachel in the middle. The flat directly above where I was standing was empty, but sound travels well in an old and echoey building. I stood still and listened carefully. Revenants have excellent hearing—Kitty likes to joke that I could hear a sparrow fart from three streets away. In fact, the entirety of revenant 'powers' can be summed up as 'normal human abilities, but without limits'. You know how people are always saying humans only use a tiny percentage of their brain power? Well, I can use *all* of it—even though it currently seemed to be doing nothing more than dredging up random information I'd forgotten I ever knew. Same goes for physical strength—I might not have been the fittest person on the block when I was alive, but my muscles no longer get stressed or tired. And because I don't need to breathe, I can never run out of breath. And the fact I'm already dead takes away much of the fear of injury that curbs human courage. These days I'll happily scale a cathedral tower without bothering to look down, because the worst that can happen is that I'll fall to the ground with a splat. And obviously, that 'splat' would be terminal to most humans— but because my undead body exists in this weird stasis, it just snaps itself back together before I've had time to say 'oops, sorry for landing in your picnic.' I'd been shocked to discover that injuries still hurt—although it actually makes sense, because clearly I still have nerves—but the healing usually happens so quickly I don't have time to think about it.

Standing there in the middle of my cafe, eavesdropping on my vampire lodger, I thought—not for the first time—about how utterly fucking bizarre my life had turned out to be. I'd bumped into an old schoolfriend a while back whilst on a flying visit to my mum, and she'd chatted about her life and kids as though I'd know exactly what she was talking about. I'd never wanted kids, but I definitely had an occasional pang of yearning for sheer, boring mundanity. Nothing more to consider each day than going to work, paying the bills and what might be on television when I flopped down at the end of the day, probably with an unhealthily large glass of wine in my hand. But here I was, being nosy about a vampire's love life and wondering whether one of the most notorious kings in British history was going to hunt me down and— what? Kill me? He'd just have to put his name on the wait list, like everyone else.

Flora's was already clean and tidy and didn't really need anything doing until the bakery delivery arrived, and that wouldn't be for another hour. I decided to polish the cutlery, and laid piles of spoons, knives and cake forks out onto one of the little round tables before going into the staff kitchen to find the cleaning cloths. Five minutes later, everything was sparkling and several forks had a faint glow about them from the friction of being rubbed so fast. I put them all back into their correct storage containers and slumped down on the floor behind the counter with a sigh. I could see my distorted reflection in the door of the dish-washer opposite. My face was a pale blob, surrounded by a carrot-red halo. I tugged at a handful of curls in annoyance and my reflection did the same. *At least I haven't had to use the Voice for a while*, I thought idly. *Things are nicer when my friends aren't scared of me.* The Voice is something I only bring out on special occasions—trouble is, I don't have much control over it. It's been happening since the day I died. Something winds me up to a point of fury and suddenly, instead of just yelling like a normal person, my voice gets this booming, ominous tone and people start expecting a large white horse to come trotting round the corner.

You could learn to channel that voice, said the city. **Not control it, exactly—allow it symbiosis.**

Don't overcomplicate things. I'd never been fond of science at school. Everything was supposed to be a known quantity that could be labelled and categorised and understood by humans. Even back then in my teens, something abut the human arrogance of it all grated on me. No wonder I'd gravitated towards history by the time I came up to Liverpool to do my degree. History is malleable and fascinating, written by the victors and the elite. However famous the myths and legends, you have to really dig into the background information to find out what *actually* happened. Reports of the time might talk of famous victories and heroic actions, but you can bet your sweet bippy they're only talking about whoever was on their side. The opposition will have similar stories, each painting their own major players in a positive light. Whoever won a battle will claim it as the only rightful result, while the loser will insist they were the plucky underdog, trodden down by cruel and misguided fools. There are two sides to every argument, as they say —and the truth is always somewhere in the middle.

You still have a mental wall up, the city went on. **There's something stopping you from becoming what you are destined to be.**

This isn't a soap opera, I said. *I'm not going on a journey of self-discovery here. I'm just trying to get through.*

You think? I'd have said yes, actually, I did indeed think, but at that moment the doorbell rang. I pushed myself up from the floor and went to open the door for Fred, who brings us our bakery delivery.

"Mornin' Lil," he said, wedging himself and his box of delights past me through the door. "I'm a bit early, so it's lucky you're here. How's it hangin'?" He placed the cardboard box on the counter and turned to look at me. "Found yourself a nice bloke yet?"

"Not yet," I said, just as an almighty crash resounded through the ceiling from upstairs.

"That your cousin again?" asked Fred. "She hasn't calmed down any, then." Fred had been at Flora's the day I'd brought Rachel home from Anfield Cemetery. Which surprised everyone—including myself—because vampires are horrible, stinky, feral creatures that you wouldn't want to meet in broad daylight, let alone on a dark street. But Rachel had done her best to save me from an ambush (which had been set up with the help of a local pharmacist—an even longer story than my usual exploits) and vampire society wasn't going to forgive her for that. So home she came. After a couple of days of listening to her wailing through the floorboards, I'd considered taking her to live with Joe Williamson in his tunnels, deep underneath Edge Hill. But Joe wasn't the most focussed of men and had a tendency to take everyone at face value, so I couldn't be sure Rachel would be kept safely away from rogue vamps if I left her in his care. Joe's soft nature had led to him being de facto step-parent to several of the city's vampiric waifs and strays—it had been one of his charges who'd knocked me off the fire escape and started my undead adventures—but he didn't always monitor what they were up to when he wasn't looking. Which was quite often, because Joe Williamson is as blind as the proverbial bat. He's known as 'the Mole Man of Edge Hill' because of his tunnelling exploits back in the nineteenth century, but given his tiny, barely sighted eyes, the name suits him on many levels. Anyway, Rachel came home with me in the back of Basil, my beloved ancient Beetle, which has smelled funky ever since. Grimm had decided to 'welcome' her by landing on Basil's bonnet in a furious ball of spitting fur, and Fred had been unfortunate enough to witness the entire stressful scene. Izzy had later told him I was acting as carer for my cousin, who had 'issues' (carefully unspecified).

"Yeah," I sighed, "that's our Rachel. She certainly makes life interesting."

Fred grinned. "It'll do you good to have family around," he said. "Must get boring here, just running a cafe every day." He tilted his head and gazed at me. "You need to get out more, Lilith," he said in a kindly tone. "Meet new people, stretch your wings a bit. Laura's getting married next year, did you know?"

"No, I didn't know that," I said, keeping my voice carefully neutral. Laura was the daughter of the bakery owners. She was also my ex-girlfriend. It hadn't been the most important relationship in my life—that honour probably went to Ajamu, my first serious boyfriend. Mum and Dad had adored Aj and were gutted when we broke up before heading off to different universities. I'd ended up giving them a weirdly parental lecture about how both Aj and I were too young to settle down permanently, but maybe we'd see how it panned out when university was over, whilst knowing damn fine we'd never see each other again. We'd made a pretence of texting each other at Christmas and birthdays for the first year or so, but then he'd met the woman he'd gone on to marry and contact petered out. Last I heard, they were living in Ludlow with a pair of perfect children and a small, yappy dog. I knew all this because Mum bumped into them a couple of years ago and thoroughly embarrassed Ajamu in front of his apparently very tolerant wife. I'd had a few relationships through my university years, but nothing to write home about. Laura was the most recent. We'd broken up the summer before I died and I knew Mum at least had hoped we'd maybe get back together. Then Mum realised her daughter was a fully paid up member of the undead underworld, and stopped worrying about my love life in favour of squeaking excitedly about my newfound immortality. Dad still doesn't know about my change in mortal status, and long may it stay that way. He doesn't hold with anything paranormal, declaring it 'a pile of cobblers' if the subject ever comes up, before going back to grumbling over his daily copy of The Guardian.

"Yeah," said Fred, "nice girl from up Crosby way. Reckon she'll be too dull for our Laura in the long run, but what do I know?" He shrugged. "Anyways, I'd best be off. There's a couple of salted caramel doughnuts in there," he nodded at the box, "figured you and Izzy might like a treat."

"Thanks Fred," I said, "you're a good 'un." He grunted an acknowledgement before heading back out onto the street and disappearing off to wherever he'd illegally parked his van. I opened the box and inhaled.

The aroma of freshly baked pastries assaulted my nose as I pulled out two carefully wrapped doughnuts from the top of the pile. Lifting the greaseproof paper away from the sticky delights beneath, I almost wept at the knowledge I would never again eat a salted caramel doughnut. Or anything else, come to that. Revenants can and do drink—we need some liquid to replace what's lost through basic evaporation. But we don't— *can't*—eat. I once asked Nik what would happen if I did swallow something, and he gave me a graphic lecture about the horrors of what happens when things go rotten inside an undead body. It had been enough to put me off any potential experimentation. Sighing, I set to laying out the pastries on the display shelves. Maybe I could just start wearing doughnut-scented perfume.

Eat, Sleep, Work, Repeat

"**M**orning, dead girl!" Izzy came banging through the door in a flurry of skirts and perfume as I was finishing my arrangements on the display counter. Today's dress had an all-over peacock print and was nipped in at the waist in the retro way all Izzy's clothes were designed. People were always complimenting her on her style, but she'd once confided in me she'd only started wearing the fifties look because it gave an illusion of curves on her otherwise slender and ramrod straight body. Izzy's perfect deportment was a constant source of envy to me, but she said it wasn't a conscious thing, she'd just got into the habit because it was one less thing for her mother to moan about. Izzy's mum is living for the day her daughter meets a nice, up-and-coming lawyer and settles down in a new-build house somewhere on the outskirts of a Shropshire village, before popping out a couple of perfect grandchildren. None of this is going to happen. Actually, I think the kids might. But knowing Iz, she'll end up adopting rather than having her own. And she definitely won't be dating any lawyers. She tried once, but said that every time she asked him how his day had been, she struggled to stay awake.

"Hey you," I said, "how's it hanging in the living world?" Me and Iz used to work together every day, but since my untimely death it's been a bit less. Undead politics takes up more time than you'd think. And that's without the seemingly endless threats of violence.

"Oh y'know," she said, coming behind the counter and dumping her bag and coat on the floor, "same as usual. Eat, sleep, work, repeat."

"That sounds really nice," I said. Izzy leaned back against the dishwasher and looked at me with interest.

"Immortality getting boring?" she asked. "Fed up with all those gorgeous undead guys already?"

"What gorgeous undead guys?" I couldn't quite look her in the eye. "There's nothing going on in that department, and you know it."

Izzy snorted—a thoroughly inelegant noise that didn't match her appearance, but was very Izzy. "Come on, Lil," she said, "what about Mister Tall, Dark and Gruesome? He's definitely got the hots for you." She was talking about Ivo, who'd briefly stayed at my flat whilst recovering from being attacked by a wraith in the catacombs of Anfield Cemetery. He'd spent a night in my bed upstairs (alone, before you ask) and then a couple of days at a corner table in Flora's, taking in the energy from the customers. It had felt a bit unethical, but I didn't have any other option at the time. And Ivo is *very* careful with how much energy he takes from humans. I sometimes wonder whether he's got that much self control in all situations. Then I stop wondering about it and go off for a cold shower. Anyway, he was back to his old Machiavellian self in no time. On the fourth day, I came back from visiting Daisy to find him gone, having told Kitty he was needed at home.

"Ivo isn't a good person," I said primly.

"Since when have you dated good people?" hooted Izzy. "Your basic requirement in a partner has always been 'as unsuitable as possible', for fuck's sake!"

"Laura wasn't unsuitable," I said indignantly, "and neither was Aj."

"You and Aj broke up over a decade ago," Izzy pointed out, "and Laura could be a right pain in the arse."

"You never told me you didn't like Laura?" I was genuinely taken aback. As far as I'd been aware, Izzy and Laura got on like a house on fire. Okay, so maybe the house fire was actually arson and someone was going to get into serious trouble, but they'd always seemed to have fun.

"Never said I didn't like her," said Izzy, picking her things up from the floor and hanging them on the hooks behind the door to the staff kitchen, "just that she could be a pain. A funny pain, to be fair. But she'd have done your head in, eventually."

"Neither Laura nor Aj were unsuitable," I said doggedly, folding my arms for emphasis.

Izzy grinned and patted my arm as she walked past me and started refilling the napkin holder on top of the counter. "Two people in over fifteen years of dating," she said. "What about all the other unfortunates?" I thought back through the relatively small number of people who'd passed through my life—and bedroom—over the intervening years. A couple of them lasted a good few months. There was Devin, a fellow waiter from the Bluecoat who collected Dungeons and Dragons miniatures. And Flis, an older woman I'd met through Izzy, after we'd gone out for a drink with her friends from pilates. Both relationships broke up without any major drama, although Flis had crossed the street to avoid talking to me the last time I'd spotted her in town. I saw Devin whenever I ventured back into the Bluecoat, though. He was still working the same job and still painting the same miniatures, and seemed happy with his lot in life. There'd been maybe half a dozen others. A couple had been only a few chaste dates that came to nothing, whilst several ended up in the bedroom, but one or both parties declared incompatibility fairly rapidly. There'd also been one or two much briefer (and more memorable) absolute shag-fests that left everyone involved with a smile on their face and absolutely zero desire to see the other person ever again. All fairly average for a broad-minded woman in her early thirties, I reckon.

"Okay," I said, "I'll allow that I don't always make the best decisions." Izzy grinned at me. "But does anyone?"

"Nah," she said, twirling a tea towel up into the air and catching it neatly, "everyone fucks up at times. Part of the fun of it all, innit?"

"I guess so," I said, walking across to the front door. I flipped the sign to 'OPEN', then fixed the lock in the unlatched position so that customers could let themselves in. It was only October, but there was a nip in the air that suggested it wouldn't be wise to wedge the door open. Cold weather doesn't bother me at all these days, so I have a tendency to forget that humans don't like it so much. I've had to develop a conscious habit of working through how a human would feel in certain situations. So I check the weather forecast and try to remember to dress for it. If I don't, I have an unfortunate tendency to wander down Castle Street in a t-shirt and sandals when there's frost on the ground. And people stare at that, even in a city.

"So?" said Izzy, expectantly. I looked at her blankly. "The divine Mister Laithlind! What are you going to do about him? Because if you don't do *something,* I will be eternally disappointed in you, Lilith O'Reilly."

"I can't do anything about him," I said. "He's our enemy."

Izzy arched an immaculately drawn eyebrow. "'Our' enemy?" she said. "Really? I'd have said it's more like Eadric's bearing a good grudge and taking the rest of you with him. Cos if you don't mind me saying," she pointed a glossily black-painted nail at me for emphasis, "you could do worse than getting it on with the Viking. He'd definitely be more fun than mister high-faluting lord of the manor, stuck up there in his tower."

"Eadric's not as snobby as he appears," I said, wondering why I was bothering to defend Eadric Silverton. If there'd been dirty work to do in the course of revenant defence over the last few months, it had mostly been me doing it. It had been me who'd had no option but to chop off his wife's stupid head, for example. And it had also been me who was sent down south to gather support from the London crew whilst Eadric supposedly sorted things at home, only for me to come back and almost immediately end up fighting an evil spirit up in the cemetery. *Then* I'd rescued both Ivo and Rachel from their respective fates worse than un-death. And that's without even mentioning the seven-foot vampire I'd had to stake through the head in order to make it up to the catacombs in the first place.

"Just because you happened to be unalived in Liverpool," said Izzy, "doesn't mean you're obliged to join the local gang. How can you be sure they're even the good guys, anyway?" I considered what she was implying.

"Mapp's on their side," I said. "And he wouldn't stick with them if they weren't legit."

"Aah," said Iz, as she carefully picked rogue spoons out of the fork box, "but Gaultier Mapp is an absolute trollop of the first order. He'd stand by anyone who made his life steady enough for him to have nothing more to think about than whether he needs a new pair of silk trousers and maybe a cleaner for those hard-to-reach corners of the ancient book market."

"The birds like Eadric," I said firmly. "Bella wouldn't tolerate anyone dodgy looking after the undead elements of her city." The Liver Birds might be relatively new arrivals to Liverpool, having only been installed in 1911, but they dominate both the skyline and the city's public image. Eighteen feet high with a twelve-foot wingspan, Bella and Bertie are identical in everything except personality. Bertie is literally a grumpy old man, who glowers over the city as if daring anyone to do anything he doesn't approve of. Bella, on the other hand, looks out onto the water and is clearly much jollier for it. I love them both, but in different ways. Bertie's good company when all you want to do is stare into the distance and think things over. Bella's better for those occasions when you need a sympathetic nod and the occasional twitch of laughter as you explain to her just what's pissing you off and why. I planned to take a tin of oil up when I was supervising the welding, in order to grease Bella's joints a bit. Sometimes she gets so carried away in silent conversation that she moves more than she probably should. I'm a bit worried people will hear the creaking one of these days and panic that she's falling.

"True," conceded Izzy. "But you can't deny that Ivo is way more— oh hi, Sean," she turned to smile at the man who'd just walked into Flora's. "Same as usual?"

"Please," said the cute-looking man with floppy brown hair and a kind smile, as he made his way to his favourite table, "that would be great." Sean Hannerty is a very successful crime writer who likes to sit in the window of Flora's whilst making research notes for the seemingly endless books he churns out. He's been our most regular customer since I first opened Flora's over two years ago. He is also the last person with whom I had a proper date, but he can't remember anything about it on account of how Mapp had to wipe his memory. It's complicated. He found himself a very beautiful girlfriend during the summer—a blonde woman called Sophie, whose casual elegance made me feel like a badly-dressed raccoon in comparison. I'd figured that was that and tried my best to stop moping about it, but the happy couple had broken up suddenly and dramatically after she'd apparently accused him of saying my name in his sleep. I knew all this because it had happened in Flora's and Izzy witnessed the entire bizarre thing. And by 'witnessed', I obviously mean 'skulked close enough to hear everything whilst trying desperately not to look too obvious. From what Iz had been able to make out, Sophie had only made the connection between me and the sleep-talking when she'd overheard Izzy talking about me to Todd, our part-timer. Iz relayed Sean's clear and obvious confusion at being suddenly accused of 'fancying that woman who owns this place'. He'd denied all knowledge, only for Sophie to declare he'd done it on several occasions and she'd had enough. She'd stalked out and he'd run after her, but the next time he'd come into Flora's, Sean had been alone He hadn't made any attempts to chat me up again, but I'd felt his eyes boring into my back from his window seat a few times. I was beginning to worry that maybe I'd messed with Sean's head more than I'd realised when I'd made my own attempt to wipe his memory. I'd botched the job —in my defence, I was new to immortality at the time and didn't know how these things worked—and had to ask Mapp to fix my mess when Sean reappeared in Flora's barely able to string a sentence together and looking like he'd been sleeping in a bin for a week. Maybe some traces of memory had survived? Being able to remember seeing a mermaid sitting on top of your date's television set whilst having a face-off with an angry cat was the sort of thing that would stick, I reckoned. Or maybe I was just such a brilliant kisser that no one else could live up to it, even if Sean couldn't remember why. Sighing, I turned away as Izzy made Sean's coffee and busied myself cleaning the tops of the syrup bottles.

Izzy took Sean his black Americano and perched it between the books he'd already spread across the table. Then she came back to join me behind the counter, an impish grin on her face. "Haven't seen the delightful Sophie in weeks now," she whispered. "Maybe it's time to make your move." When I didn't reply, she frowned at me. "Lilith," she said firmly, in a low voice, "there is no point in being immortal if you don't *do* something with your life. Afterlife. Whatever you call it. Right now," she prodded me right in the chest with a sharp nail, "you have all the time in the world. And you are *wasting* it." Luckily for me, a group of tourists came into the cafe then and I escaped any more uncomfortable conversation. The rest of the day was uneventful but busy, and Izzy didn't get another chance to lecture me on my shortcomings. I spoke to Sean a couple of times, but only briefly—once when he asked for a second coffee, and again when he said goodbye as he left towards lunchtime. As I watched him strolling casually down the street, I thought about what Izzy had said. I really did have all the time in the world. So why wasn't I having more fun?

Jamaica? No, I Asked Nicely

"At least *consider* getting yourself back out there again?" Izzy was still pecking my head as we closed Flora's for the day. We used to shut a bit earlier between October and March, but these days business is brisk enough that we stay open until at least five every night, all year round. Sometimes it's later, if Mapp's running one of his endless craft groups. What had started out as a weekly meeting of the Renshaw Street Knitting Club rapidly grew into a confusing schedule of what Mapp insists on calling 'the yarn arts', in what he likes to think is a mysterious tone of voice. I've had to limit him to three groups a week, because otherwise innocent customers get caught up in discussions about the best ways to learn amigurumi. Too many people have found themselves holding a crochet hook instead of a cake fork.

"I'd love to start dating again," I said, as I locked the front door and turned the key that kicked the ancient shutter system into life. "I'm just scared of accidentally killing someone." The shutter clanked loudly before moving slowly downwards with an ominous creak.

"So date someone who's dead already," said Izzy, fastening her coat. "Save yourself the worry." She grinned at me. "If you're not going to let Ivo have his no doubt *very* wicked way," she said, "then perhaps consider your friendly neighbourhood landlord of all he surveys."

"I thought you weren't keen on Eadric?" I said, checking that Billy wasn't in his doorway opposite. The last thing I needed was the local ghost hearing all about the dire state of my love life. Not that Billy would ever mock—it was just all way too embarrassing for words. I was supposed to be a glamorously sexy member of the undead realms, for fuck's sake, not a faintly tragic thirty-something who lived with her aunt and a cat.

"I don't dislike Eadric Silverton," said Izzy, "I just think he's boring. Ivo seems like much more fun. And it's about time you had some fun. Laters!" She twirled round and headed off towards Button Street and the tiny flat she'd been living in for the past decade. Maybe I could persuade Eadric to let Izzy move into the Albert Dock flat, as it was apparently going begging. She could supervise Daisy in return—at least she could use the fish. The shutter had finally closed itself, so I turned and walked the few steps round the corner of the building to the fire escape and headed up to my own flat. Distracted by thoughts of Eadric Silverton in nothing but a bathrobe—what can I say, at least I consider *all* my options—I was halfway up before I noticed movement in the furthest corner of the carpark next to Flora's.

Calling it a carpark is overly grandiose for what is essentially an abandoned patch of scrubland, but I park Basil there for safekeeping and that makes it a carpark in my book. To my absolute astonishment, Rachel-the-vampire was sitting on what appeared to be a folding chair, next to a small table. She was dressed in grey leggings and a baggy black t-shirt, and had what looked distinctly like a pair of children's plimsolls on her feet. Alan was with her, sitting on a matching chair and grinning up at me. "A'right, Red?" he asked. He was dressed in his idea of smart-casual, which comprised a black suit over a white shirt with a pointy collar that was as sharp as the boots on his feet.

I squinted down at them. "What's in the glass?" I asked Rachel. She was holding a wine glass that was half filled with a red liquid that I *really* hoped was wine. The vampire looked embarrassed and hunched slightly in her chair. Al patted her knee in a vaguely possessive way.

"It's fine, girl," he told her. "Red knows the score."

"What score?" I asked suspiciously.

Alan turned his brightest, full-watt stage smile on me. "She needs to feed, yeah? And that cat of yours has been helping her out. I just thought," he tapped Rachel's glass with his fingernail and it made an audible clink, "she'd maybe enjoy it more if things were a bit more civilised."

"That's rat blood," I said, nodding at the glass, "isn't it?"

"Got it in one, Red," said Alan, nudging Rachel in amusement. "Chin chin, as they say." Rachel shyly lifted her glass slightly and then took a sip. I tried not to retch, and it turned into a cough.

"I'll leave you to your romantic evening," I said, and raced the last few steps to the flat before either of my resident weirdos could reply.

"Evening Lil," called my aunt, as I banged through the door and dumped my things on the kitchen table. "Had a good day?" I found her sitting in my living room, with Grimm—as always—installed on her lap. It had taken Kitty a while to get the hang of looking vaguely human, but these days most people wouldn't give her a second glance. The transparency she was prone to at the beginning has almost worn off, and you'd have to be looking really closely to notice the gap caused by her hovering fractionally above the chair, rather than on it. Grimm blinked at me slowly as Kitty scratched his neck just the way he likes it.

"You're spoiling that cat," I observed, and I swear Grimm narrowed his eyes at me. He's been developing some unnervingly human habits recently, and I'm not entirely sure I approve. "Did you know Rachel's outside with Alan?" I asked. Kitty raised her eyebrows questioningly. "Drinking blood from a wine glass, no less. And you can stop staring at me!" This was to Grimm, who was definitely grinning. "How many rats does it take to fill a wine glass, anyway?" The cat shrugged and flopped over onto his back so that Kitty could tickle his belly.

"You can't deny it's solved the rodent problem," said Kitty. "Our Grimmy's a *clever* ickle pusscat, aren't you? *Yes*, you are!"

"How's your history knowledge?" I asked, dropping onto the sofa opposite. "Kings and politics, that sort of thing."

"What's going on now?" Kitty narrowed her eyes at me. "Your lot aren't going to try to overthrow the monarchy, are they? Are you?" She looked genuinely worried.

"You know what I think about kings and queens and their stupid bloody thrones," I said. "They're only there by an accident of birth, and modern society would be better off without them."

"Have you told Eadric Silverton that?" asked my aunt. "Because it's my thinking he's also a ruler of sorts. You think you'd be better off without him?"

"Not the same thing at all," I said, but it wasn't quite true. Elizabeth —the real Queen of London, but only if you know your way round the underworld as well as the underground—once told me that all territories need a leader. Someone to look to for guidance and reassurance. Someone in charge. "It's not just about monarchy with us," I rallied, "it's as much to do with admin as anything else." Back when I was still new to the whole 'undead world hidden in plain sight' scenario and only knew Eadric as someone who lived—literally—up in a high tower, I'd assumed he didn't do much except wander around the roof of the Liver Building, looking down on his subjects. Turns out that immortality involves a whole heap of paperwork—most of it fake—if you don't want the humans finding out that the owners of the biggest property company in the area have a combined age of about twelve-hundred. Eadric makes up the bulk of that, to be fair. Nik's far more youthful, at a mere two-hundred-and-thirty-something years old. Eadric even has a driving license, although I'm assuming he has to re-fake it now and then to avoid being questioned as to why he's the youngest-looking eighty-year-old in history. I'd avoided getting too involved in the business side of things, even though I was clearly being absorbed into the Silverton empire whether I liked it or not. It was one thing learning to deal with sudden and unexpected immortality, but quite another to get to grips with the idea that every level of society had a certain amount of people who knew damn fine that the paranormal world was not only real, it also required replacement birth certificates on the reg.

"Why are you thinking about royalty," said Kitty, "when you dislike them so much?"

"Because," I sighed, "I think one of them's about to come back from the history books and bite me right on the ass."

"Not literally, I hope?" Kitty raised a neat eyebrow.

"Who the fuck knows," I said, putting my feet up on the coffee table and ignoring the dirty looks from both my aunt and our bloody judgmental cat. "Get this," I said to Kitty over the top of my boots. "William the *fucking* Conqueror. Live and kicking, probably lurking his way up to Liverpool as we speak."

"Well," said Kitty, "he can't actually be very *live*, now can he?"

"Stop splitting hairs," I grumped. "The long and short of it is that one of the most famous kings of all British history is back in the 'hood. And going by the panic it's causing up at the Liver Building, I don't think they're expecting it to be a particularly sociable visit."

"Well, it's got nothing to do with you," said my aunt, firmly. "You stay well out of it, Lilith O'Reilly." She frowned at me. "You *will* stay out of it, won't you?"

"Believe me," I said, "I'd like nothing better than to stay the fuck out of pretty much everything to do with undead politics. Unfortunately for me, it never seems to work out that way. Coffee?" I got up and headed to the kitchen.

"Yes please," called Kitty at my retreating back, "same as usual." I gazed out through the kitchen window as I waited for the coffee machine to dispense two espressos. Kitty never even drinks hers—she just doesn't like being left out. But making and drinking (or ignoring) cups of tea and coffee are a reassuringly human thing to do. I purposely didn't look down into the carpark, because I really didn't want to know what rodent-based activities Alan and Rachel might be getting up to. I wondered what the success rate for ghost/vampire relationships might be, or even if any of them had ever tried before. Alan's a ghost in the same way Billy is—solid as you like and perfectly capable of touching and being touched. Neither of them had any of Kitty's fragility, or the faint holographic shimmer she gives off if she's trying to make herself invisible. What they do all have in common is a freakish ability to teleport. No kidding, Kitty once popped up inside a car I was driving and I damn near drove through a hedge in shock. The sound of off-key singing wafted up from Harrington Street and I peered through the window to see a group of women walking along arm-in-arm, with not a care in the world. I missed that feeling. I really, *really* missed it.

~

Izzy picked up on the second ring. "Fancy going to the pub?" I asked. There was a brief silence.

"What's prompted this?" she said, eventually. "It's not like you to want to socialise with no good reason."

"What better reason," I said, sprawling across my bed, "than finally realising I need to have more fun in life?"

"And death." A snort at the other end. "Yeah, go on then. Gimme half an hour to get changed and make myself presentable, then I'll come over. Assume we're going to the Pilgrim? Damon's supposed to be staying here tonight, I'll have to let him know where we are."

"Not the Pilgrim," I said. "Let's go somewhere different for a change. What about that place on Jamaica Street?"

"It's a fair walk," said Izzy doubtfully.

"Come on," I said, "it's only up in the Baltic. It's not that far." The Baltic Triangle is a small corner of Liverpool city centre that has an attitude disproportionate to its size. Formerly an industrial area— for either the whaling or timber industry, depending which history you read—it sits just below Chinatown and is bordered by Wapping, Park Lane and Parliament Street. Most people know it as the location of those big green graffiti'd wings, which every woman who ever visits Liverpool is seemingly obliged to pose in front of for photos. And yes, somewhere in the depths of the Facebook account I gave up using years ago, there's proof of me doing exactly that. Designated as officially 'up and coming' by the local council a few years back, the old warehouses of the Baltic now mostly house terrifyingly trendy dive bars and the sort of street food vendors that look like they rocked up out of someone's kitchen but have probably been given five stars and deemed 'the place to go' by a food critic from the Guardian. The Duck and Swagger pub is, on the surface, the absolute opposite of all this, being a traditional pub with traditional beer and traditional football on the traditional widescreen televisions bracketed high up on the walls. It was designed exactly that way when it was built as part of the very modern Baltic Hotel next door just a couple of years earlier. The ladies' toilets even have ye olde traditional graffiti'd wings on the wall, so that gaggles of screechingly drunk young women can pose in front of them with the words 'Baltic Bitches' proudly emblazoned above their heads in matching pink scrawl. The entire place is so artificially ridiculous that I can't help but love it. And Izzy and I had only managed a couple of visits before an abrupt fall from a tall building had changed my life forever. "It'll be fun," I said. "I'll carry you if you get tired."

"No thank you," said Izzy. "I get travel sick."

"Are we going to the pub or not?"

"Of course we are," she said. "How can I turn down the first night out with my bestie for literally months? Be over as soon as I'm decent." With that, she rang off. I felt a pang of guilt. There was no denying I'd neglected Izzy over the last few months. Yeah, I'd been busy with the whole 'being dead' thing, but she really was my best friend and I hadn't spent much time with her. And the way she'd coped with my unexpected transformation in the last year had been nothing short of astounding. Most people would have run a mile at the discovery that their friend had become a walking, talking zombie. But Izzy had not only taken it in her stride, she'd also accepted the cast of weirdos that had come with my new status. Not to mention the extra work at Flora's. Sure, I'd upped her wages a ridiculous amount to make up for it when I'd realised just how low-cost my undead lifestyle was, but she was still ridiculously tolerant of the strangeness that surrounded me these days. I got up off the bed and stuck my head around the door to the living room. Kitty was on the sofa with Grimm curled up on her lap, as usual. What was less usual was that the television was on, and they appeared to be watching an old episode of *Neighbours*. As far as I knew, Kitty had yet to master the remote control. They both turned their heads to look at me.

"Have you ever seen this, Lil?" asked Kitty. "It's so much fun! Charlene's my favourite, I think. She's very good. Do you know who the actress is at all?"

"Uh huh," I said, glancing over to where Scott was attempting to chat up the tomboy Charlene. "She's done quite well for herself over the years. I'll play you some of her music sometime."

"Ooh," said Kitty, "she sings as well? Clever girl."

"She certainly is," I agreed. "I'm going out with Izzy tonight, if that's okay with you?"

Kitty's face lit up. "Of course it is," she said enthusiastically. "It'll do you good to have a night on the town." She frowned. "Are you sure you'll be safe, though? If this William's planning to come up here, isn't it risky to be going anywhere too far from home?"

"It won't be William coming up," I said. "At least, not until they've tested the waters. More likely to be his envoy—someone they can risk sacrificing. An envoy who will no doubt be a well-dressed creep with a mind full of nothing but politics." Just like Ivo Laithlind. Who betrayed his lover, his daughter *and* his best friend, all in the name of power. I was going to have to practise my interactions with humans if I was ever going to date again, because there was definitely no one on the deceased side of my social circle I could risk getting jiggy with.

"Well," said Kitty, "I'm sure you know what you're doing." Bless my great-aunt and her trusting ignorance. I had absolutely zero idea what I was doing from one day to the next, but so long as no one actually realised that, it was all good. "What are you going to wear?"

"What's wrong with this?" I looked down at the leggings and baggy jumper I'd had on all day. "It's still clean. Ish."

"Pshuh," puffed Kitty, "being dead does not mean having no standards, Lilith O'Reilly. Go and find something pretty to put on." I scowled, but turned back into the bedroom all the same. "And do something with your hair!" called Kitty after me. Gazing into the wardrobe mirror, I had to begrudgingly admit she had a point. My clothes were perfectly adequate for working in Flora's, but 'adequate' was about the sum of it. And there was what looked distinctly like a coffee stain down my chest. Sighing, I took everything off and dumped it on the chair that served as a laundry basket, before tying my hair up into a pineapple on top of my head and wrapping myself in a towel.

"I'm getting in the shower," I said to my flatmates, who ignored me entirely. "Won't be long." My shower might take an age to warm up, but once it gets going, it's pretty decent for something that looks like it was installed while ol' Vicky was still on the throne. I rooted my shower cap out from the back of the shelf and pulled it over my topknot. Whatever Kitty said, my hair takes at least an hour to dry and style properly and I didn't have time. The unsuspecting public would just have to cope with it as it was. As I scrubbed myself, I wondered why I didn't have showers more often. Probably because I don't really need them. Revenants don't sweat, so we don't get whiffy in the way humans do. Ergo, less incentive to bother washing. I do like a soak in the bath—I'm not a complete skank—but the quick scrubbing urgency of showers is more for necessity rather than pleasure. I definitely felt better for standing under the flowing water, though. I have to shower at human speed—if I forget and start splashing round too energetically, water comes out of the tub and soaks the floorboards—but it doesn't take long, anyway. There isn't much to do when your body hair doesn't grow and you don't get B.O. Staring down at my toenails, I thought idly that it would be nice to have a pedicure at some point. Although if the therapist buffed too much dry skin off, I'd be living with sore patches for a *very* long time.

Switching the water off, I stepped out and dried myself down vigorously. One thing I had noticed since I'd died was that, deceased or not, I still got dry skin occasionally. Maybe it was just a slow erosion process, and I'd eventually be a different shape? Hopefully it would wear off my thighs first and leave my cleavage alone. I walked out into the living room and found Izzy on the sofa, sitting next to Kitty. She was wearing a short fitted dress over tights and Mary Jane shoes, and had a pink, fake fur jacket draped over her lap. "Shift your arse then," she said, glancing over at me briefly, before turning back to an ancient episode of *The Price Is Right*. Kitty had clearly found one of the golden oldies channels. Or maybe it was Grimm's choice—although he looked more the murder-mystery type to me. Probably sat watching it thinking how he'd do the murders better and never get caught. I shifted my arse, as instructed. Having seen Izzy's outfit, I figured I'd better up my game from the 'jeans and a nice top' I'd vaguely planned. I wasn't even sure why I'd suggested this night out, other than to stick two metaphorical fingers up at everyone who seemed to think my life was duller than dishwater. It currently felt like one of those walks you go on because people keep insisting it's good for your mental health. You head out with zero enthusiasm and a whole heap of resentment, only to begrudgingly realise it really has made you feel better. Hopefully, a trip to the pub would do similar. There was no denying I didn't have much of a normal life anymore. While that was kind of understandable cos of the whole being dead side of things, eternity was going to be terminally fucking boring if I didn't remind myself how to have fun occasionally.

In a fit of bravado, I pulled a dress out of the wardrobe that I'd never actually worn outside the confines of the flat. A long, v-necked maxi dress in dark bottle green, I'd bought it for a friend's wedding several years ago. Then I'd decided it was far too low-cut for a wedding and I didn't want to spend the day worrying about whether my tit-tape would hold. So the beautiful green dress had been shoved into the back of the wardrobe and I'd worn a perfectly nice flowered one instead. I was a bit sick of being 'nice' right now, I decided. I pulled the dress on over nothing more than knickers and a pair of trainer socks—if I wore my Converse, I wouldn't feel too far out of my comfort zone. Swishing around in front of the mirror, I thought it looked like something Elizabeth of London might wear. And Elizabeth definitely wouldn't waste time worrying about whether her neckline was too low. I twisted my hair into the messiest bun the world had ever seen, and shoved on some quick eyeliner and mascara. It would have to do. I picked up my sneakers and went into the living room.

"Swit *swoo*!" crowed Izzy when she saw me. "Bloody hell, Lil—that's a version of you we haven't seen in a good while." She grinned as I sat in the armchair to pull my shoes on. "You look amazing, babe," she said, and I felt myself blush. Having tied my laces, I looked up to see Kitty staring at me, a look of wonderment in her eyes.

"What?" I asked, feeling self-conscious. "Is it too much?"

"No, no," said Kitty, and I realised she had ghostly tears in her eyes. "It's just that you look, well, *yourself*, Lil. A normal young woman, going out on the town with her friend." She clapped her hands together in glee. "I'm just so happy to see you going out, is all."

"Gawd," I said, trying not to show how touched I was, "I clearly need to go out more often."

"You do!" exclaimed Kitty. "When did you two last go out together?" Izzy and I looked at each other. Our last venture out on the town had ended down at Pier Head, killing a half-dead zombie and disposing of his body. Which was not an experience either of us was in a hurry to repeat.

"Too long ago," said Izzy firmly, getting to her feet. She turned to look down at Kitty. "You could come with us, if you like?" For a terrifying second I thought Kitty was about to say yes, but then she looked down at Grimm and shook her head.

"No," she said. "It's very kind of you, Izzy, but I think me and Grimm here are going to have a movie night together. What do you think, Grimmy?" The cat looked up at Iz and gave her a slow blink. "There you go," said Kitty happily, "Grimm thinks so too. Maybe next time." I somehow managed to hide my relief. Not that I'd have minded taking Kitty out with us. Despite being my great-aunt, she's actually only three years older than me. And she has a much better sense of style, helped enormously by that annoyingly useful ghostly ability to change her appearance more or less at will. But she has a tendency to disappear and reappear without warning, and I wasn't sure it was late enough in the evening for the punters in the Duck and Swagger to be drunk enough not to notice. Maybe next time we could just go out later. I grabbed my leather jacket from the back of the door.

"Come on then," I said to Izzy, "let's see how drunk we can get you before Damon turns up."

"If I throw up," said Iz, "you're holding my hair."

"It's a deal," I said, opening the back door and stepping out onto the fire escape. "Let's go have some fun."

Let Me Entertain You

"Holy Mary, mother of God," said Billy, as I stepped off the fire escape onto Harrington Street. "That's some look, Red."

"Thank you," I said, dropping into a mock curtsey in the middle of the street. "Presentable enough for a night out?"

"I should say so," he said. "Ain't seen nothing like that in a long time."

Izzy came up beside me. "Hey Billy," she said. "She scrubs up okay, don't you think?"

Billy grinned. "She does indeed," he said. "It's a lucky Liverpool tonight, to be in the presence of women as lovely as yourselves."

"Get on with you," I said, embarrassed now. "We're just going to the pub."

"Mind you're careful now," said Billy. "Don't want the menfolk fainting in your presence."

Shaking my head, I pulled Izzy's arm. "Come on," I said. "First one's on me." It's only a fifteen minute walk from Harrington Street to the Baltic Triangle, even at human pace. There was no one else on Park Lane as we walked along the back of John Lewis, so I entertained Izzy by bouncing up onto the high wall of the car park and running along the railing at the top, my long skirt trailing behind me in the breeze.

"Reckon that would work as a parachute?" asked Izzy. I gathered the bottom hem of my dress and jumped off the wall onto a bollard, which would have been a neat move had I not let go of the skirt. It flapped up around my waist and there was a half-hearted cheer from a group of blokes walking along Liver Street in front of us. I dropped sheepishly to the ground and gave them a curtsey, just for the show of it. The weather was dry but cold, and Izzy and I laughed at the sight of lads wandering round in jeans and t-shirts, alongside girls in tiny dresses and a lot of chilly-looking bare skin. "Remember when we used to say we'd wear a beer jacket to save carrying an actual coat?" said Izzy, as we turned onto Jamaica Street. "Froze our asses off for the first hour or so, until we were pissed enough not to care."

"The amount of cheap vodka we used to get through," I said, "it's a wonder we didn't end up dead from hypothermia in the gutter. These days I'd be happy to get even vaguely pissed."

"Never mind," said Izzy, pulling open the pub's front door and ushering me inside in front of her, "you can have fun watching me."

Two hours later, I was doing exactly that. I'd bought us both a drink to start with, but just hung onto my first one whilst refilling Izzy's glass regularly. We'd somehow become attached to a group of people on a night out from a local office, and had sung happy birthday to a short, middle-aged woman twice so far, whilst she giggled drunkenly and flopped all over the much younger man sitting next to her. He didn't seem to mind. Izzy got up to go to the loo, leaving me with a bloke in his fifties who had a straggly moustache and sweat stains in his armpits. He told me his name was Gareth, and he was the firm's accounts manager. After I'd had to remove Gareth's hand from my leg for a second time, I excused myself and said I was off to find Izzy but would absolutely be straight back, of course I would. Gareth stared after me as I wriggled my way through the packed bar to the door that led to the stairs down to the toilets. I had to wait at the top for three girls to make their wobbly way up, two of them propping up the third. They thanked me as I held the door to the bar open for them. As I turned back to head down to the

Ladies, a man was walking up towards me. He was in his late thirties at a guess, and although he was wearing a t-shirt and jeans, they reeked of tastefully unobtrusive quality. His hair was dark brown, with reddish hints that showed up under the bright lights of the staircase. As I watched, he absentmindedly ran his hand through, ruffling it slightly. The stubble on his chin had light flecks in it, and looked like it was there because he genuinely hadn't had time to shave, rather than being an affectation. He looked up at me as he got closer and did a gratifying double take—which was when I saw the silver edge to his brown eyes. However much this man looked like an indie musician having a night off, he was actually a revenant. As far as I know, there's no rule saying you can't be both, but I was pretty sure it was quite rare. Ifan would fit the bill, if it wasn't for the fact he's actually still alive. Just. And it wasn't as though I expected to recognise every immortal in the neighbourhood —I knew there was a few dotted around who I'd yet to meet—but I was pretty sure I'd have remembered meeting this one. His face broke into an easy, open smile and he held out a hand. I stared at it blankly for a second, before recovering myself and shaking it politely. "Well, well," he said, "it's not often I bump into my own kind on a hotel staircase. How strange."

"You're in Liverpool," I said. "There's plenty of strangeness around." I risked a breath, to check he really was an immortal. Just a tiny one, because if he was human after all, there was a reasonable chance I might suck the life out of him. Inhaling carefully, I picked up a potent scent of warm, woody citrus that I thought might be frankincense, but nothing to suggest he was anything other than determinedly deceased.

"So I hear," he said. "I'm Liam." He looked at me expectantly.

"Lilith." He nodded. "And I'm trying to find my friend," I said. "So if you'll excuse me?"

Liam stepped politely backwards. "Of course," he said. "I hope you and your...*friend* have an enjoyable evening." I skittered down the stairs a bit too fast, hoping the human punters were all too drunk to notice, not daring to glance backwards until I was at the bottom. Liam was nowhere to be seen.

I found Izzy doing someone's hair in the Ladies. She was re-pinning the woman's blonde curls, whilst also shouting encouragement to the rest of the party, who were posing in front of the pink graffiti wings. "Heyyyy, Lil," she called, "come hold this?" I dutifully held the woman's hair up whilst Izzy deftly fixed it back together. When she was satisfied, she twirled the woman round to look at herself in the mirror above the sinks. "There you go," she said, "you're gorgeous. Never forget that." The woman squeaked and clapped at her reflection. After turning to give Izzy a wobbly hug, she tottered off to join her friends, who swept her off out of the loos in a cloud of perfume and hairspray. "What's it like being sober?" Izzy asked me. "Cos I've forgotten. Hang on, I need the loo." She left the cubicle door open whilst having a wee, so she could keep talking. "Damon will be here soon," she said, "is that okay?"

"Of course it is," I said. "Why wouldn't it be?"

"I worry about you being on your own all the time," said Izzy, as she rearranged her clothes and flushed the loo. She walked over to the sink next to me and started washing her hands. "Of course you've got all this," she flapped her hands around, sending water droplets flying, "*weird* shit to deal with, but you're still here, you know? You're still *living*, even if you're not actually alive." Someone came through the door behind us and went into the first stall. "It's about time you made more of it," Izzy said in a low voice, leaning towards me so she wouldn't be overheard, "instead of doing nothing but dealing with the bullshit that seems to surround the Silvertons."

"I'm fine," I said. "I'm out now, aren't I? It's not my fault I can't get drunk."

"Me neither, love," called the woman in the toilet stall, "Drink like a fish, but always the last standing." There was a bang and a brief '*oh shit*' and then the toilet door opened and a dark-haired woman in her twenties appeared. She was dressed in a sequined jumpsuit and was awkwardly pulling the shoulders straight as she emerged. Never go out drinking wearing anything that has to be completely taken off to go for a wee, is my general rule in life. "Mostly standing, anyway," she grinned, before bouncing off towards the staircase without washing her hands.

"There's a weird man here," I said to Izzy, when I was sure we were alone.

"Yeah," she said, squinting at me, "we're in a pub in central Liverpool. It's filled with weird people."

"A *weird* weird man," I said, cursing to myself as two girls in their late teens skittered in through the door and both went into the same toilet cubicle with much giggling. "One of my lot," I said in a low voice.

"Ooh, how exciting!" Izzy clapped a hand over her mouth. "Sorry," she said, fractionally more quietly. "Is he good looking? Have you spoken to him? Would he like to be your very loyal subject?" She grabbed my arm and began pulling me determinedly towards the door.

"What are you doing?" I hissed, dragging back.

"We're gonna go find him and you can chat him up. Do you good to get back into the game."

"I can't *speak* to him, Iz!" She was still pulling at me—but believe me, when a revenant decides not to move, it's like trying to shift half a tonne of granite. "I don't know who he is!"

"Lil," said Izzy, turning to face me (although I noticed she propped herself against the door frame in order to stay upright), "you deserve some fun." She hiccuped gently. "And however much Ivo would like to get into your undead pants and I would very much like you to let him, there's no getting away from the fact he's a power-hungry scrote."

"Ivo isn't getting into my pants," I said, "*ever*. Power-hungry or not."

"Yeah," said Izzy, "whatever you say. Anyway, let's go find mister spooky tits and I shall tell you whether I approve."

"I don't think he'll be in the pub," I said, as we went back up the stairs. "More likely he's staying in the hotel and just nipped through." Izzy stopped so suddenly that I was three steps ahead before I realised she wasn't next to me. I stopped and turned to look down at her. "What's up?"

She frowned up at me. "Why was he down here?"

"How should I know?"

"It's just the loos," she said. "And pardon me for touching on a personal subject, but since when have any of you lot actually needed to go for a piss?"

"Never," I said. "Maybe he pretends, same as I do."

"Or *maybe*," said Izzy, "he'd spotted you across a sweaty bar and was lurking in the hope of bumping into you. How romantic!" With that, she stomped determinedly past me and pulled open the door to the bar. "Follow me," she said. "We're going on a man hunt."

The Duck and Swagger is tiny and you can see pretty much every corner from wherever you might be sitting. So our hunt was both very short and very lacking in undead men of any description. Having made me wriggle behind her all the way through the crowded pub, Izzy insisted on wriggling right back to where we'd started. "He's not here," I said, as she leaned back against the door for the toilet staircase. "Sorry to disappoint."

"I can't imagine you ever disappointing anyone," said Liam, as he pulled the door open from the other side. Izzy staggered and he caught her before she fell. "There you go," he said, propping her as she regained her composure.

"You've got good hearing," she said accusingly, then relented. "Thank you." She put a hand out to balance herself against the wall. "I appear to be more drunk than I thought I was." She turned to fix me with a beady look. "Funny how that always happens."

"Don't blame me for your terrible life choices," I said.

Izzy made a snorting noise. "Huh," she said, "s'about time you started making some better ones of your own, eh Lil?" She gave what I assume she thought was a subtle wink, but which in fact came across like demented gurning. "M'going for another wee. You," she prodded Liam in the chest, "can entertain my friend."

"My absolute pleasure," said Liam. Izzy snorted again and headed down the stairs, holding onto the bannister carefully. "She's nice," he said to me, nodding his head towards Izzy.

"She is," I agreed.

"So," said Liam, "how would madam prefer to be entertained?" There was a distinct twinkle in his eye.

"You can start by telling me who you actually are," I said.

Liam grinned. "Straightforward," he said. "I like it. Liam O'Connor," he made a sweeping bow, "at your service."

"That's a very Irish name for someone who sounds pure British boarding school," I said.

"Quite," agreed Liam. "My real name is long gone, I fear." He smiled. "But this one has served me well for a long time now."

"What are you doing in Liverpool, Liam O'Connor?"

"How do you know I'm not from here?" he asked. "You can't know everyone in this fair city."

"Let's just say you strike me as someone I'd know if you'd been around for any length of time."

"So suspicious," said Liam, but he smiled as he said it. He had a friendly, open face that invited interest. "But as you are being straight with me, I shall do you the honour of replying in the same manner. I am indeed a visitor to this fair city," he said, bowing slightly, "but this is far from being my first time here. Nor, I hope, will it be my last." He tilted his head as if judging how much information he should give me. "I am, shall we say, on a diplomatic mission."

"Where from?"

"From elsewhere," said Liam. "We've heard stories about certain...*events* in the area. This has been a cause for concern, especially as some people feel we should all be working more closely together for protection. Therefore, it was decided I should attempt to find out exactly what's going on, before anyone higher might be tempted to intervene. Mine is a friendlier face than some of the alternatives, I can assure you of that."

"What do you think's been going on?" I asked. "And why is it any of your business?"

"Lilith," he said, "with apologies for my earlier pretence of ignorance, I am well aware of who you are. Your activities are the talk of *many* towns." We both fell silent as a member of the bar staff came through the door, carrying empty glasses. She smiled gratefully as we both stepped backwards to let her through to the kitchens behind the bar area. "And it is our business," he said when she'd gone, "for the simple reason that we don't generally go around drawing attention to ourselves."

Marvellous. "Who's 'we'?" I asked, although I was pretty sure I already knew the answer.

"I've travelled from Hereford," said Liam. Of course. "We are a neighbouring territory, and there has been some concern about the state of things so close to us. But having met you," he smiled, "I will report back that everything is absolutely fine." I should have bloody known it. The first undead man I'd met who I'd genuinely consider getting to know better, and he turns out to be one of Billy The Sodding Bastard's lot. Eadric would be well pissed off if he knew I was consorting with the enemy, right in the city centre.

Eadric Silverton would absolutely not approve—

Shut up, I mentally hissed. *You promised to leave me alone tonight.*

We cannot stand by and watch you risk your own safety. We—

You are not my bloody parents. Fuck off.

But—

No. Shut up and leave me. NOW. Ooh, that was clever. My inner voice had turned into The Voice, despite still being inside my head. I'd have to practise that. It might come in handy. *AND DON'T COME BACK BEFORE TOMORROW.* Heh.

"Are you alright, Lilith?" Liam was gazing at me with a curious expression on his face. Fucksake, now the hottest man I'd met in a literal lifetime was going to assume I was absolutely batshit. Same old, same old.

"I'm absolutely fine," I said. Luckily, Izzy chose that moment to come back up the stairs from the loos.

"Heyyyyyyy, you two," she grinned. "Made your introductions?" She swung off the top of the bannister and Liam caught her again before she toppled over. "Such a gentleman," she said. "Ooh!" a slight hiccup. "Here's my maaaaaaan, come to save me." Damon came through the door from the bar and rolled his eyes in amusement at the state of Izzy.

"Want me to take you home?" he said.

Izzy nodded vigorously, and the effort almost sent her sprawling again. "Please," she said. "I appear to be," she squinted as though concentrating, "a tiny bit squiffy."

"Good," said Damon. "It's about time you two started having fun together again." He winked at me, but I felt a pang of guilt. Although I'd never been particularly sociable, Izzy and I did used to have occasional nights out together, back when I was still human. As far as I knew, Damon wasn't aware of my undead status. And without context, it probably looked like I'd simply found other people to hang out with and left Izzy out in the cold. "Although Lil can clearly hold her beer better than you." He turned to me. "You coming with us, Lil?"

"I thought Lilith and I might go somewhere quieter," said Liam. I looked at him and he smiled. "Somewhere we can chat properly."

"Maybe you should give her your number," Damon said to Liam, "and she can call you another time. *If* she's interested." Gawd. First night out in forever and we were already at the 'alpha males locking metaphorical horns' stage.

"I'm fine," I said to Damon, making my mind up on the spot. "I'm not pissed and I know what I'm doing. I'd like to have a chat with Liam alone, if it's all the same to you."

"I'm not your dad, love," said Damon. "Just looking out for you, is all."

"I know," I said, leaning forward to give him a peck on the cheek. "You're a lovely man, Damon. I hope Izzy appreciates you properly."

"I'll appreciate him properly," Izzy snorted, "when I'm slightly less pissed." She wobbled and caught hold of Damon. "Don't s'pose you could carry me home, babe?"

"Your chariot awaits, m'lady," said Damon. He scooped her up and she clung round his neck, a radiant smile on her face. "We'd better find a bucket for next to the bed." Liam held the door open to the bar and we both watched as Damon negotiated the crowd with Izzy in his arms. She waved happily to the office crew, who were still at their table. The birthday girl now appeared to be asleep in the lap of the man sitting next to her. Gareth looked over and smiled hopefully as he spotted me through the open door. Then he saw Liam and his face fell into an expression of almost comic disappointment.

"Was someone maybe hoping he was in with a chance?" said Liam, who'd obviously also seen Gareth's reaction.

"I didn't come out on the pull," I said. "And even if I had, I would not be getting it on with a sweaty accounts manager. I'm sure he's a very nice person, but—"

"He looks like an idiot," interrupted Liam, "if you ask me."

"Gareth definitely needs practice in the lady department," I admitted. "Bless him."

"Let's have a drink," said Liam. "Come on," he said in response to my raised eyebrows, "we can hide in the corner of the pub and pretend to be normal people. No overlords watching over us for once. It'll be fun."

"You make it sound like we're bunking off like kids," I said.

"That is *exactly* what we're doing," said Liam with a grin. His eyes crinkled at the corners when he smiled, which was often. Up close, I could see the faintest of silver streaks in his red-brown hair. His big brown eyes gave him a puppy-dog air, even with the silver glint at their edges. "I can't remember the last time I sat down and talked properly to someone I didn't already know."

"The novelty wears off," I said. "I've met way too many new people this last year. Not all of them were very nice."

"Oh, but I am," said Liam with a wink. "Promise." He held open the door to the bar and gestured me inside. "After you, m'lady." I laughed and walked through the door, even as I was shaking my head at the ridiculousness of the situation. Gareth was still sitting at the table with his work friends, and I gave him a polite smile as I walked past. He looked like he might cry, and I wondered—not for the first time—where some blokes get their confidence from. There's nothing wrong with sweaty accountants—if that's your thing then all power to your sexy elbow and that—but however bad the body odour levels, they still seem to assume they've got a chance with anyone they happen to set their beady eyes on.

By some miracle, a group of people were leaving a small table in the corner just as we approached. I slid into the vacated bench seat before anyone could beat me to it. "Drink?" asked Liam.

"You know I don't drink," I said.

"Yes," Liam replied slowly and carefully, as though talking to a child, "but we'll draw more attention to ourselves if we don't buy at least one round. If only because the management won't appreciate us taking up an entire table if we're not drinking at the bar."

"Red wine," I said. "Doesn't matter what sort." Liam nodded and turned to fight his way to the bar. I watched as he wriggled through the crowd and almost immediately got the attention of the nearest barman. I try not to be shallow when it comes to potential partners, but Liam really was very attractive. And he seemed honest, which was a big plus point in my book. He could have lied about where he'd come from and I wouldn't have been any the wiser. Presumably Eadric would know exactly who he was, but I wasn't going to check in for Eadric's approval every time I got chatted up. Not that I got chatted up very often, anyway. At least—I glanced over to where Gareth had now turned his attention to one of the women in his party—not by people whose attention I actually appreciated.

"Here you go," said Liam, passing over a large glass of red. "Bottoms up." I clinked glasses with him, then we both put our drinks down on the table without drinking anything. To my surprise, Liam slid onto the bench seat next to me, although he left a careful distance between us. "Let's do some people-watching," he said with a grin. "See if we can guess who's going to get lucky tonight."

"Her," I said confidently, nodding towards a small, dark-haired woman who was standing with her back to us at the bar.

"Really?" said Liam. "She doesn't appear to be flirting."

"Which just shows how out of touch you are," I said. "What is it with you ancient blokes?"

Liam shrugged. "We get out of practice, I guess," he said.

"I very much doubt that," I said. "Anyway, look at the woman with her." The other woman was taller, older and blonder than the first. She was also gazing down at her drinking partner with the sort of starry-eyed look more often seen on smitten teenagers.

"Aah," said Liam, one eyebrow rising a fraction. "I see. What about him?" I followed his gaze to where a man in his forties dressed in sharp trousers and a heavy shirt unbuttoned at the neck was talking to a woman of roughly the same age. She was wearing a long floral dress over flat sandals and touched the man's arm briefly as she smiled at something he'd said.

"Already married," I declared. "Or at least in a very long-term relationship."

"And are you in a long-term relationship, Lilith?" asked Liam. I turned to look at him and found nothing but genuine curiosity in his eyes. "Or any relationship at all, for that matter?"

Oh well, I thought—in for a penny, in for a pound. "Nope," I said, "my love life's deader than I am. Which is saying something."

"That's a shame," said Liam. " Although I'd bet good money I've been...unattached, shall we say, for far longer than yourself."

"It's been a couple of years since I got naked with anyone, put it that way," I said. "Pretty sure I've forgotten how everything works."

"Try going more than eighty years," said Liam. He laughed when he saw my expression. "I'm picky," he said with a shrug. "Anyway," he picked up his glass and took a sip, swirling the wine round his mouth with evident delight, "I don't meet many single women who are, shall we say, on the same level as me."

"Physically or metaphorically?" I asked, unsure where this conversation was going.

"Physically," Liam grinned. "Not on an aesthetic scale—I think that's more a human thing. More just your basic 'both as dead as each other' situation. I'm not sure if you know this, but it's quite difficult to date a human. They ask difficult questions. And you have to pretend to be breathing when you're not, because otherwise they have an annoying tendency to panic that you're dead. Also, if you *do* accidentally breathe, there's the whole 'oh god this tastes amazing maybe I could just suck the literal life out of them' angle. Which can be awkward."

"Yeah," I said ruefully, "I know all about that one." Liam raised a questioning eyebrow. "I haven't killed anyone," I said. "Or at least, not by kissing them."

"I'm very glad to hear that."

"But I came close to it once," I said. "I kissed a human I liked very much, and I wasn't sure I was going to be able to stop."

"You did stop, though," said Liam. His eyes crinkled at the corners as he smiled at me again. Liam smiled a *lot*. It was nice—I'd spent the last few months with people who were mostly very stressed about things, often for good reason. When I was around humans, I had to play pretend in order to fit in, and when I was with revenants, the world was a dangerous place. It was nice to just be chatting with someone for no other reason than having fun.

"I did, yes," I said. "But I damaged him and Ma—" I stopped myself explaining Mapp's part in it just in time, "—a friend had to help me out. And I haven't bothered dating since."

"Do you think we could actually get drunk eventually," said Liam, "if we tried hard enough?" Thrown by the change of topic, it took me a second to catch up. Liam swirled his glass and looked into the wine as though scrying for portents of the future. He turned the glass a fraction too vigorously and wine splashed out and onto the table.

"I think it would take a very long time," I said, mopping the spilled wine with a clean napkin someone had left on the table. "But I'd be prepared to experiment." I looked up at Liam. "I miss having fun."

"Then I think we should do our absolute best to make sure you have more fun, Lilith," said Liam. He held up his glass as if to give a toast. "Here's to fun," he said.

I looked at him for a few seconds before picking up my own glass. "To fun." I clinked in agreement.

"I'm staying here," said Liam suddenly. "In the hotel. Fancy escaping the rabble?"

"Are you propositioning me, Liam O'Connor?" I already knew what my answer was going to be. It was easy for the Silvertons to warn me off people from other territories, but as Izzy had pointed out, how could I be sure Eadric and Nik even had my best interests at heart? We all got on well enough and they looked out for me when needs be, but I had no doubt their loyalty would always depend on what was good for the territory as a whole, rather than me as a person. If I was deemed a threat at any point, Eadric would get rid of me by any means necessary. Okay, so he might feel pretty shit about it, but he'd still do it. You don't get to rule over a good chunk of an entire country for almost a millennium by being soft-hearted. The only people I'd met from other territories were Elizabeth and Jude, from London. And Elizabeth had made it clear that any support she offered was to me personally, not Eadric as local ruler, which made me think things were maybe not as cut and dried as the Silvertons liked to imply. It was time I made my own decisions. And possibly my own mistakes. But I wouldn't know until I tried.

"That would be incredibly inappropriate," said Liam, "not to mention politically dangerous."

"Because your boss wouldn't approve?" I asked.

Liam grinned. "It's your boss I'd be worried about," he said. "I gather Silverton's very protective of his lark."

"He doesn't show it very well," I said. "And he's not my boss." Something else occurred to me. "Why do people call me the lark?"

"It's meant affectionately," said Liam. "From my side it is, anyway. I think. Although I can't speak for other territories any more than I can speak for those who rule my own."

"Who rules you?" I asked him.

"Are you ruled over?" asked Liam, neatly side-stepping the question. He was definitely under the impression I didn't know about Big Bad Billy, I decided. Which hopefully gave me some advantage, even if it was only that he wouldn't be able to surprise me with the big reveal.

"No, I bloody well am not," I said. "The Silvertons are obviously the people I go to with any problems. And they've been very helpful so far, to be fair. But they don't own me."

"I'd prefer to think of us both as emissaries for our respective territories," said Liam. "If we work together, then perhaps we can improve the current situation for all concerned. And," his brown eyes twinkled, "have some fun while we're at it."

"How do you hide your, erm, *special* status from Izzy?" asked Liam. We were sitting at opposite ends of the velvet sofa that was wedged into his small hotel room, and 'opposite ends' actually meant 'squashed up together desperately trying not to touch knees'. The room would have been dark even in daylight with its exposed brick walls and red and black colour scheme, but was undeniably cosy.

"Wouldn't you have preferred to stay somewhere grander?" I asked, looking around the room.

"You don't like it?" Liam's eyes crinkled again as he watched me taking the room in.

"Actually," I said, "I do like it. It's cute and comfortable and fun. But it seems aimed at younger people coming into town for the nightlife, not undead diplomats."

"Are you saying I'm old, Lilith?" He pulled a mock-offended face.

"How old are you, exactly?"

Liam's face twisted into a smile. "How old do you think I am?"

"Crack on with your bullshit," I laughed. "We both know you could be anything from," I looked him up and down speculatively, "forty and just turned, or nearer a thousand, but very well preserved."

"Well," said Liam, "as you asked so nicely, I'll tell you. This body," he waved his hands up and down himself, "is technically forty-three. But I've been around for many centuries."

"Shares in Oil of Olay? Never mind," I said, seeing Liam's blank expression, "I'm never going to make it in stand-up. As for hiding things from Izzy," I went on, "I don't. She's known from the start."

Liam looked startled. "And she hasn't told anyone?" he asked. "How can you trust her not to betray us?"

"Us?" I frowned at him. "Izzy's nothing to do with you."

"She is if she's likely to tell people about us," he said, getting up and walking over to the audio speaker tucked into the corner of the room. He pulled open the front of it to reveal a mini-bar. "Possibly," he said, "you were right about this hotel being designed for younger people." He pulled two mini champagne bottles out and starting hunting round in a drawer underneath the cabinet. "Ha!" he said, producing a handful of cardboard straws. "We can pretend to drink to our future collaborations."

"There'll be no collaborating on anything if you threaten any of my friends," I warned him, "living or dead."

"I'm not threatening anyone, Lilith," said Liam, sitting down next to me. He passed me a bottle and a straw. "I am simply concerned about the amount of human connections you appear to have."

"Can you stop using my full name?" I asked him. "It feels like I'm being spoken to by a teacher at school."

"What should I call you, then?" he asked.

"Lil," I said, "or Lili. Some people call me Red."

Liam gazed at me for what felt like a very long time, and I was pretty sure I was blushing. "I think," he said slowly, "I'll go with Red. It suits you." He held his bottle out. "Fancy a simultaneous champagne pop?"

"Thought you'd never ask." Years of waitressing has made me good at popping corks. I deftly unwrapped the top and held my thumbs on either side. "Ready?" I asked Liam.

"As I'll ever be," he said with a grin.

"One," I counted, "two...three...*go!*" My cork launched with perfect precision, landing on top of the speaker-fridge. Liam's was less accurate, shooting up into the air with enough force to hit the ceiling, and sending champagne spurting out of the bottle and all down his shirt. I squawked with very inelegant laughter and got up to grab a towel from the tiny en-suite bathroom. As I walked back into the room, Liam was taking off his shirt. It took all my mental strength not to squeak again, but somehow I managed it. Liam wasn't buff—which was lucky, because that's never been my type—but he was certainly fit as a butcher's dog, as Izzy liked to say. I handed him the towel and sat back down, determinedly looking anywhere but at the half-naked man in the room.

"It's been a while," said Liam. "I'm clearly out of practise."

"You and me both," I said, before I could stop myself.

"Well," said Liam slowly, "maybe we should practise." I looked at him and it was like locking eyes with a shark. Exciting and terrifying and, well...yeah, mostly just exciting.

"Yes," I said with a grin, "I think we probably should."

The Vampire
Preservation Society

"Do you think we should maybe practise a bit more," Liam said, "just to make sure?" I rolled over to face him on the hotel bed. He turned to look at me, a crooked smile on his face. His hair was sticking out in all directions, and I leaned over to smooth down some of the more wayward strands. Catching hold of my hand, he kissed it, his stubble scraping gently against the skin of my palm.

"What's your boss going to say if he finds out?" I asked.

"I think," said Liam, "I would like to keep this between us. Just for now."

"But what *would* he say?" I persisted.

Liam grinned. "My biggest concern," he said, "would be that others would want to fight me for you."

"I'm not keen on the idea of being fought over," I frowned. "I can make my own decisions as to who I want to spend time with."

"Red," he sighed, "you forget I come from a much older time, with much older customs. Believe me when I say that fighting for you would be an honour. But it would come with no obligation on your part."

"Huh," I flopped onto my back, "you oldies are *weird*."

"Not so much of the old, thank you," he said, rolling onto his front and flinging a possessive arm across my stomach. "I'd like to think I still have the stamina of a man half my age." Turns out I needn't have worried about the workings of the undead male body. Everything functions just the same as it always did—better than most, in Liam's case. I'd rapidly discovered that immortal athleticism also stretches—literally— to being able to bend into positions that would have been physically impossible back when I was human. If only because I'd have risked throttling myself with my own ankles. It also makes those tediously long sleepless nights *way* less boring.

"That would still make you several hundred years old," I pointed out, turning my head to look at him. "Practically ancient." His eyes were closed, and he had a faintly self-satisfied smile on his face. Me, I was still trying to get my head around the impact that never getting tired and never needing to breathe has on your sex life. If I hadn't noticed the sun coming up through a gap in the blinds, we'd probably still be at it now. I wondered briefly how much paranormal activity a hotel mattress could take before its luxury coiled springs collapsed into submission. Reaching over, I trailed my fingers down Liam's spine. His skin was pale and marked with faint silvery scars. I traced one of the more noticeable ones with the tip of my finger, following it from the base of his left shoulder blade down to his right hip. It was wider in places, and ragged. It looked like a rip, rather than a cut. "I need to go," I whispered. "Izzy will worry if I'm not back at Flora's by the time she gets there."

"Can't you text her?" asked Liam, his voice muffled in the sheets. "Tell her you're taking the morning off?"

"I have to go," I repeated, pulling away reluctantly and kneeling up on the bed. "I've got things to do," I lied, "and places to be." I wasn't going to let anyone think I was that easily won over. Treat "em mean, keep 'em keen, as they say. "You know how it is." I pulled away and began the awkward hunt for my clothes. We'd undressed each other with such speed that I actually found one of my sneakers in the bathroom sink. Liam turned onto his back and lay spreadeagled on the bed, watching as I got dressed.

"Can I see you again?" he asked.

I walked over to the bed and bent to kiss him on the forehead, dodging out of the way with a laugh as he made a half-hearted attempt to grab my backside. "Yes," I said. "You can absolutely see me again."

"Not a word to anyone in the meantime?" he said.

"Not a word." Feeling brighter than I had in months, I blew him a kiss and left.

"Do you think anyone will ever work out just how far these tunnels go?" I asked the man standing below me.

"Well," he said, "if they do find out, I'd be pleased to know." I shifted on my sandstone seat to look down at him. The low, wide ledge had been carved out of the bedrock almost two centuries earlier, during the creation of the arch-roofed cavern in which it sat. Standing in front of me, shadowed in the light from the roaring fire behind him, stood the architect of the whole ridiculous thing. Joe Williamson—aka the Mole Man of Edge Hill—was peering up at me through his pebble glasses, a benign smile on his face. I'd called in on him on the way home from the Baltic, dropping through the hatch in the crypt of St Luke's and practically skipping up the tunnel to Joe's favourite cavern. So far he'd been too polite to mention my outfit, which was somewhat unlikely for a casual wander underground. And Joe's expression was rarely anything *but* a benign smile. I sometimes wondered if Joe was firing on all his mental cylinders, but there was no denying he'd been an absolute force of nature back when he was alive. It was Joe's philanthropy that had inadvertently led to a warren of tunnels—some tiny, others awe-inspiringly cavernous—snaking underneath a good chunk of the south-eastern area of the city.

"Do you really have no idea?" I asked. The tunnels had got out of hand even before Joe died, his addiction to burrowing underground being far greater than his efficiency in drawing up proper plans. Even though the tunnels' official custodians were digging through decades of landfill to map them out, I'd assumed Joe himself would have a rough idea where it all went.

"Not really," he said, and there was a wistful note to his voice. "I suspect I did back then," 'back then' being when he was still a living, breathing surface-dweller, "but you know how memories fade." I nodded, and decided not to tell him about my own memories getting sharper by the day. I'm not that cruel. And anyway, I think he probably got the better deal.

"How many tunnels are there on our side?" I asked him. "That you remember, at least." 'Our side' meaning the section of tunnelling known only to those who've found themselves one way or another in the afterlife. Blocked from accidental human discovery by several land-falls that Joe had conveniently arranged almost two centuries earlier, it was further protected by Joe's connection to someone high up at the city council. Whether the person involved knew who Joe actually was, I couldn't be sure. I suspected they did, because how else could he persuade the authorities to go to the effort of keeping entire chunks of the city centre off limits for roadworks? Whatever the politics behind it, the section of tunnels already known to the general public was run as a tourist attraction accessed from Edge Hill, while the rest of it was left in peace for Joe and his gang of merry vampires.

"There's this one, of course." He waved a hand around the tunnel we were in. "And your own access route, although obviously it comes to rather an abrupt end these days." The tunnel that led back to Flora's had originally carried on underneath Harrington Street, through the remains of an old basement nightclub and on towards Mathew Street. At that point, it dropped into a natural—and bloody enormous—underground cavern, which was situated, appropriately enough, underneath the site of the original Cavern Club. This cavern under the Cavern had been blocked off from my side when Maria had dumped half the car park—not to mention my beloved car—down into the access tunnel. "Oh, and the side tunnels in which my charges live." Joe still had a few of what I called his 'foster vampires' hiding out in the tunnel system. I'd once asked him where they came from, but he'd just looked confused. Apparently, it had never occurred to him to question them. I thought they were probably just strays who'd somehow avoided being co-opted into the rather more dangerous vampire contingent who'd tried to off me in the summer.

"Are you sure they're safe to have around, though?" I said.

"I prefer not to judge people for their lifestyle choices," said Joe. "If anyone—human, vampire, or random mythological creature—requires sanctuary, then they are welcome to find it in these tunnels."

"Even the murderous ones?"

"Did you eat meat when you were alive?" asked Joe. He still had the same smile on his face. I really like Joe—honestly I do—but fuck *me*, he can be irritating. Especially when we both know he's got the moral high ground.

"Yes, Joe," I sighed, "I did. Steak and chips, bacon sarnies, the lot." Oh, how I missed bacon sandwiches. The salty crunch of the well-crisped rind against the soft squidge of the bread. And it had to be the cheapest white bread, not the fancy stuff. 'Plastic bread', Izzy calls it. With brown sauce. And now I'd never eat one ever again. I sighed heavily.

"Then it's not for you to judge the dietary habits of others," said Joe.

"And you think these tunnels," I waved a hand towards a small opening high on the wall that led to the side tunnels, "are the only ones your lot have access to?"

"As I said, Lilith," Joe did a little shuffle of annoyance in the dust, "I don't rightly know what goes where these days."

"You must have *some* idea," I persisted. "It would be helpful even if you could only show me a vague area on a map."

"Well now," said Joe, "that's the thing. I've never really known where things are on the surface. And the rock falls from when Mrs Silverton had her funny turn have confused things even further." 'Funny turn' was something of an understatement for Maria's deadly rage, given she killed one of Joe's pets, attempted to exorcise Billy and caused several million pounds' worth of damage to the city's infrastructure. Parts of Mathew Street were still fenced off whilst the foundations of several buildings were being made safe again, and Abercromby Square now has a permanent dip in the middle.

"Are there any bits we should be worried about?" I asked. "Do you think some areas might fall in?"

"Oh lord no," said Joe. "As you have seen for yourself, Lilith, these tunnels are incredibly strong and well built."

"They collapsed in two different places when Maria went rogue," I pointed out.

"I would call that wilful destruction," said Joe, a hurt tone in his voice, "rather than a lack of structural integrity."

"Of course," I soothed. "I'm just concerned about where these new vampires might be hiding out." I gazed around at the cavernous room we were in. I was used to Joe's excavations these days, but the sheer scale of it all was still incredible.

Joe looked pained. "You know my own friends are good people," he said. "Regardless of their origin."

"I know you feel sorry for orphan vampires," I said, "but whether I approve of it is another question entirely."

"Don't you have one living in your own building right now, Lilith?" Joe asked.

"You know I do," I said, "but Rachel's different."

"How is Rachel different?" asked Joe. He spoke kindly and patiently. But then Joe always sounds like that.

"She saved my life," I said. "She warned me about the vampires, and when they did try to attack me, she helped fight the bad guy. Who really stank, by the way. Even more than they usually do." I pulled a face.

"How did you know they were going to hurt you?" asked Joe, still in that annoyingly reasonable tone of voice.

"They clearly weren't there to talk about puppy dogs and flowers, Joe!"

"Maybe it's time you gave everyone the benefit of the doubt, Lilith," he said. "Not just those you deem acceptable." Me and Joe are never going to agree on his 'all vampires are worthy vampires' schtick, so I don't know why I bother.

"Okay, okay," I said, pushing myself off the ledge and dropping lightly down onto the tunnel floor. "I'll leave you to your good deeds. But if you remember anything about where the tunnels might go then you let me know. Promise?"

"I will do my best, Lilith," said Joe primly. "As always."

I left Joe gazing after me as I disappeared at speed down the tunnel that leads to Harrington Street. I'm pretty good at it now and have my own little routine for the trip, which involves propelling myself off the left-hand wall with my feet in order make the sharp turn to the right that bends the tunnel halfway along its length. I then bounce up to touch the St Luke's hatch, before putting my head down and doing the last half-mile or so as fast as possible. This time I even managed to stop before my head hit the wall of rubble that now marks the end of the tunnel. As soon as I clambered out of the hatch into the car park next to Flora's, my phone pinged. Sliding it out of my jacket pocket, I swore as I saw the two missed calls from Eadric, followed by a text message. Nothing good ever comes of Eadric Silverton needing to contact me urgently. The text message said nothing more than '*call me*', so after I'd closed the hatch and made sure it was padlocked, I did just that. He picked up on the second ring. "Could you pop over, Lilith?" Eadric said. "There's someone here I'd like you to meet."

"Don't tell me," I said, scuffing my trainers in the dirt, "Ol' Billy Boy's wanting to talk business."

"How do you know that?" he asked, surprise audible in his voice.

"Met one of his envoys last night," I said, already wondering how I was going to keep a poker face in front of Eadric. There was no way I was going to admit to last night's gymnastics with Liam—I just hoped my partner in crime felt the same way. It was unlikely that either of our supposed leaders would look kindly on such inter-tribe fraternisation. At least, not before the head honchos had agreed terms. Which I really hoped they did, because Liam was extremely talented in certain departments and I was definitely up for a rematch in the very near future. I grinned to myself as I walked, thinking about some of the more athletic events of the previous evening.

"What was their name?" asked Eadric. From the clunking sound behind him, I suspected he'd walked into a different room. Perhaps he didn't want to be overheard.

"Can't remember," I lied. "We didn't chat much." That bit was true, at least—there'd been far more interesting things to do than sitting around talking. I started walking down towards the Liver Building.

"Well, we've got just the one visitor today," said Eadric quietly. Definitely trying to avoid eavesdroppers. His voice dropped even lower. "And it's the Bastard himself." I stopped dead in the middle of Castle Street, forcing a Tesco delivery van to brake suddenly. I gave the driver the benefit of my middle finger as I stalked to the other side of the road. I'd assumed Liam had come up to Liverpool alone, purely to scout things out. But nope, the merry king of all old England had been hiding in the wings all the time. Ugh. Although it was definitely a relief to know I wouldn't have to stand in the same room as Liam and the Silvertons and somehow keep a straight face.

"Am I really going to meet William the Conqueror?" I asked, dodging traffic on the Strand and walking slowly down the side of the Liver Building. I wasn't sure whether to be excited (William the actual bloody Conqueror!) or terrified (William the actual bloody Conqueror!).

"Yes," said Eadric, and I could have sworn I heard him sigh. "Yes, you are. Please do your best not to cause all-out war."

"Oh, ye of little faith," I said, hopping over the gate to the basement steps and spooking a pigeon. "Fucksake!" I flapped a hand at it, sending it spinning across Canada Boulevard. Its progress was stopped by a bollard and I was relieved to see it hop back onto its feet with a faintly stunned expression on its feathery face. "Oops."

"What are you doing?" asked Eadric.

"Wrestling a pigeon," I said truthfully, bending down to unlock the door to the Silverton's private entrance. "Be up in a sec." Cutting the call before Eadric could ask any more questions, I stepped into the basement and locked the main door behind me. The lift was already at the bottom waiting for me, so I stepped in and pulled the old shutter gates closed before me. As it clanked slowly upwards, I wondered how grim William might actually look. It couldn't be anything pleasant, given what happened to his corpse. I hadn't been kidding about him going pop when they wedged him into his grave. It was one of the few things I've always remembered from older history. On the other hand, there was no way he could have been wandering around for centuries with his insides hanging out. Maybe he'd been stitched back together at some point, like a medieval Frankenstein's monster. Regardless, it probably wasn't considered polite to retch in the face of a guest. I practiced my polite face as I rose slowly upwards. When the lift finally reached the Silverton's floor, I pulled the gate open and stepped out, still determinedly poker-faced.

"What on earth are you doing?" asked Eadric Silverton in a low hiss. He was standing in the doorway to his main reception room, clearly waiting for me.

"Practising keeping a straight face," I said. "Does he smell of rot?"

"What are you talking about?" asked Eadric. "And what on earth are you wearing?"

I looked down and saw that, as well as showing an awful lot of cleavage, my dress was also filthy where the hem had dragged in the dirt of the tunnel. "Thought I'd dress for the occasion," I shrugged. I could hear Nik talking in the other room, and another voice too low to pick up properly.

"For god's sake, Lilith," said Eadric, standing aside so I could walk past him, "please do you best to not humiliate us. Just this once."

I narrowed my eyes at him as I walked past. "Absolute cheek of it," I muttered. "I am perfectly capable of managing in polite society. However stinky it might be." As I stepped into the room, Nik turned towards me.

"Afternoon, Lil," he said. A man stood with his back to us, gazing out of the window across the Mersey. "We'd like you to meet our guest," he went on. "This is William of Normandy." The man at the window turned to face me, his hand outstretched and a grin on his face.

"Nice to meet you," said Liam O'Connor.

Caution: Risk Of Exploding Revenant

I stood rooted to the carpet, rigid with horror. Liam was still holding his hand out for me to shake and Nik just looked plain confused. "William?" I asked slowly.

Liam nodded. "The very same," he said, dropping his hand. "You'll understand I prefer to travel under a pseudonym. Safety first, as they say."

Eadric came to stand next to Liam. William. *Jesus fucking Christ I had sex with William the Conqueror*, screeched a panicked voice in the back of my head. *I got naked and jiggy with one of the most famous kings in British history ohmygodohmygod—*

We tried to warn you.

SHUT UP.

"Everything okay, Lilith?" asked Eadric. He gave a faintly embarrassed laugh and turned to Liam. "Lilith was under the impression you would look as you supposedly did at the time of your death," he said. "The truth is clearly something of a surprise. Isn't it, Lilith?" He looked at me with a *'please for the love of all that is holy do not fuck this up for us'* expression in his eyes.

"YOU LYING FUCKING BASTARD!" I yelled. Before anyone could stop me, I kicked Liam as hard as I could. My aim was excellent and he folded like a pack of cards, curling up on the floor and making quiet gasping noises. Nik and Eadric were both staring silently at me, expressions of pure horror on their faces. I pushed past them and dragged Liam to his feet.

"As I said," he hissed up at me through gritted teeth, "I travel under a pseudonym." He was still clutching himself. Good.

Eadric came to his senses first. "What the *hell* are you playing at?" he asked, grabbing me and pulling me away from Liam. "Have you lost your bloody mind? William is an honoured guest of this city, Lilith O'Reilly."

"He's a lying, good-for-nothing bastard, is what he is," I growled, pulling my arm free. "And you can get your hands off me this instant, Eadric Silverton." Liam had seemingly recovered himself and was clambering to his feet, watching us with a look of amusement on his face. I stepped forward and shoved him hard, and he stepped backwards. "What the *fuck* were you playing at?" I said. "'*Oh I'm no one important, don't mind me, why not come up for a nightcap*' YOU ABSOLUTE FUCKING SHITHEAD!" I slapped him hard before he could stop me. Eadric stepped forward, but Liam put up a hand to stop him.

"I'm fine, Silverton," he said, and now there was an air of authority in his voice I hadn't heard before. "Lilith has good reason to be angry with me."

"Oh my god," I turned to see Nik watching us and clearly struggling not to laugh, "you're not telling me...you two..." he trailed off and waved a hand at us in a vague gesture.

Eadric just looked stunned."Oh, don't look so bloody shocked," I snarled at him. "People do have sex, you know."

"Excellent sex, to be fair," said Liam and I whirled round to glare at him.

"Under dishonest circumstances," I said sharply. "You are a lying bastard and you can fuck off back to your own stupid bloody territory right now."

"I think it might be best if you leave, Lilith," said Eadric.

"And have this fuckwit involved in how we run the place?" I said. "Over my very dead body, Eadric Silverton."

"That's enough," said Eadric. He put a hand on my arm again and I stared down at it, wondering how my head hadn't exploded from rage. "We'll talk about this another time."

"DON'T TOUCH ME." Woop, there it was. The Voice itself. Eadric was clearly getting used to it, because he didn't move his hand. "GET OFF ME." He reluctantly let go and I stalked towards Liam, who was finally beginning to look nervous. "Get out of my city," I said to him, "and do not come back."

"We should talk," said Liam. He had a strange expression on his face. "Properly." He looked over at the Silvertons and then back at me. "Alone."

"I am not going to talk to you," I said, "whether alone or otherwise. You need to leave. Now."

"What if I refuse?" asked Liam.

"Lil—"started Eadric.

"Shut up, Eadric," I said. "This has nothing to do with you. I don't like liars and I never have. And *Wil*liam here is the grandaddy of all liars."

"Just because we went to bed together," said Liam, "there's no reason to—"

"Get out," I said.

"Or what?" Liam was looking amused now, which wasn't doing anything for my temper. "Going to make me?"

And that was the point at which I threw William the Conqueror out of a very high window. Technically, it was 'through' rather than 'out', the window itself being closed. Nik and Eadric could do nothing except stare in horror as I grabbed Liam with a strength even I hadn't known I possessed, before launching him as hard as possible. The glass was reinforced with iron bars, which slowed his flight and thus saved the general public from witnessing a man hitting the pavement at high velocity. Instead, Liam dropped downwards, landing on the lower roof of the building with a crunching thud that was audible from where we stood, a floor above him. I stalked over to the broken window and leaned out. Below me, Liam was getting to his feet and brushing himself down. A creaking noise made me look up to where Bella was peering over at the chaos.

"It's okay, baby," I called up to her, "Mummy's just throwing out the trash." She gave me a long, slow blink of acknowledgement and slowly creaked upright again. When I looked back down, Liam was gone.

～

"Ha!" I ducked back into the room and turned to face the Silvertons. "It's hammer time, baby." I even did a little gleeful shuffle-dance. How *dare* he lie to me like that? And on my own territory, as well. The absolute cheek of it.

Oh, said the city, ***so you want nothing to do with the politics, but suddenly it's your territory when you've got a point to prove?***

Yes. Shush now. The city shushed, but I was pretty sure I could hear muffled grumbling just on the edge of hearing.

"And what are we supposed to do now?" asked Eadric. He was standing in the centre of the room with his hands held out as if in supplication. Nik was sitting in an armchair with a huge grin on his face.

"About what?" I asked. "There's nothing to do about anything. We had an unwanted visitor and I got rid of him. End of story."

"Aah," said Nik, "that's where you're wrong. William won't simply go away, just because you've told him to. If it was that simple, English monarchy would have a very different history." He was still smiling. "It was certainly satisfying to watch though, I'll give you that."

"Lilith," said Eadric slowly, "you just threw one of the greatest kings this country has ever known out of a very high window. He isn't going to forgive that."

"His greatness depends which side you're on," I said. "And I'm not going to forgive him for being a lying bastard."

"How did you, erm, meet him?" asked Eadric.

"In the pub," I said, and heard Nik choke back an inelegant snorting noise.

"In the pub?" Eadric looked genuinely incredulous. "You just happened to bump into William the Conqueror in the *pub*?"

"How was I supposed to know who he was?" I said indignantly. "He told me his name was Liam O'bloody-Connor! Izzy did say it was a bit convenient that a hot dead guy just happened to be in the same pub as us, but, well…" I trailed off, but then thought of something else. "Hang on a minute," I said, "what happened to him being old and fat and going pop?" I looked from Eadric to Nik and back again, but their expressions were blank. "William the Conqueror was a grumpy old fat bloke when he died," I went on, "remember? Not a decent-looking bloke in his forties with a barbershop haircut and designer clothes. So who, exactly, was *that*?" I pointed to where a breeze was blowing in through the broken window.

"That," said Eadric, "was the real William of Normandy. He'd used a stand-in for years, for security reasons. Then he died, and the stand-in was forced to keep up the pretence for the rest of his life. It happened whilst I was still alive, so of course it wouldn't have occurred to me that William himself might not have been quite as dead as I'd assumed. And I'd left his," Eadric hesitated, "*employ* by then anyway, so all I knew was hearsay. The reality of the matter has been a very recent discovery."

"What," I said, "the fuck?" I stood there in stunned silence for a long moment while this new information sank in. "You're telling me that all those stories about William and his Domesday Book and his general asshattery were actually all down to a stunt double?"

"No," said Eadric patiently, "the Domesday Book was definitely William's doing. I helped collate some of it, remember. He set up the stand-in later, after one too many assassination attempts. And then the real William died, and was presumably most surprised to wake up again shortly afterwards. The stand-in William was becoming increasingly unpopular, so the real deal apparently decided to make the most of immortality and just left the country to it."

"And thus, the monarchy proves itself useless yet again," I griped. "Nice to see they started how they meant to go on."

"Lilith," said Eadric patiently, "you forget just how old some of us are. Nik here is a youngster compared to myself or William." Nik twirled an elegant hand in a regal wave. "And Ivo is, as you know, even older."

"Well, maybe some of you could have used the extra time to sort out the country's ridiculous political systems, is all I'm saying. Fight poverty and inequality. Do some good with your eternal lives."

"Says the woman who spends most of her time ricocheting round the city causing mayhem," said Nik. "Instead of volunteering at the cat rescue centre, or whatever it is you think would be the best use of your time."

"Grimm would get jealous if I spent time with other cats," I said. "And I absolutely do not ricochet around the city creating mayhem, *thank* you. I don't find mayhem, mayhem finds me. I'd be very happy for mayhem to piss off and concentrate on someone else for a while."

"Well, that's not going to happen if you insist on throwing people out of windows, is it?" said Eadric. He sounded weary. "We have been in this territory for centuries, Lilith. Centuries of peace and quiet and hardly anyone knowing we even exist. Then you come along and, well…" he trailed off.

"We are not going over this again," I said. I knew what was coming. The whole '*well something happened when you died and now you're going to have to deal with the consequences*' schtick was getting tedious. "I can't help that everything's gone tits up recently, anymore than I can help the fact that a sodding vampire pushed me off a sodding roof. I'm here now and I realise I'm not what you expected, but I can't be something I'm not."

"Oh," said Nik drily, "I have no doubt you will only ever be one hundred percent Lilith, through and through."

I glowered at him. "And what, exactly, is that supposed to mean?"

"For what it's worth," said Nik, "I think William deserved what you just did to him." Eadric opened his mouth to say something, but Nik stopped him. "No," he said, "hear me out. Lil meets someone who takes her fancy and he tells her his name is Liam. Bit close to William if you ask me, but then that would only occur to someone who knew the connection. And he always was an overconfident little shit, from what I've heard. She thinks he's a safe bet, and no one can deny she deserves a bit of fun. But the fun turns out to be wrapped up in the body of her territory's potential enemy, which she didn't know on account of him being a deceitful rogue." Nik shrugged. "Reckon I'd put someone through a window if they pulled that trick on me."

"Thank you, Nik," I said, "finally someone who remembers that women's rights actually exist." He tipped an invisible hat at me and picked up a book from the side table. "Why is everyone so scared of him, though?"

"Don't ask me," said Nik. "Like the man said," he gestured at Eadric, "I haven't been around long. Not compared to our lord and master, here." He made a show of going back to reading.

I opened my mouth to say something, but Eadric beat me to it. "I'm no one's lord *or* master," he said, "before you start. Merely a figurehead. And an administrator." He sighed. "Which never seems to get any simpler."

"You *are* in charge, though," I pointed out. "There's no point denying it." Eadric moved to sit behind his enormous mahogany desk, which only made him look even more official. I walked over to the broken window and peered out. There was no sign of dead kings seeking vengeance. Yet. "I'm not saying you're not perfectly capable of being in charge," I said, turning to look at Eadric. "But why all this ridiculous background bickering about territories that no one in the living world even knows about? I've been dead six months now, and most of that has been with a background of grumbling about who owns which bit and where. Who even *cares* who's in charge?" I walked across and leaned on the desk, facing Eadric. "Seriously," I said, "who cares? Because I bloody don't."

"I care," said Eadric quietly. "Because I don't want people—*our* people, Lilith—being oppressed. Not by me, and not by anyone else. I do my best to stay out of the way, but others wouldn't. I can promise you that, should William gain control of other territories, he would rapidly force many into subservience. Is that what you want?"

"Why would he do that?" I asked, thinking beyond my earlier fury, back to the previous evening with the person I knew as Liam. He'd been cute and funny and flattering, and had seemed genuinely interested in me. He'd seemed to *care*. But now I was supposed to just accept that he was a duplicitous shit-heel and crack on with it. My head was throbbing from the strain of trying to keep on top of the ridiculousness that seemed to be par for the course these days.

"Why would who do what? And *hello*, my darlings!" Gaultier Mapp swept into the room—'swept' being the operative word, as he was wearing a full length cloak over what appeared to be a formal evening suit. "Aah yes," he said, seeing my raised eyebrows, "rather dramatic, no?" He did a twirl in the middle of the room. "I'm off out for dinner with Heggie and the ever-delightful Kitty, so I thought I'd make an effort for once."

"As if you ever don't make an effort," I said, grinning at him. "All you need is a white mask and Sarah Brightman singing on top of one of the towers." Of all the very weird and sometimes wonderful people I've met since the day I fell off the fire escape, Gaultier Mapp is my favourite. I'd never tell him that, though—his ego's big enough to fill an entire room as it is. A tall Black man with cropped hair and the sort of eyelashes women spend a fortune to achieve, Mapp likes to dress, well—*experimentally*, is probably the best word for it. He is also over eight hundred years old and originally from Herefordshire, although you'd never know that from hearing him speak. He has that sort of mid-range accent that's hard to pin down, with an occasional twang of Scouse that comes from having spent decades living in Dingle. These days he mostly hides out at his shop up on Renshaw Street. It's supposed to be a bookshop, but as well as the towering stacks of hardbacks that are constantly threatening to turn into a paper-based tsunami, Mapp likes to buy and sell curiosities. I once asked him to explain what exactly constituted a 'curiosity' and he said it was anything that made him curious. Which is probably why the entire place looks like a compulsive hoarder set up shop in the back of Doctor Parnassus's caravan. I half expect mice to come dancing out from a mouse-organ every time I venture to the back of the store. "Did you know we had unwanted guests in town?" I asked him.

Mapp frowned slightly. "There are always *potential* guests," he said, "wandering the streets of this heathen city. It's why I like the place so much." He swung himself round and down into an armchair that matched the one Nik was currently sprawling on. "Whether or not they're wanted," he went on, "depends on individual circumstance."

"Lilith met William last night," said Eadric.

"She did more than meet him," snorted Nik from behind his book, "she checked him out very thoroughly indeed." I gave him my patented hard stare, but he couldn't see me through his book, which, going by its cover, was yet another Mills & Boon. Nik might have left poetry far behind him, but he just can't bring himself to drop the cheesy romance. I'm fully expecting him to pull a *Shirley Valentine* one of these days and run off with a waiter from that Greek place up on Duke Street.

"Shut up," I hissed, but it was too late.

Mapp's eyes lit up. "You did *not*?" he crowed. "Lilith O'Reilly, you dark, dark horse!" His eyebrows waggled alarmingly. "Tell me *all* about it, you little minx!"

"I'm not telling anyone anything," I said, "which is more than can be said for Liam sodding O'Connor."

"Oh, he's gone back to his old name then," said Mapp.

"You're telling me it's not fake?" I asked incredulously. "Liam *O'Connor*?"

"Of course it's fake," said Mapp in an annoyingly reasonable tone of voice. "But it belonged to a real person way back when. William's been using that name on and off for centuries now. I do hope he's dropped that terrible faux-Irish accent, though. He never could pull it off properly."

"Why are you going out for dinner?" I asked, belatedly registering the start of the conversation, "when none of you eat?"

"Heggie does," said Mapp. "Kitty and I just have wine, and I drink it for both of us."

"Heggie eats?"

"It would be stranger if he didn't," said Mapp, "surely?"

"But I thought Heggie…well…"

Mapp laughed, a deep, rumbling noise from deep inside his chest. "Darling," he said, "Heggie is human. Always has been. He eats and drinks like a human, and he'll get old and die like one, too. Which is utterly tragic, of course. But there isn't much I can do about it."

"But," I didn't know where to start with this new information, "I don't want Heggie to get old and die! I thought he was one of us!"

"He *is* one of us," said Mapp. "He just happens to be alive. Now," he clapped his hands together and looked between me and Eadric, "what are we to do about the vampires?"

"What vampires?" I asked. By the looks on Eadric and Nik's faces, they were thinking the same thing.

"The ones that were spotted up in Kenny last night," said Mapp. He meant Kensington, the area of Liverpool wedged between Everton and

Edge Hill that even in this age of gentrification still has what estate agents like to call 'character'. "The real deal, no less. Thankfully, the locals are assuming it was either a student prank or would-be muggers."

"How do you know they were real?" I asked.

Mapp looked at me with one eyebrow arched sharply. "Are you telling me I wouldn't know a vampire from a spotty teen, Lilith O'Reilly? And me with all my centuries of experience? Not to mention my literary background in that sort of thing."

"Mapp," I said patiently, "you wrote that book in the twelfth century. Sorry to break it to you, but it isn't on the general school curriculum these days."

"Education isn't what it used to be," Mapp sniffed. "Anyway," he went on, "they're the real deal. As real as any of us here in this room. And they're not the friendly type, I can tell you that much."

"Are they the same ones who attacked me up in Anfield?" I asked.

"That's the assumption," said Mapp. "Joe's lot don't come out much these days. Learned their lesson when they took you on, didn't they?" He grinned at me. "So yeah, got to be the Anfield lot. Right area, as well."

"The fact they jumped me in Anfield doesn't mean that's where they're based," I pointed out. "They could be anywhere." Vampires don't turn into bats, and they don't fly—but they can move as fast as revenants and they do it in shadowy flickers like characters from a horror movie. What we were currently calling the Anfield vampires had made it clear they wanted rid of me before I could upset their plans too much. They didn't explain themselves very well—all the vampires I've met so far have issues with speaking properly; they'd never get a role in a *Buffy* remake. But I got the distinct idea they were planning to take over the city. Or the world. You know, in that undramatic and subtle way vampires have had since the dawn of time. But before they could chomp me with their nasty yellow teeth, I'd impaled their scary leader with a tree branch through the head. Doesn't matter what the mythology says—a stake through the brain kills most things, already dead or not.

"True," said Mapp. "And gods only know where they might have made their lair. This city is complicated underneath the surface, as you well know. Both metaphorically *and* physically. They could be anywhere."

"Word on the street is that they're wanting to go public," said Eadric unexpectedly. "At least, that's the impression Elizabeth has. I spoke to her yesterday, before William turned up."

"She already knew?" I asked. Eadric nodded. "Then why hasn't she mentioned it before?"

"Territories are autonomous, Lilith," he said. "It's not Elizabeth's responsibility to keep us informed of activity further south, any more than it's our job to update her on things happening in our own region. God knows," he went on, "it would be embarrassing if others discovered the sort of ridiculous behaviour that somehow keeps happening up here."

I scowled at him. "Doesn't matter who or what is causing ridiculousness," I said. "You all need to be talking to each other in order to stay safe."

"No one's refusing to talk to each other," said Eadric. "We just don't feel the need to involve everyone in our private affairs."

"You all seem interested enough in mine," I pointed out.

"Aah well," said Mapp, his brown eyes twinkling at me, "It's more interesting than *Emmerdale*."

THE UNSAVOURY
HABITS OF MERMAIDS

"Hey love," Mum sounded brighter than anyone had right to be at—I checked the clock next to my bed—six in the bloody morning. "You around today?" I'd been practicing zen-like meditation, hoping to get a break from the endless memories that were still dropping into my head 24/7. I wasn't quite yogi standards just yet, but I'd managed to drift off into a very nice daydream in which I had nothing to worry about except floating. And then the phone rang. Pushing myself upright on the bed, I put it on hands-free and stared at it in confusion.

"I'm around *every* day," I said, "as you well know. Why do you ask?"

"Well," she said, "your dad's going to a classic car show with Brian the post," 'Brian-the-Post' being a friend of my parents who works for Royal Mail, "so I thought I'd treat myself to a day out."

"You haven't been up here in years," I said. "How come you've suddenly developed an urge to do the tourist thing?"

"Well," Mum said in a hurt tone, "if you'd rather I didn't come to see you—"

"No, no," I interrupted hurriedly, "it would be lovely to see you. I've got the day off from Flora's, anyway. What time are you likely to be in town?"

"Well, I've promised to go visit Geor—Nikolaus, first," she said, "so it'll be sometime—"

"Oh, so *that's* why you're coming up," I snarked at the phone. "Visiting your pretentious little friend up in his fancy little tower, is it?" Mum started laughing. The cheeky fucking mare. "And don't laugh at me!"

"Oh Lil," she snorted, "you're so funny." I huffed at the phone. "Yes, I'm visiting Nik. I'd like to talk to him about...*things*, and he's been kind enough to invite me up to visit."

"And you couldn't give me more warning than this?" I clambered off the bed and shoved my feet viciously into my slippers. A ripping noise came from one of them and it flapped against the floor as I stalked out of my bedroom and into the living room. Kitty was sitting on the windowsill, dressed in a silk vest top and long floaty skirt over bare feet. She gave me an enquiring look, and I shrugged helplessly in return.

"It was only decided last night," said Mum. "I thought you'd be pleased." I walked into the kitchen to find Grimm staring accusingly at the closed door of the cupboard in which I keep the cat food. I pulled it open and left him to it. Unlocking the kitchen door, I went outside and sat on the top platform of the fire escape, the city still mostly dark below me. I heard cartons falling out of the cupboard behind me and the faint hiss of a cat who's looking for his favourite flavour and been left disappointed.

"I'll go shopping later," I said in the vague direction of the kitchen door, "I promise." There was a distinct huffing noise and the sound of a foil lid being dragged slowly off a carton. "I *am* pleased," I said to the phone. "You took me by surprise, that's all."

"You know I've wanted to chat to Nik for ages," said Mum reproachfully.

"Yeah, I know," I said, feeling mean. "It's just weird, you know? All..." I waved my hands in the air in a gesture she couldn't actually see, "...*this*, isn't necessarily something I want my parents involved in."

"Well, I'm not your parents," she said, "am I? I'm your mother. And an O'Reilly too, don't forget." As if I was ever going to forget that my own mother is actually as spooky as all fuck, despite still being of the living and breathing variety. Not that I knew that when I was still alive, of course. Oh, no—it took a fall from a very high building and the reappearance of my dead aunt for my own bloody mother to admit that actually, she's been seeing dead people for as long as she can remember and of course it doesn't matter that I no longer need to breathe because why should a minor case of death come between family, anyway? And she is indeed an O'Reilly, same as me—and same as Kitty and my grandma and every other female member of my mum's side of the family, going back who knew how many generations. Growing up, it had somehow never occurred to me to find it weird that me and mum had a different surname from my dad, despite my parents having been married since they were in their teens. I just accepted the fact that women in my family keep their own name.

"Mum," I said, "do you think it's the O'Reilly bloodline that carries the weirdness gene?"

"Who are you calling weird?" asked my mother. "Yes," she said, before I could answer, "I'd imagine so. Maybe we should prod the family tree properly at some point."

"Huh," I said, "might be best left un-prodded, in all honestly. God knows what freakishness we might find. What time will I see you?"

"I'm going to have a cuppa," she said, "then set off. Your lovely landlord has given me special permission to park underneath the Liver Building, so that's exciting." I rolled my eyes so hard it was a wonder they didn't pop out and spin off down Harrington Street. "Anyway, Nik says I'm to ask you if you'd like to come over around lunchtime. That should give us plenty of time to chat before you turn up." Before I turn up and start annoying people, is what she was too polite to say. As I stared down at the street below me, Billy appeared from the Button Street end and started setting up his patch for the day. I waved as he turned and spotted me.

"Yeah," I said to Mum, "that's fine. It'll be nice to see you."

"On your home turf for a change," said Mum, "how nice is that?"

"Lovely," I agreed. "You just have to promise you won't fall for Eadric's charm. And whatever he says, I am *not* moving to Albert Dock."

"Honestly, Lilith," she said, "you are so ungrateful at times. Some people would give their eye teeth for a rent-free flat, let alone a penthouse in one of the most beautiful spots on earth."

"Yeah," I said, "but most people aren't being bribed with said flats because they've found themselves dead and unburied, are they?"

"There is that. Anyway, love," she went on brightly, "I'll see you later."

"Later." She rang off.

I shoved the phone into the waistband of my leggings as I made my way down the steps to where Billy sat. "You're up and at 'em early this morning," he said. "Got plans?"

"I do now," I said. "My mum's visiting."

Billy tilted his head to look at me. "You don't seem very enthusiastic," he said. "Do you not get on with your mother?"

I slumped down onto the pavement next to him and leaned back against the wall. A jogger appeared out of the misty morning gloom from the Button Street end. He eyed us curiously as he passed—the woman in ripped slippers and the homeless bloke in a sleeping bag. I made a show of flipping my middle finger at him and he picked up speed. "Dunno what you're looking at!" I called after him.

Billy grinned. "You're a funny one, Red," he said. "Can't make head nor tail of you half the time, honestly I can't."

"Well, that makes two of us," I said. "Because right now I have absolutely no fucking idea what I'm doing."

"Doing with what?" asked Billy.

I turned to look at him, my head still back against the wall. "Life, Billy," I said. "Life, the universe and everything. It's supposed to be finite, you know? All this," I waved my hands in the air, "is supposed to be for a set amount of time, and then we die. That's what keeps most people going, isn't it? The fear of dying before doing everything they want to do." I sighed and closed my eyes. "So what incentive is there to do anything when we're never going to run out of time?"

There was a long silence, then Billy spoke. "I reckon," he said, "things will still happen, even if we do nothing." I cracked open one eyelid to peer at him. "Think about it, Red," he went on. "Even if you and I did absolutely nothing—literally just sat here all day and night forever, doing nothing more than watching people coming and going—things would still happen around us. And those things would affect us. Your Izzy would still open Flora's and serve customers, same as she always does. But it would be changed by your absence. Doesn't matter who does the bulk of the work in there," he ignored my frown, "the place is affected by your presence."

"I have absolutely no idea what you're talking about," I said.

"Look at it this way," he said earnestly, clearly warming to his topic, "everyone's a spider and their cobwebs tangle up with each other, whether we like it or not. Even if one of those spiders disappears into thin air, its cobwebs are still there."

"Nope," I said, "still not getting you."

"Then you'll just have to work it out for yourself, Red," said Billy. "But your existence gives balance to the world—to all the worlds—and so does everyone else's. You can't escape it any more than I can."

"I don't *want* to escape it," I said. "I just don't want to have to think about it all the time!"

"With great power," said Billy, "comes great responsibility. Or something like that, anyway. I don't quite remember."

"That's a line from a bloody comic, Billy." I shook my head at him. "And life isn't a comic book."

"I thought it was a film," he said.

"Closing line of number fifteen in the *Amazing Fantasy* series by Marvel Comics," I said. "Came out in nineteen-sixty-two. Stan Lee didn't come up with it himself, he was paraphrasing something that originally appeared in political decrees during the French Revolution. Seventeen-ninety-three, or thereabouts. Wasn't Voltaire either, however many people make stupid memes crediting him with it. And don't ask me how I know all that," I scrunched my eyes up and rubbed at my temples, "because I haven't a fucking clue. I've got enough random trivia in my head to keep a quiz team busy for years."

"How does it work?" asked Billy.

"How do you mean?" I opened my eyes to find him looking at me with genuine interest. "My endless, headache-inducing fount of pointlessly random fun facts?"

Billy nodded. "Yeah," he said, "that sort of thing. How did you come to know it all in the first place?"

I puffed out my cheeks and huffed into the chilly autumn air, gazing down towards North John Street. The streets were getting busier now, office workers and early shoppers beginning to replace the deliverymen and self-righteous joggers. "As far as I can tell," I said, "it's all stuff that I've actually heard or learned. Even if I've just caught a snippet of a television programme or skimmed an article in a magazine, stuff like that. A bit like having a photographic memory, but to a ridiculous degree."

"Could be useful, though," said Billy.

"Not unless you want to know stuff like the timeline of the members of The Damned," I said. "Dad was into them, so I guess I picked that stuff up from him. People are often surprised to discover Gary Holton briefly replaced Dave Vanian as lead singer for a Scottish tour in nineteen-seventy-eight. Is that the sort of useful information you're talking about? Or I could probably quote you the lyrics of most Taylor Swift songs, if she's more your thing." That was thanks to local radio, which Izzy often had on in the background at Flora's.

"What about politics?" asked Billy. "Or history of the monarchy? Maybe theories of the undead, that sort of thing. Stuff that might actually be useful."

"Some of it's coming back," I said. "But slowly. I could give you a list of American Presidents and be reasonably sure it was in the right order, but I couldn't tell you what any of them looked like."

"Aah," said Billy, "but that'll be because there was no such thing as cameras back then, won't it? You can't know what people looked like if there's no photos of them."

"Maybe," I said, "we'll just have to wait for them to rise from the grave." I grinned at him. "Imagine the fuss if Roosevelt turned up?"

"People would just assume it was someone in costume," shrugged Billy. "No one would believe it was real."

"But we'd know," I said, "wouldn't we?"

"True enough," he agreed. "Heard any more of Laithlind's daughter?" The sudden change of conversation threw me. Mab was the daughter of Ivo and Maria—yes, Eadric's best friend and his wife, because this stuff is never not complicated—and had tried to kill me up at Anfield cemetery back in the summer. And did I mention that Mab had been in contact with her father for over a century without him bothering to tell her that her mother was still alive? At least, she was alive until she pushed me that one step too far. Which is why, in all fairness, Mab has good reason to dislike me. Anyway, I survived the encounter, obviously, but Mab escaped with help from her idiot father and I'd been left to explain the damage. Mostly to Eadric, who'd had to pull major strings with his contacts at the council in order to get the northern catacomb stabilised and fenced off from public access. I was supposed to go down there at some point and help clear it out. It's basically the undead version of community service.

"Nope," I said eventually, "no sign. Or at least, not that anyone's telling us."

"Perhaps it's better to live in ignorance," said Billy. "At least for now."

I nodded, still gazing down the street. Maybe I'd go see if Daisy was around, a swim might do me good. "Yup," I said, "you're probably right." Which just goes to show how wrong we can both be.

Daisy could usually be found bobbing about in the river at this time in the morning, if you knew where to look. She likes watching the ferries going in and out, although I've had to have words with her about clinging onto their bows in order to joyride her way over to Seacombe. Luckily they don't start running until after seven in the morning, so only a few months of the year are dark enough for her to get a jaunt in before it's light enough for passengers to spot her clinging to the front of the boat. According to Todd, who was on board the ferry the last time it had happened, a passenger saw her and screamed, causing panic to spread. Someone found the captain and told him he had to stop and call for the lifeboat. Todd swore he overheard the captain saying, 'Aah, she'll give up soon, let her have her fun.' Which just goes to prove my suspicions that more people round here know about the weird stuff than are letting on.

Of course, the one morning I could have used the distraction, there was no sign of Daisy as I wandered along Kings Parade. I considered running along to Otterspool to see if she was lurking there, but it was late enough now that the river front was dotted with people on their way to work. And they'd definitely notice if someone ran past them fast enough to cause a draught. Weirdly, I can get away with the speedy running in busier places, because people are less likely to notice me appearing and reappearing. Sighing, I turned back towards the Strand—which was when I spotted the police boat. It was almost all the way across on the other side of the Mersey and still enough that I assumed it must be at anchor. Did police boats even have anchors? I wasn't sure. But it certainly didn't seem to be heading anywhere. Instead, it bobbed around in the water whilst several people on board peered over the side. Now, the one thing Daisy loves more than ferries is police boats. She finds it amusing to swim underneath them and knock on the base of the hull, in order to give those onboard a fright. I've never known her do it to the coastguard boat—I get the distinct impression she respects them more. My eyesight's good enough these days that I can see what's going on the other side of the river, so I leaned against an iron railing post and settled in to watch the drama. One of the people on the boat held a long stick, which they were using to poke about into the water in front of them. God, I really hoped Daisy wasn't pushing her luck by playing dead in the water again. Asrais do look *basically* human, if you squint a bit. They have long limbs that are out of proportion with the rest of their body and they're also incredibly pale. Daisy's hair is so blonde I thought she might have albinism the first time I'd met her, but she's got blue eyes and surprisingly dark eyelashes. She also has webbed fingers and toes. She certainly wasn't someone the police were going to ignore. I was just debating whether to swim over and get underneath the boat in order to pull her away when a splash from the water below made me look down. Daisy was treading water and grinning up at me. The tide was higher than usual, so at least I didn't have to shout. "What are you *doing*?" I hissed, leaning over the heavy chain link fence. "You'll be seen, you idiot!" I love Daisy to bits, you understand, but she can be *really* hard to manage at times. She gestured over towards the police boat. "I know," I said. "What were you doing?" Daisy shook her head vehemently. "Wasn't it you in the water by them?" She shook her head again, then dropped it to one side and did a good impression of someone being dead. "A body?" She nodded, then pointed to herself. "Your body?" She nodded again. "But you're here in front of me," I pointed out, "so it can't be your body they're looking at." Daisy gave me a long look—one I've learned to interpret as her considering just how stupid I might actually be. Then she mimed 'dead' again, before holding her hands up in front of her face and chomping at nothing, as though holding invisible chicken drumsticks. This was followed by another sharp point toward the boat, along with a very cross expression. Looking over to where something ominously human-sized was now being dragged out of the water and onto the boat, I put two and two together and really wished I hadn't. "You're not telling me you'd stashed a *corpse*?" Daisy grinned and nodded again, looking very pleased with herself. I felt sick. As long as I'd known her—which to be fair was only about six months—Daisy had had a habit of stashing food in the hidden crevices of the many horrible things that lurk at the bottom of the Mersey. She'd use anything —sunken boats, cars, even the occasional concrete blocks that looked suspiciously like they'd once had human feet embedded inside. I've only been right down to the riverbed once, and that was enough for me— these days I stay nearer the surface, where the worst you're likely to encounter is a grumpy pike. Daisy did once try to introduce me to a family of porpoise, but they just seemed confused. "Where did you find it?" I asked her. It's actually rare for bodies to be found around in the Mersey itself—the currents are so strong that everything gets washed out to sea pretty quickly. To my horror, Daisy pointed at me, then over towards Pier Head. Right where me and Izzy had dumped a body, back in the spring. Someone had been foolish enough to assault me just after I'd died—I didn't actually know I was dead at that point, so it had come as just as much surprise to me as him when I'd sucked the literal life out of him. That was also the first time I'd met Ivo Laithlind, when he came to my rescue as I stood staring at the corpse with no idea of what to do next. He'd helped me throw the body into the canal to make it look like a drunken accident, and that should have been the end of it. But the gruesome groper had made a second appearance the next night, emerging from Canning Dock just as me and Izzy were settling down for some late night chips. It had been like something out of a zombie movie, but with even less personality. Anyway, me and Iz had made sure he was properly dead and then dumped him in the river, hoping he'd get eaten by fish before anything incriminating floated to the surface. Then we'd gone home for a vomiting session (Izzy) and explanations re the whole 'dead but not dead' thing (me).

And now here was Daisy, apparently telling me she'd tucked my unfortunate attacker away as a snack stash, but he'd now been found by the police. "Shit," I hissed to myself, "shit, shit, *shit*!" Daisy made a low chirruping noise and tilted her head to one side in an expression of concern. "It's fine," I reassured her, "nothing to do with you. I just hope they can't connect him to me, that's all." As I spoke, I saw the police boat turn and head towards us. Daisy waved at me in a recognisable 'don't worry' kind of way, and mimed biting her fingers off. "Oh god," I said, leaning my head against the iron post, "are you telling me you've eaten his fingerprints?" She bounced in the water with enough enthusiasm to make noisy splashes. "You're the best friend a girl could have, Daisy," I said with relief, wondering whether the fact I can't vomit was making me feel better or worse. "Promise you'll stay well away from the police, though?" I asked her. "Just while they're investigating the body. Or what's left of it." I wondered—not for the first time—what the *fuck* had become of my life. This time the previous year, I'd been doing nothing more than making endless pots of tea for customers and griping to Izzy about my non-existent love life. Now, I spent my time arguing undead politics with people who were born before Britain was even a nation state, swimming with mythical creatures and getting jiggy with thousand-year-old kings. Okay, so it was just the one king and only the one time, but you can totally see why my brain was a bit fried. I sighed and clambered to my feet. "I'm going to go see my mum," I said to Daisy, who gave me an uncomprehending look. "Don't get into trouble." She grinned and nodded vigorously, before executing a perfect backflip that sent her flying down into the water without a single ripple. "I'm in enough trouble for both of us," I said to the empty surface of the Mersey, before turning to walk reluctantly towards the Liver Building.

~

I walked along the waterfront all the way along, rather than cutting across George Parade as I'd normally do. The police boat was chugging steadily, and I slowed my pace so it would get to the landing point before I did. By the time I'd reached the ferry terminal, the police boat was pulling up at the concrete jetty steps. A small, unmarked van was reversing up to the edge, its rear doors already open. A pair of special constables were busily roping off a perimeter with police tape. One looked up as I approached and I recognised her as a member of Mapp's knitting group, albeit a very human one. I once asked him if he was worried people would guess his secrets if they all started chatting a bit too much, but he said no. "It's all knit and purl and does my bum look big in this crocheted skirt," he'd said. "Not 'oh that's a neat hem, now do you mind me asking if you're actually a zombie?'"

"Need to walk round, love," the constable said, before recognising me. "Oh, hi Lil!" She finished tying her end of the tape to the fence post and came over to me. "It's all going on this morning," she said, nodding down to where the boat had been moored so the people from the van— I assumed staff from the nearest hospital morgue—could attempt to look respectful whilst lugging the corpse off the boat and up the steps. They'd taken a body bag down with them, but there wasn't anywhere flat enough, so it had been draped over a stretcher instead. A police officer was stationed either side of the stretcher, walking up the steps alongside it in order to hold the sheeting down.

"Caught anything interesting?" I asked, trying to sound curious but indifferent.

"Body of a man," said the constable, whose name I now remembered was Jenny. "Been in the water a good while, apparently. Can't imagine there'll be anything very recognisable left." As she said this, the stretcher and its bearers reached the top of the steps behind her. I glanced over her shoulder towards it just as a gust of wind made the sheet flap up at one end. The nearest police officer swore and grabbed it quickly in order to hide what was underneath, but not before I'd seen the remains of straggly ginger hair hanging from the top of a horribly green-looking human skull. Jenny caught my expression and turned to see what I was looking at. "Christ," she said, "and I haven't even had breakfast yet. I'd better go help," she patted me on the arm, "you have a good day now." I caught one last glimpse of a distinctly rotten-looking toe poking out from the end of the stretcher, before Jenny blocked my view.

MY MOTHER, THE
FANGIRL

"Good morning, Lilith," said Eadric politely, as I stepped out of the lift. He was leaning against the doorframe that led into the main rooms and had his arms crossed across his chest.

"Uh oh," I said, "why do I feel as though I'm about to be lectured by the headmaster?"

Eadric raised one elegant brow. "I think we've established beyond all doubt," he said, "that no matter what I say, you will do whatever you consider best. Regardless of whether it is actually the best thing to do."

"In that case," I said, "why bother now?"

"Because I have to *try*, Lilith!" Eadric pushed himself upright and sounded as though he was struggling to hold his temper. "I have done my best to look after this territory for centuries and, however useless you think I am, I do have some awareness of how these things work."

"And?" I narrowed my eyes at him. "You think I should just accept being taken for an absolute fool by Liam fucking O'Connor? Despite him admitting in front of you that he'd deceived me?"

Eadric's playing the long game, said the city. **He's been playing it a very long time, now.**

Then it's about time he started scoring some bloody goals.

It's not always about the scores, Lilith. Sometimes it's about how we play.

Do not *start that again*, I warned the city. *I have had just about enough of people and their opaque quotations.*

But we're not people.

Yes you are, I pointed out, *you're a* lot *of people. And as it's my head you've taken up residence in, I get final say on when you should shut the fuck up.*

But you—

Shut the fuck up, I said. *Final answer.*

"Lilith," said Eadric, this time attempting to keep a reasonable tone to his voice, "I realise that none of this is easy for you."

"Yeah," I said, "you've been saying that for months now. But you still can't seem to give me any leeway for being new to it all."

"When someone dies," Eadric said, "but keeps living, they usually take some time to get used to it. They move away, so they'll never have to watch their loved ones get old and die. They start a whole new life somewhere else."

"Quitters," I muttered under my breath.

"Regardless," said Eadric, "this is the usual way of things for one simple reason—it works. Someone dies, and is mourned by those who cared for them. Then life moves on. And the dead person also moves on—elsewhere. It fits the expected human narrative whilst making things more manageable for the revenant concerned. You," he nodded at me with just the hint of a smile crinkling the corners of his mouth, "have refused to do anything at all that might help smooth things over. And it is making life very difficult for all of us."

"All of us?" I asked, "or just you?" I stepped forward, so we were less than a metre apart. "I get that you don't want to ruffle undead feathers, Eadric, but I will not be used as a pawn in your games."

"I don't play games," said Eadric. "I never have, and I'm not starting now."

"And neither do I," I said, holding his gaze. Voices were audible through the doorway into the Silvertons' rooms. Nik was obviously busy impressing my mother with his knowledge of Romanticism and the many ways of tying a cravat. "I want to be left alone, Eadric. I want to work at Flora's and chat to the customers and then go up to my flat at the end of the day and sit with my cat and my auntie in front of the television. That is the sum total of my ambition in this life, and you can't change my mind."

"But you don't *have* a life," said Eadric quietly. "You're dead, Lilith. Dead but immortal and stuck here forever, whether you like it or not. Just like the rest of us. You can insist on living with the ghost of your aunt and your very strange cat," I narrowed my eyes at him, "if you choose to do so. But what you cannot change is the fact that you are dead."

"This isn't a stupid movie," I said, sulkily, "it's my *life*."

"Your *after*life," said Eadric. "Which is already proving to be more ridiculous than any movie would ever dare to be. Lilith," his tone was kinder now, "hasn't it occurred to you, not even once, that there must be a reason for you still being here, long after you should have died? You know now that immortality is real, at least for a chosen few. The spirit of the city has taken up residence in your *head*, Lilith! As far as I know, that hasn't happened to anyone else in all the centuries I've been on this godforsaken planet. Yet you still insist on pretending it's everything else that's unusual and unnecessary?"

"Everything becomes normal when it actually happens to you," I said. "Eventually."

"Indeed," said Eadric. "Which is why you should perhaps give some thought to what I am saying to you now, rather than dismissing me out of hand. The fates are more powerful than humans could ever imagine. Yet they gaily joke about them all the time, little knowing the danger they're putting themselves in. Luckily for humanity, the fates have more important things to deal with and cannot allow themselves to be sidetracked by human silliness."

"Don't you dare try to tell me the fates have a capital 'F' and sit up on clouds looking down on everyone," I scowled.

Eadric smiled. "They don't sit on clouds," he said, "I'll give you that. But they're real, and they're powerful. And dangerous, if you don't take them seriously."

"So why are they taking such a close interest in me?" I asked him. "There's nothing about me that could be important to anyone, let alone the bloody Fates." I wiggled my index fingers to emphasise the last word.

"I have no idea," he shrugged. "Perhaps their intention is for you to take over my place at the head of this city at some point in the future. Regardless," he ignored the horrified expression I was pulling, "they clearly know something we don't. Which is why," he gave me the full 'firm but fair headteacher' look, "I'd be happier if you'd listen to me occasionally."

"And what?" I asked him. "Learn from the master until you can safely retire and have me sitting here as your little puppet? You can stop this patriarchal bullshit right now, Eadric Silverton. I might not do things the way you'd like, but that isn't my problem. Surviving the afterlife is. And if I have to take this ridiculous city along for the ride, then I will. But I will *not* be told what to do by men who think they hold all the power. Not even you. Am I making myself clear?"

"Crystal," said Eadric, and I could have sworn he was trying not to smile. "Although perhaps you will consider listening to advice, instead?" His face tightened briefly. "Because however strong and determined you might be, Lilith, you can have no idea of the future that lies ahead of you."

"Oh, I don't need to worry about that," I said airily, as I headed through the door to find my mother, "I'll just hire you as my chief advisor."

"It's one thing telling Eadric I'll just do things my own way," I said, "but I'm pretty sure I don't actually want to end up in charge of all this ridiculousness." I scowled down at the people walking along Canada Boulevard, far below me.

"Oh, I don't know," said Mum, "think of all the fancy outfits you could wear!" I narrowed my eyes as she tried not to laugh. We were sitting at Bella's feet, looking out over the river. Mum had accepted Nik's assistance up onto the dome with good grace, and had even let him clip her to one of Bella's legs with a safety harness. The giant bird was humming quietly to herself, the low vibration rumbling down through the metal. Bella's always happier when she's got company. And even more so when it's company like my mother, who had spent the past half hour telling her what a good girl she was. Faintly aggrieved noises drifting across from the other tower suggested Mum was going to have to clamber across and give Bertie the same treatment before she left, or there'd be an avian ruckus by bedtime. "Come on, love," Mum said kindly, leaning over to pat my knee, "it could be worse."

"How?" I asked. "I've spent the summer being attacked by various supernatural creatures that are apparently only too real and now I'm informed I might end up being responsible for the lot of them." I shifted my weight slightly and gave Bella a friendly scratch on the back of her leg. She wriggled happily above us, her copper wings creaking alarmingly. "That doesn't sound like fun to me."

"You could be dead," said Mum. "Properly dead. Like your brother." I glanced across to where she was staring out towards Birkenhead. "That would be worse, I think." Cally would have been thirty by now. Actually nearly thirty-one, I realised. His birthday was at the beginning of December and mine was the end of January. Luckily for us, they'd been far enough away from Christmas that only our gran ever dared giving us presents that were 'for both birthday and Christmas, as they're so close together'. But then Cally had died and would forever be eight years old. He'd never had a second chance. Not like I had. No befriending strange mermaids for Cally, nor climbing famous landmarks in order to chat to the bird sculptures in the sky.

"Yeah," I said, "I know. I'm an ungrateful brat." I sighed. "How am I supposed to manage it, though?"

"Taking charge?" asked Mum, turning to look at me finally. I'd expected her to look tearful after mentioning Cally, but her eyes were dry. She looked determined, somehow.

"Yeah." I wedged my elbows onto my knees and rested my chin in my hands. "It's not like I was born to it, is it? I'm not a royal princess, knowing all my life that someday I'll be in charge. At least princesses have time to get used to the idea."

"I think plenty of princesses would probably rather not become monarch," said Mum. "It's a huge responsibility, isn't it?"

"Uh huh." I stared gloomily out over the river and wondered

whether Daisy had room in her pod for a human mermaid. Maybe I could don a wetsuit and just disappear permanently into the Mersey.

"Not many would choose to do it if they had other options, love," said Mum. "But it's rare for anyone in that position to *have* other options, isn't it? Queen or nothing, is how it usually goes. And the 'nothing' means letting everyone down in the process. Just look at the mess with Edward and Mrs Simpson."

"Why should he have given up someone he loved, though?" I asked. "I've never understood it. He didn't *ask* to be put in charge of the country; it was just an accident of birth. And people didn't like Wallis just because she was an American *and* a divorcee. It's always the woman's fault," I went on, "even if she's done nothing wrong. Society lies in wait for women who know their own minds. And it trips them up as soon as it gets a chance."

"A bit like your namesake," said Mum. I knew the story, of course. Adam's first wife and made from the same clay as her husband, Lilith was kicked out of the Garden of Eden for refusing to be subordinate. Her replacement was created from Adam's rib in order to give him a real sense of ownership, and Lilith was left to the mercies of the biblical storytellers and the judgmental mythologists. Depending which history you read, Lilith is either the origin story for feminism or a murderous harpy whose bitter and twisted nature made her a very unsuitable babysitter. You don't need to be a genius to figure out which version is best remembered.

"Why did you choose it?" I said. "My name, I mean. Why call me Lilith?"

"Don't you remember me telling you?" asked Mum. "You'd have been about seven, I think. Someone at school had been teasing you for having an unusual name and you came home in tears, asking why you couldn't have been called Summer or Becca, like everyone else. Actually, we'd half-considered calling you Autumn, but decided at the last minute it was too twee. Could have been worse, though," she glanced across at me, "your dad wanted to call you Eloise."

"I like Eloise," I said, thinking it would have been an easier name to live with than bloody Lilith.

"Yeah," said Mum, "but three of our friends had already used it for their own daughters, so we thought we'd better go for something different. And then Granny Ivy said you should be called Lilith."

"Gran suggested it?" I was surprised—Ivy had been a dour woman who'd never struck me as someone with any form of romanticism lurking in her soul. She was Kitty's older sister, although she'd died long before Kitty had reappeared in my life. Knowing Kitty now, it was hard to believe the two of them had even been related.

"She did," said Mum. "Apparently it was the right name for you. That's exactly what she said—'it's the right name for that girl'. And mum rarely showed much interest in what I was doing, so I thought I'd better make the most of it."

"I'm not sure what I could possibly have in common with the biblical version," I grumbled.

"Oh, I don't know," said Mum. She was grinning. "I think you might have inherited her independent streak."

"Oh, isn't this lovely?" Mum said, as she wriggled into a seat wedged in by the serving counter in Flora's. "I haven't been in here for so long, Lil! It's lovely to see it so busy." Izzy had Todd working with her and he was being his usual efficient self, charming customers with his faintly camp chit-chat. Kitty waited for Mum to get comfortable, then perched on the chair next to her. We'd gone back to the flat so Mum could say hi to her long-dead aunt, and then decided Kitty might as well just come down to the cafe with us. She looks solid enough these days that you'd have to watch her carefully for a good while to notice the faint glow she gives off if the light's hitting her at certain angles. Izzy brought cappuccino for Mum and an espresso for me, waggling her eyebrows at Kitty as she put the cups down on the table.

"Are we risking it yet?" she asked, nodding at the cups.

"I don't think so," said Kitty. "I had a little bit of Mapp's wine the other night and it went straight through me." When Kitty's says something's gone straight through her, it isn't a euphemism for stomach troubles. "Got the seat cushion damp. I'm sure the staff thought I'd wet myself."

"Maybe next time," said Izzy with a grin.

"You're working wonders with the place, Isobel," said Mum. She's known Izzy for more than twenty-five years, but still insists on using her full name. "Have your parents seen it?"

"Nah," said Izzy, "I'm avoiding family visits until Zombie Girl here has kicked the city into touch a bit."

Rude.

Truthful, though. You're all over the place at the minute. Should be ashamed of yourself.

We're still waiting for you to live up to your fated role.

I'm dead. Bit hard to live up to anything when you're not alive.

Semantics won't save you now.

Clearly. I let out an audible sigh, and Mum looked concerned.

"You okay, Lil?" she asked.

"She's fine," said Izzy airily. "Just having silent conversations with the spirit of this entire city. As one does."

"Not the entire city," I snarked back. "Just its people. And we weren't going to mention it, remember?"

Izzy shrugged. "It's not the weirdest thing about your life these days, to be fair."

"You talk to the city?" Mum's expression was curious rather than disbelieving. "How?"

"It's in my head," I sighed. "Whether I want it there or not. And it's bloody rude at times."

We prefer to think of ourself as high-spirited, thank you.

"Also delusional. Anyway," I picked up my coffee cup and smiled brightly at my life-giver, "how was your chat with darling Nikolaus? Did he bore you to tears with his stories of Greek sunsets and the saucy taverna waiters?"

"You're so mean to him," said Mum with a smile. "He's a sweetheart." I snorted. "Lil," Mum said, "I don't think you realise just what an incredible person Nik really is."

"I have no doubt about Nik's well-deserved place in the annals of history," I said, "I just like taking the piss. Don't forget we're talking about a bloke who, when he had to pick a new name, went with that of a deckhand he'd been having a fling with. A deckhand who'd left him for a fisherman. And you also have to remember that I now live in a world where Emperor Constantine could walk through the door right now, and it still wouldn't be the strangest thing that's happened to me this week." Before Mum could answer, the door to Flora's opened behind me and her face lit up so brightly that for the briefest second I panicked that maybe a legendary Byzantine ruler really had decided to pop in for a latte.

"Is that," Mum leaned across the table and dropped her voice to a loud and unsubtle hiss, "Sean Hannerty? The crime writer?" Bollocks. I made a show of turning to check an invisible something on the floor next to me and peeked at the man standing at the counter.

"Yup," I said, sitting up straight again, "That's our Sean, alright." Mum opened her mouth to speak, but wrangled it into a smile instead. I felt Sean's breath tickling the back of my neck as he came to stand behind me at the table.

"Hey Lil," he said, "it's not often we see you this side of the counter. Although you've been noticeable by your absence anyway, just recently. How's tricks?"

'Yeah sorry Sean, been busy fighting the forces of evil and trying not to get chopped into pieces by my countless unseen enemies,' is what I didn't say. Instead, I settled for just trying not to look like a complete idiot. "Been busy," I said. "You know how it is." I could feel the blush creeping up my throat towards my chin. Other women get prettily flushed cheeks when they're feeling self-conscious. I develop what looks like a dodgy rash, which starts at my cleavage and ends somewhere around my jawline. It clashes with my hair and makes me look like a farmhand who's been out harvesting all week.

"You'll have to excuse my daughter," said Mum, holding her hand across the table for Sean to shake. "She appears to have forgotten how to behave in polite society." I scowled at her, but she's had decades of training and ignored me. "I'm Helen, Lilith's mother. And this," she nodded towards Kitty, who grinned impishly, "is my sister, Kitty." I narrowed my eyes at the pair of them, but they determinedly didn't meet my gaze. "Why don't you come sit with us?" she went on. "My husband's a huge fan of your work, he'll be *so* excited to hear you're a friend of our Lil's."

"That okay with you, Lil?" asked Sean, the faintest tremor of nerves in his voice. If only I could explain that of course it was okay, it was just that I tended to lose all coherence when he was anywhere near me. Especially when I thought back to the time he'd kissed me, after our first date. A kiss that Sean couldn't remember and I'd never forget. Mostly because we then discovered Daisy had broken into my flat and was chomping on fish whilst perched on top of my television. It's a long story, and I generally try to consign it to the 'let's pretend it never happened' section of my mental filing system.

"Of course it's okay," I managed, moving to the next seat to make room. "Take a pew."

"Your grandad used to say that," said Mum, looking at me with interest. "Funny how you must have picked little things up over the years without realising. You say a lot of things like my parents these days, I've been noticing it for a while now. I'm surprised you remember it all."

If only you knew, I thought. But settled for "Yeah, brains are weird." Sean smiled at me and seemed about to say something, but at that moment Todd arrived and put a coffee down on the table.

"It's on the house," he said to Sean. "Izzy says it's about time Lilith socialised a bit more."

"Oh, did she now?" I said, turning to glare at my eternally annoying best friend behind the counter. She ducked, but not before I saw the grin on her devious face. "How very *thoughtful* of her."

"Are you writing anything at the moment, Sean?" asked Mum, before things could get any more awkward. She and Kitty were both looking at him with bright, interested eyes.

He flushed slightly. "Oh," he said, "you know. Supposed to be. I should be sending the next one to my agent in a couple of months, but right now it isn't much more than a heap of notes and some files on my laptop." Sean's notebook habit was legendary, if only within the confines of Flora's. He had a favourite table in the front window, and a set routine. It involved laying out paper and pens, making notes for approximately ten minutes and then gazing thoughtfully out of the window until he'd finished his coffee. Some days he'd manage three coffees over four hours and write only a couple of sentences, but on others—the muse having clearly struck him along with the first hit of caffeine—one Americano would last nearly two hours and he'd scribble intently until he'd almost filled an entire notebook. Until he'd mentioned the laptop, I'd half imagined he maybe wrote entire novels in longhand on paper.

"Can you let us into any secrets?" asked Mum, leaning forward. "Little titbits I can take back to Lil's dad, just to prove I've really met you?"

Sean laughed and, to my shock, put an arm around my shoulders. "More than my life's worth," he said. "My agent would kill me. Why not take a pic of me and Lil together? That should be proof enough." Mum looked like she might burst with excitement as she scrabbled around for her phone.

"Squidge together then," she said to me and Sean, whilst wiping the camera lens on her Breton-striped M&S t-shirt. "Try to look as though you like each other."

"Who says we don't?" grinned Sean. I'd been determinedly keeping my mouth shut so I wouldn't be tempted to take a breath, but then Sean leaned in towards me and I couldn't resist. God, he tasted good. He was still using fruity shampoo, but had swapped his usual Calvin Klein aftershave for Gaultier.

"Le Male?" I asked. Sean looked startled, then recovered himself.

"My aftershave?" I nodded. "Yeah," he said slowly, "it is. Decided to change things up a bit. I always liked this one way back when. Clever of you to guess." He smiled, and his face crinkled at the edges slightly.

"I, erm," I stumbled. "It's nice."

"Thank you," said Sean, a wide grin now on his face.

"Why don't you give Lil your number, Sean," said Mum, her eyes twinkling, "That way she can send you the pic."

I swear to god I am going to spontaneously combust from sheer mortification in a minute.

Ohhhh, said the city, **you want to talk to us now you need moral support.**

Well it's about bloody time you started earning your keep, I muttered silently, *instead of just hanging out in my skull and annoying me.*

Charmed, we're sure. Anyway, we like him.

Who? Sean?

Who else? We don't see any other potential love interests in the room. Outside is quite different, of course.

Different how? Sean had pulled his phone out from his bag and was opening the contacts section.

"Fancy giving me your number, then?" He smiled, fingers poised over the keypad.

It took me two goes to rescue my own phone, which had slipped from its usual home in my waistband and gone wandering down my thigh beneath my leggings. I then had to remember how to find my number, whilst Mum and Kitty stared at me as though I was bringing shame on the O'Reilly name. Wouldn't be the first time.

Never mind what's outside, said the city, **you need to learn how to behave in basic social situations first.**

If I'm so shit, I held the phone out to show Sean the number, which he copied into his own, *then why does Eadric seem to think I'm going to be his replacement?*

If it's fated, Lilith, then we have no choice.

Gee, thanks.

"I was beginning to think you'd got another job and just left Izzy running this place," Sean said. "Especially when she got Todd in."

"No," I said, thinking quickly, "I've just been busy working on something. Expansion. You know." I really hoped he didn't ask what sort of expansion I meant, because other than putting tables out on my crappy car park, there wasn't much further Flora's could spread. "Lots of paperwork, chats with the landlord, that sort of thing."

"Isn't this place owned by Eadric Silverton?" asked Sean, surprising me. "Interesting chap."

"He's just my landlord," I said, noncommittally, "not much interesting about that."

"I looked into his company once," said Sean. "I'd been thinking about setting one of my books in and around the Liver Building and, well, I'm a sucker for research rabbit holes. It's a strange company. Seems to have been around literally forever, but Silverton himself could only be, what? Forty?" I wondered if Eadric knew a crime novelist had been investigating him and if so, whether he'd count it as a security risk.

Although Sean couldn't be the first person to have looked into the origins of Silverton Properties.

"I don't know about his age," said Mum, "but he's certainly eye-catching. Don't you think so, Lil?"

"Can't say I'd noticed," I said, giving her my patented 'wtf' eyebrow waggle. "He's just the person I pay rent to."

"Single as well," said Mum. "You want to get in there, love." She nudged Kitty, and they both snorted.

"How do you know he's single?" I retorted. "Asked him, did you?" I didn't know what the fuck she was playing at, but I really needed her to pack it in.

"You've met him, then?" asked Sean.

Fucksake.

She knows what she's doing, said the city. I swore I heard it chuckle quietly.

"I called in with Lilith earlier," said Mum. "He's very nice. And the views! Our Lil's very lucky to be able to go up there occasionally. It's much different from doing the official tour." She sat back and smiled at me with an expression of satisfaction on her face.

"I'll have to use that number of yours sooner rather than later, then," said Sean to me. "Before you fall for the charms of your mega-wealthy landlord."

Told you.

"I've never been interested in wealth," I said weakly.

"Then I'll just have to distract you with my other talents," said Sean.

"What the hell was *that* all about?" I demanded, after Sean had finished his coffee and left with a round of goodbyes and promises to keep in touch.

Mum grinned across the table. "I just think you need to get your life going again," she said. "Now you've got all the time in the world."

"You don't understand," I said. "It's not safe! I nearly killed him last time, I can't risk it again."

"Lil," said Mum, "you're thirty-three next birthday and I can't remember the last time you had any romance in your life. Cut loose a bit, love."

"If you're that interested," I said, "I had sex a couple of days ago, *actually*." It came out louder than I'd intended and a couple at the next table turned to look at me in surprise. "Bloody hell," I said, hunching in my chair, "just when I think my life can't get any more mortifying."

"Is that why you didn't come home the other night?" asked Kitty, grinning widely. "What fun! Who's the lucky boy, then? Girl?" She lowered her voice. "Dead or alive?"

"Dead," I sighed. "And male, for your information. Not that any of it matters. I won't be seeing him again."

"Anyone we know?" asked Mum.

"Only from history books."

"Come on," said Mum, "you can't tell say that and not give us the details. Who was it?"

"Have you forgotten I'm your daughter?" I scrunched my face up. "This is not a comfortable conversation."

"It's different these days, Lil," said Mum. "You being immortal changes things, don't you think?" We all stared at the table for a long minute, contemplating eternity and the End of Days. At least, I was. Mum might have been considering what to have for tea, for all I knew. And Kitty looks happily vacant most of the time, regardless of what's actually going on around her.

"His name's Liam," I said, giving in to the inevitable. "You'd know him better as William. William the Conqueror." They both blinked at me in surprise, wide-eyed disbelief etched clearly across their faces.

"Nooooo?" said Mum, stretching it out as if to give herself more time to think. "*The* William the Conqueror?"

"Pretty sure there's only ever been one of them," I said, and then caught myself. "Officially, anyway."

"But how?" asked Kitty.

"Well," I started, "when two people like each other very much—"

"Yes, yes, no need to be facetious," said Kitty tartly. "I mean, how did you meet *him*, of all people?"

"In the pub," I said. "And yes, I know, what the fuck, etcetera

etcetera. He was staying at the pub I was drinking in, we got chatting, one thing led to another. I didn't know who he was."

"I know you're an adult and can make your own decisions, love," said Mum, "but don't you think it might be better to find out who someone is before getting into bed with them?"

"You can take those judgey knickers off right this minute," I said indignantly. "I knew he was—" I considered my words for a second "—one of my lot, and that was enough for me. Revenants don't carry diseases and I can hold my own if anyone attacks me, so why shouldn't I have fun for once?"

"Okay, okay," said Mum, "I'm sorry. For what it's worth, I wasn't judging your choice of activities. It's more just basic concern for your safety. Like you say, he wasn't who you thought he was. Although I can kind of understand why he'd be under a pseudonym," she went on, "on account of how booking a room might be difficult if you've got one of the most famous names in history. Anyway," she beamed, "when are you seeing him again?"

"Hopefully never," I scowled. "He's a lying, deceitful toe-rag and I want nothing to do with him."

"Don't be too hasty," said Mum. "Better to keep your options open. And right now, your options are a wealthy writer or a famous king. Not bad going for a cafe owner from Liverpool."

"I've got enough on my plate," I sighed, "without my love life getting complicated. Again."

"Oh, I think it'll get far more complicated before too long," said Mum with a grin. "What fun!"

There's Not Enough
Sage In The World
For This Shit

After a quick visit upstairs to say hello to Grimm and pass judgment on my tastes in home decor, Mum finally decided she'd had enough of making my life difficult and should probably head off home. "I'll walk you to your car," I said. "Someone needs to make sure you don't decide to run off with your poetic boyfriend."

"You're not serious?" Mum stopped in the kitchen doorway and turned to look at me as I picked up my bag. "You think...ohhhh Lilith..." She started laughing, her hand up to her face. "I haven't got the hots for Nikolaus, if that's what you're implying," she said, when she'd finished snorting. "He's a *friend*, Lil. I'm allowed friends, right?"

"Of course you are," I said, feeling sheepish. "And I didn't really think you have a thing for Nik. Not really. Well," I paused, "maybe a tiny bit."

"I love your dad, Lil. Always have, always will. I wouldn't leave him for anyone, not even the most famous poet in the world. The honest answer is that I'm thinking of doing a PhD, and Nik has kindly offered to help me write the proposal." I was less surprised at the news my mother was going to attempt a doctorate than others might have been. Having left school with a decent amount of O-levels, Mum had worked part time throughout our childhoods. Usually bar or shop jobs that could be fitted around school hours. Then, maybe a year or so after Cally died, she signed up to do a degree with the Open University. I'd assumed at the time it was just to give herself a distraction and she'd get bored fairly quickly, but she was a committed, grade-A student from the start. Turns out my mum loves learning, just for the sake of it. Her bachelor degree was the 'open' type—a hotchpotch of subjects that she chose purely based on what she fancied learning each year. Me and Dad had gone to her graduation and cheered as she waved proudly at us from the stage. When I'd left home for university, she'd taken a part-time Masters, but this time it was more focussed. She graduated with an M.A. in literature from Chester only a year after I got my own history degree. And that was more than a decade ago now, so the news was probably overdue.

There was just one thing bothering me. "Are you telling me," I narrowed my eyes at her, "you're writing a proposal for a literary PhD with the help of one of the most famous authors in history?"

"I can't help it if I have interesting friends," she said, scrunching her face up at me, "now can I?"

"I'm pretty sure that's cheating," I said, shooing her out onto the fire escape. "Insider knowledge and all that."

"Primary sources are invaluable for research," Mum said primly. "You should know that well enough."

"When I did *my* degree," I said, walking down the steps behind her, "my primary sources comprised an online subscription to the newspaper archives and a lot of visits to the university library."

"I guess," said Mum, "you could argue those are really still secondary sources? You're still reading someone else's interpretation of the history, don't forget." She stepped out into Harrington Street and turned to look at me, a cheeky grin on her face.

"Find out who that last poem was really about," I said. "That'll earn you some brownie points with your tutors."

Mum snorted. "Earn me a sectioning, more like," she said. "Fancy being able to get it all from the horse's mouth, but with no way of telling anyone about it."

"Then you'll just have to look forward to feeling privately smug for the rest of your life," I said. "Swings and roundabouts, like."

"Maybe you could publish it all in centuries to come," said Mum as we waited behind a group of tourists to cross the Strand. Listening to them chatting among themselves, I thought the woman wearing the hijab was probably the daughter of the family, with her own child in the pram she was pushing. An older couple stood next to her, a boy of about six between them. Presumably the older brother of whoever was in the pram. The older couple each held one of the boy's hands; concerned grandparents ensuring he couldn't accidentally step out into the traffic. "It's weird to think we'll never do that," she went on. When I turned to look at her, she was gazing at the multi-generational family with what I thought was a wistful look in her eye.

"That would never have happened anyway," I said. "Sorry."

"Oh I know," said Mum. The pedestrian light finally turned to green, and we crossed the road at an uncomfortably slow pace behind the family. "I guess I was just used to it still being a possibility, however unlikely it might actually have been. I sometimes wonder if it's not grandchildren I'm worried about missing out on, mind. Maybe it's more that the O'Reilly line will end with you. I thought we'd go on forever, somehow."

"We will, though," I said. "Have you forgotten that your only daughter is immortal? I might be the last O'Reilly standing, but I'll be here til the end of time."

"Yes," said Mum quietly. I turned to look at her as we reached the Liver Building and stopped at the gateway down to the private entrance. "That's what worries me."

It was getting dark by the time I'd said my goodbyes to Mum and started the walk back to Harrington Street. The air was damp with mist and the background sounds of the city seemed muffled as I headed up Brunswick Street. Busy with thoughts about what my immortality meant to my friends and family, I almost didn't notice the shadows flitting above my head. Luckily for me, instinct took over and, leaping onto a shiny silver Porsche that had the misfortune to be parked close by, I bounced off its roof and up onto the balcony of the India Buildings. The vampires had obviously planned to hit me hard and fast, but they slammed down onto the tarmac instead. I watched from my perch as they pulled themselves upright and shook in unison, like a pair of dogs emerging from the sea. I thought the taller one was possibly female and the other male. Not that gender's ever relevant to vampires—they're all just bundles of nastiness wrapped up in bad skin and teeth. Rachel was the only exception I'd met, but now she'd dropped the vegetarian lifestyle for a meatier one, I wasn't sure I'd turn my back on her, either. At least, not without first making very sure any small furry creatures were locked safely out of reach. "Seriously?" I yelled down at them. "Can't you leave me in peace just for a little while? Give me a month off for good behaviour, maybe?" The shorter vampire made a growling sound and stepped forward. "Don't you *dare*!" I looked around for potential weapons and came up blank. The balcony backed onto large, plate glass windows—thank gods the offices had closed for the day, or the staff would have really had something to discuss at tea break—and was constructed from unhelpfully smooth Portland stone. "What's Joe going to say when he finds out?" I glared down at the pair of would-be undead attackers. "He'll send you to bed early without your tea, I reckon."

"No," hissed the female. "Us-now-only-us." She did the usual vamp thing of running her words together, as though she'd forgotten how to speak properly and was having to concentrate.

"You and whose fucking army?" I demanded. "You don't get to run around in this city without learning to behave yourselves first. I am a reasonable woman," glancing down, I realised the male had disappeared from view, "but you are beginning to test my patience." I whirled round and smacked the other vampire as hard as I could as he tried to jump me from behind. Pinwheeling over the balcony, he crashed onto the bonnet of a battered VW Golf parked on the other side of the street. It had one hell of an alarm system for an old car and what sounded like an air raid siren went off, the noise ricocheting off buildings and swirling around above the hazard lights that were now also flashing. He rolled off and underneath the car, dropping out of sight as the taller vamp made her move. Seemingly defying the laws of gravity, she ran on all fours like a gigantic four-legged spider, straight over the top of the Porsche. Its own security system finally kicked in—clearly VWs are better prepared for attempted theft than their more expensive cousins—and the entire street was suddenly a migraine-sufferer's worst nightmare. Lights started coming on in the building behind me, presumably cleaners or caretakers wondering what on earth was going on. Suddenly, the female vampire was in front of me, just a few inches away from my face. I yelled in shock, and it was loud enough to make her hesitate for the fraction of a second it took me to regain my senses. Grabbing her arm, I swung her round with such force that I felt her shoulder dislocate. She gave a short scream before somersaulting forwards, pulling me off my feet and snapping her arm back into place. I landed on my backside and looked up to find her looming over me. She had a long, thin face and eyes that were bigger than they really should have been. There was a quiet thud behind me, which I took to mean the other vampire was, quite literally, watching my back. "What do you actually *want*?" I asked, and for a second the vampire's face was blank. Then she smiled, showing her tiny sharp teeth.

"You," she hissed. With that, she lunged forward. I ducked sideways fast enough that she hit her friend behind me instead, and they tumbled along the balcony until they fetched up hard against the carved stone finial and landed in a heap. Hopefully, the impact had knocked the pair of them out. I hopped onto the balustrade and looked down for a handy car roof to break my fall. It was clearly my lucky night, because an old red transit van was parked on my side of the street, just fifteen feet to my right. If I pushed off hard enough, I should be able to reach it. I crouched slightly, pressing my fingers and the balls of my feet hard against the stone as I prepared to leap. Which was, of course, when the other vampires emerged from the shadows. There was at least twenty of them, of all shapes and sizes. I was pretty sure I recognised a couple from the Anfield incident earlier in the year. I scowled at them all in turn, just to make my feelings clear. "You have *got* to be kidding," I shouted down at them. "Can't I have just *one* night off from this stupidity?" Deciding discretion really was the better part of valour, I turned and started climbing upwards instead. If I could get to the top of the building, I might make it home across the rooftops. The upper floors of the India Buildings had clearly been built without any consideration for those of us who sometimes feel the need to run vertically. The stone was smooth and the windows featureless, with no useful gripping points. Risking a glance down, I saw the vampires on the street beginning to climb up towards me. Launching myself upwards, I somehow scrabbled high enough to grab the first window ledge with my fingers. Swaying my legs from side to side in an attempt at building momentum, I was just about to swing my feet up onto the ledge when something heavy caught hold of my ankle. I looked down to find the female vamp clinging to my foot. "I am having a *very* difficult week," I said, scowling down at her, "and you are *not* helping." I kicked out as hard as possible. She somehow clung on, her nails digging into my leg. "Oh, for *fuck's* sake!" I yelled, and managed to smack her straight in the face with the heel of my other foot. I'd swapped my usual Converse for DMs in deference to the wet weather—even immortals find soggy socks unpleasant —and I heard a crack as the toughened sole connected with her cheekbone. With an angry howl, she dropped backwards off the building and crashed down in the middle of the road. A few of the pack dropped down and ran over to her, but I could hear the rest skittering up the building below me.

Just then, an engine growled in the mist. I turned to look as a familiar black car came hurtling up the street, its brakes squealing as the driver skidded to a halt. "Lilith!" yelled a voice from inside. "Jump!" I launched myself without thinking, landing on the car's roof and swinging myself in through the open window. In front of us, the female vampire was dragging herself to her feet, helped by two of her creeptastic minions.

"Hang on," said my rescuer, flooring the accelerator. The vampire didn't even see the car until it hit her. I watched it playing out in front of me almost in slow motion, the impact making her legs visibly snap and bend backwards even as she was thrown into the air. One of her helpers managed to get out of the way, but the other wasn't as fortunate. I felt the muffled crunch as a wheel went over his leg and he screamed loud enough to wake Beelzebub himself. Although Beelzebub probably had better things to do than stand around watching undead gang fights. Especially when at least one of the gangs really would have preferred being at home with a nice cuppa.

"Thanks for coming to the rescue," I said, turning to my saviour in the driver's seat of the Alpha.

"You're welcome," said Eadric. "Oh, and you can pay the repair bill." He swung a right onto Fenwick Street. "I'm pretty sure there's an imprint of your foot on the roof."

"How did you know I was in trouble?" I asked Eadric, who was sitting, rather incongruously, in the battered armchair in my living room. He was leaning back comfortably with his legs crossed and was currently jiggling a pointy shoe at Grimm, with whom he was engaged in a staring competition. The cat would win, of course—he always did. Kitty sat next to Grimm, her benevolent smile resting on each of them in turn. I'd been astounded when Eadric had said he'd come into the flat with me, just to make sure I was safe. I obviously tried my best to talk him out of it—no one appreciates their landlord making a surprise visit in the middle of the night—but he refused to budge. He'd even produced a key fob from his pocket that lowered the safety bollards on Harrington Street, so he could drive right up to the side of the building and park the Alfa next to my Beetle. Kitty's face had been a picture when I walked into the flat with Eadric Silverton in tow. To my relief, Billy hadn't been in his usual spot, so that was one less person knowing my business.

"Bertie warned Nik," said Eadric, not taking his eyes off Grimm. "Who came to tell me."

"Why didn't Nik come down and help me himself?"

"Because the vampires might not have listened to him." With an audible huff of annoyance, Grimm turned sharply away from Eadric and began clawing at Kitty's legs. In return, she just laughed and scratched him indulgently behind the ear. Eadric looked up at me. "And he doesn't like fighting."

"But you do?"

"Luckily," said Eadric, "no violence was necessary. At least," he'd obviously remembered the vampire he drove the car into, "not on a personal level."

"And you think the vampires would have listened to you?" I asked.

"Possibly." He unfolded himself from the chair and turned to Kitty. Grimm had flopped over onto his back and was offering his soft fluffy belly for scratches. The cat's head turned slightly in order to peer up at Eadric, one upside down amber eye glinting in the low light. "It was very nice to meet you, Kitty," Eadric said, giving her a polite nod. "And yourself, of course." This was to Grimm, who I was pretty sure nodded back. But it was difficult to tell, on account of Grimm being upside down. "And you don't think that cat is strange," said Eadric to me, a smile pulling at the corners of his mouth. "Which says something about your standards for what counts as strange, no?"

"Why would the vampires listen to you and not me or Nik?" I persisted, as I followed Eadric out onto the fire escape. A movement from the street below caught my eye—Billy was back, and rearranging his bedding nest in the empty doorway. Bollocks. Eadric caught my expression and turned to follow my gaze.

"Billy knows I'm your landlord," said Eadric. "You don't have to explain things to him."

"He'll want to know anyway," I sighed. "He's my friend."

"You're very lucky," said Eadric, "to have so many friends. Your popularity will serve you well."

"Serve me well for what?"

"For whatever happens in the future," he said. "I think you're going to have a very interesting future, Lilith." To my surprise, he spun around on the spot, a hand in the air to gesture at the city surrounding us. "All of this," he said, "just waiting for you."

"This is *your* city," I insisted in a low voice. I really didn't want to explain any more to Billy than I absolutely had to. "Not mine."

Ours, said the city. **You are part of us, Lilith.**

"Huh," I said aloud. "We'll see about that."

"See," said Eadric with a grin, "the city agrees with me."

"About what?" I asked, but he was already halfway down the steps, his shoes ringing sharply against the metal. "Eadric?"

He stopped at the turn for the first floor and looked up at me. "I've known this city for a very long time," he said, "and I know what it wants. The city wants you, Lilith. Not me. It was never me."

"But—" I could feel panic rising in my throat. "But I don't want to be responsible for an entire city! I *can't* do it. For heaven's sake, I barely remember to feed my cat!"

"And yet still he survives," said Eadric drily. "He just needs to know you're around. For security, I guess. And I strongly suspect the city is the same. It just needs to know you're here." I opened my mouth to speak, but before I could get any words out, Eadric had taken the last flight of steps at high speed and was already in his car. I stood at the top of the fire escape, staring downwards blankly as the Alfa growled its way back out onto the main road, the barriers rising behind it to once again make Harrington Street a secure little world of its own.

"Want to talk about it?" Billy was sitting on the pavement looking up at me. Without saying a word, I pulled the kitchen door closed and headed slowly down the steps. When I got to street level, I walked silently over and dropped to sit down next to him, pulling a spare sleeping bag up over my legs. Billy sat silently whilst I hugged my knees, deep in thought.

After a few minutes, I turned my head slowly to look at him. "We keep doing this," I said, "don't we?"

Billy arched an eyebrow at me. "Doing what?" he asked..

"Sitting here," I said. "Just thinking."

"Aah," said Billy, "a bit of thinking never did anyone harm, I reckon. Sometimes it's just nice to have company for it."

"But what if you don't know?" I asked.

"Know what?"

"What you're thinking," I said. "My mind's so full of...." I shook my head, "...of *stuff*, that I don't even know what it is, half the time."

"Meditation not working out for you, then?" he asked. I turned to look at him, suspicious that he might be taking the piss. But he was still facing forwards, gazing into nothing in particular and apparently quite serious.

"I've got so many mental leaves on my sodding mental river," I said, "that soon it's going to clog up entirely and people will be thinking beavers have moved in."

Billy laughed, then. "That, Red," he said, "is what I'm pretty sure literary types would call a *very* tortuous simile."

"How would you know about literary similes?" I smiled, despite myself. Billy had always been the easiest of company, right from the start of this ridiculously unexpected adventure.

"You're making the classic mistake," he said, "of assuming a nobody like me knows nothing about the cultural side of life. I might live on the streets, Red, but that doesn't mean I don't have a brain."

"That's not what I meant! It's just that—"

"It's fine," said Billy. "I'm used to it, believe me. But you'd be amazed by what's to be learned from just sitting quietly out here on the street."

"Like what?" I was curious now. And I was embarrassed, because he was right—I'd assumed he didn't think about anything very much. Which was ridiculous, because Billy spent hours and days at a time sitting in his spot opposite Flora's, and doing absolutely nothing would send anyone mad. And I was pretty sure Billy was one of the least mad people I'd ever met.

"How people work," he said. "How they play games with each other and compete and win and lose at life and love and business. It all goes on round here, Red." He smiled again. "You end up privy to all kinds of unexpected things when people forget you even exist. Which," he said, clapping his hands against his knees for emphasis, "is how I know my similes from my metaphors. So what are you going to do to help clear the path for your poor, cluttered river?"

I stared blankly at him for a moment, confused by the sudden u-turn in the conversation. "I think," I said eventually, "I'm going to have to learn to swim. Or else I'm going to sink entirely."

CABBAGES AND KINGS

It had been close to midnight by the time I'd left Billy to spend another night quite literally on the tiles. He'd kept an eye out as I walked back up to the flat—just in case any rogue vampires were on the prowl—before waving goodnight and wrapping himself up like a ghostly burrito. It was now just gone four in the morning and Kitty and I were in the middle of a *Twilight* movie marathon. Her choice, not mine. She'd seen it mentioned on a television programme and got a bit overexcited. "Apparently there are sexy vampires in it," she'd announced gleefully. After giving her a brief lecture on the unsexiness of the average real vampire, I'd given in and found the entire series on a streaming service. We'd got as far as *Eclipse* and I was making coffee whilst explaining to Kitty through the doorway why Victoria suddenly looked like a completely different person. I turned back to the coffee machine and jumped as something moved outside the kitchen window. Rogue vampires would have just burst in without warning, and Izzy would text rather than walk over in the middle of the night. Rachel could get out onto the fire escape from her flat, though. Maybe she was out hunting for a spot of early breakfast.

"Just nipping outside to see what our friendly, neighbourhood rat-sucker's up to," I called to Kitty.

"Won't you lose track of the movie?" she asked.

"Aunt Kitty," I said over my shoulder, "I've watched these films so many times I can recite the scripts word for word." I also have an entire list of reasons the entire storyline is unethical, abusive and generally terrible, but I didn't think she'd be interested. And it's never stopped me watching them anyway, because I am a massive hypocrite when it cometo lightweight, sparkly entertainment. I unlocked the door and stepped outside, where I narrowly avoided tripping over the wooden box that had been left on my doorstep. Made of a dark, glossy wood, it was maybe ten inches square by six inches deep, and had been tied with a blood-red ribbon. I looked around hoping to spot whoever had left it, but both the streets and the rooftops appeared to be empty. After prodding the box gingerly with my foot in order to ensure it wasn't going to explode, I picked it up and took it with me back into the flat.

"What's that?" asked Kitty, looking up as I walked into the living room. Grimm didn't take his eyes off the television, apparently mesmerised by the CGI wolves that were bouncing around the screen like cartoon puppies.

"No idea," I said, sitting down in down the armchair with the box on my lap. "But I don't think it's heavy enough to be a human head."

"Well, thank heavens for small mercies," said Kitty. "And you're sure it's for you? Hang on." She bent down to Grimm and whispered something in his ear. He got up from her lap and made a very slow jump over to the coffee table, where the remote control for the television lay next to a copy of *Vogue* that Izzy had left for Kitty. To my astonishment, Grimm pushed the remote towards Kitty until it was close enough for her to lean over and press the pause button. The film froze just as Edward was looking professionally worried about Bella being in danger yet again, and his strangely alien face leered out at us as Kitty sat back again and looked over at me. "What?" she asked, Grimm already rearranging himself back into her lap. "You know I can touch things these days."

"What I didn't know," I said suspiciously, "was that you've been training my bloody cat at the same time."

"Oh, that wasn't me," said Kitty brightly, "Grimmy's learning all by himself! Aren't you, baby?" She scratched him under his devious little chin as he gazed serenely at me with his big amber eyes.

"I'm not sure I approve," I said. The cat's eyes visibly narrowed slightly, before he went back to staring at the television screen.

"I'm not sure he really cares, in all honesty," said Kitty. "But never mind the cat. Get and open that box. Maybe it's a gift from one of your admirers."

"Most of my *supposed* admirers are undead psychopaths," I said, still not making a move to open the box. "I can't think of anything that might fit in this box that would actually be a nice surprise."

"Maybe it's chocolate," offered Kitty. "From that lovely Sean, maybe?"

I raised my eyebrows at her. "In a wooden box?" I asked. "Not to mention the fact I wouldn't be able to eat them."

"He doesn't know that though," she pointed out. "Anyway," she sat back and folded her arms, "you won't know until you open it."

"If I find a note inside reading 'Congratulations on opening my box, love from Pandora'," I said, "you are going to be responsible for whatever happens next." Grimm shifted slightly on Kitty's lap. I wasn't sure cats should know how to flip a middle finger—or even if it was usual for them to be able to extend a single claw—but he was definitely giving the impression of trying. Sighing, I held the box down with one hand and used the other to pull the tail end of the bow. It unfastened itself neatly, and the ribbon fell backwards off the box in an unnaturally theatrical way. Lifting the lid revealed a heap of red velvet. "It's just fabric," I said to Kitty. "No, hang on," I tentatively touched the soft surface of the velvet and felt something hard underneath. "It's covering something."

"Give me a minute," Kitty said to Grimm, pushing him gently off her lap and onto the sofa. He immediately rolled onto his back and lay there like a saggy old cloth cat—baggy, and a bit loose at the seams. But I loved him, despite his duplicitous nature. "Come on then," said Kitty, now standing next to my chair, "let's see what it is." Trying not to bite my lip like a ridiculous movie heroine, I carefully lifted the velvet away from the box. There was another layer underneath, and I fought the temptation to just tip the contents out onto the table in a panic. For all I knew, it could be the dusty remains of one of the killer vampires, just waiting to reanimate and behead me in my own living room. And no, I'm not being overdramatic—shit like that *happens* in my life these days.

Forcing myself to move slowly, I carefully pulled back the second layer of fabric to reveal a circlet of dull, bronze-coloured metal with large fleur-de-lys around the top edge. Reaching out a tentative finger, I lightly touched the metal. And then I snatched my hand away in a panic and sat staring at it in mute horror.

Pick it up, said the city.

No.

It's yours.

I don't want it.

That doesn't make it any less yours.

No.

It will happen eventually. You can't stop it. No one can stop it.

We'll see about that. I thought I heard a weary sigh deep inside my head, but the city didn't say anything else.

"What is it, Lil?" asked Kitty. Both she and Grimm were watching me carefully, although Kitty's clear concern was balanced somewhat by Grimm's evil leer. *I should turn you over to the sodding Volturi,* I thought to myself. The cat made an audible snorting noise and held my gaze, even when I narrowed my eyes at him. "Please can you two stop bickering?" she went on. I was confused for a second, then realised she was referring to me and Grimm. "Isn't that," she said, pointing at the box, "a crown?"

"Gold star to you," I said distractedly. "What I want to know is, why has it been left here? And who by?"

"Aren't you going to take it out?"

"I'm not sure that's a good idea," I said.

How will you know, if you don't try?

Carefully avoiding sudden moves as if trying not to scare it, I put both my hands on the crown. Rather than picking it up straight away, I let my hands sit lightly against the metal whilst I got a feel for it. The warmth developed slowly. To begin with, it was nothing more than a faint tingling sensation in the very tips of my fingers, the pressure increasingly slightly as if the crown was pushing itself up towards me. I slid my hands down and around it and finally lifted it out of the box. It was battered and ancient, the settings around its base bereft of their stones. I could feel it encouraging me to hold it up—fully aloft, above the heads of those who should worship it. The warmth was increasing now, crawling up my arms and making me feel as though I must be surrounded by a Ready Brek glow.

It wants you.

Why?

That's not our problem to work out. It's yours.

Before I had chance to snip back at the city, my hands were moving to place the crown onto my head without conscious thought. I forced my head backwards away from the crown. There was one last push and then the crown's power subsided slightly, as though it had been testing my strength. "Oh *shit*," I said, putting the metal circlet carefully back into the box and placing it down on the table. I could feel the chair hard against my back as I instinctively pushed myself away from the gift box. "Oh shit, shit, *shit*."

"What on earth's the matter?" asked Kitty. She leaned forward as if to touch the crown.

"NO."

"Okay," said Kitty carefully. She stepped backwards and sat back down next to Grimm, who was fully upright and fluffed up, his laser eyes beaming fury at me across the room. "What's wrong with it?"

"Nothing," I lied, not taking my eyes off the box. "But I don't want it."

"It's just a silly hat, Lil," said Kitty, a fraction too brightly. "Maybe it's from your mum. A bit of a tease."

"This isn't from Mum," I said, not taking my eyes off the box. "This thing shouldn't even exist. It *doesn't* exist."

"What doesn't exist?" asked Kitty. "You're talking in riddles. How can it not exist if it's sitting right there on the table? Are you telling me it's a ghost? A ghost tiara?"

"No," I said slowly, "it's not a ghost. Or a tiara. I'm pretty sure it's St Edward's Crown."

～

Despite the trouble caused by his hopelessly non-existent arrangements for the future of the throne, Edward the Confessor was declared a saint a mere century after his death in 1066. For all the criticism of him for inadvertently causing trouble to hit England like a ton of bricks in the form of the bloke I'd recently turfed out of a very high window, Edward's multiple offers of succession to different people could, with the benefit of historical distance, be seen as a clever political move. If someone isn't sure whether to fully support you, then offering them the British throne often works as a tasty incentive. By the time of the English Civil War, five hundred years after Edward's beatification, his crown had become not only the centrepiece of the British crown jewels, but also a holy relic. Which meant little to Oliver Cromwell, who declared the jewels to be symbolic of 'the detestable rule of kings' and had them broken down. The jewels themselves were sold off, and the gold melted down in order to be turned into coins. When Charles II was restored to the throne after Cromwell's death, a new version of the original crown was made for his coronation, and it's that one which is still in use to this day. The crown sitting on the coffee table in my scruffy living room looked nothing like the ostentatiously ornate version I'd once seen on a school trip to the Tower of London when I was thirteen. Then, I'd marvelled at the glittery stones and even bought a tiny replica on a keychain that I lost within a week. Which was probably just as well, because by then Izzy had lectured me all about the colonialism and theft involved in many of the jewels and explained in great detail why it wasn't cool to decorate one's duffel bag with a symbol of patriarchal imperialism, however sparkly it might be. That crown had looked impressive— but this one *felt* impressive. "It can't be," said Kitty, staring at the crown as though it might jump up and bite her. I wouldn't have bet against it at that point.

"I know," I said. "Yet here we are."

"What on earth are you going to do with it?" she asked, still not taking her eyes off it.

"I'm going to take it to Eadric," I said, getting up from my seat. "He can keep it up in his tower until I find out where it came from."

"It can't have just been hidden all this time," said Kitty, stubbornly. "Everyone knows it got melted down!"

"Yup," I agreed. "But like I said. Here we are."

"And you're sure?" She dragged her gaze away from the crown and looked at me. "It couldn't just be a fake?"

"Fakes don't feel like that, Kitty," I said. "Fakes don't have the power that thing has."

"Who would give you such a thing?" she said.

"Someone who doesn't like me very much, I suspect." I was already dragging my boots out from underneath the chair. I tied my laces quickly and got up to hunt for a suitable bag.

"Please can you stop doing that?" asked Kitty faintly.

I stopped in the doorway through to the kitchen and looked back at her. "Doing what?" I asked.

"Racing around at a thousand miles per hour," she said. I belatedly noticed the curtains swishing as if in a breeze, and the magazines scattered across the room. "It can't be good for the floorboards."

"It needs to go," I said, grabbing an old Lidl carrier bag from under the sink and bringing it into the living room. "This will have to do." I picked up the box and shoved it into the bag quickly, with as little contact as possible. Slinging the bag over my shoulder, I looked over to where Kitty was sitting on the sofa with a worried expression on her face. Grimm was still staring at the television, which had now powered down to a screensaver background of slowly bouncing stars. "Eadric's in charge," I said. "He can look after it." I was out of the door and away down the fire escape before she could reply.

"Absolutely not," said Eadric, who was pacing the floor of his office so energetically that he was wearing a trail on the carpet. "It's not staying here."

"But how does it even *exist*?" I wailed, glaring at the shopping bag that was currently sitting on Eadric's vast mahogany desk, with its sides pushed down to reveal the open box. The lid to said box was currently on the floor somewhere in the opposite corner of the room, after Eadric had flung it in horror when he realised what it had been concealing. "And who would bring it to Liverpool, anyway?"

"It's either Laithlind or William," said Eadric. "No one else would dare. More to the point, no one else could have had the opportunity to take it before it was melted down."

"You think that's what happened?" I asked. "Someone snuck it away before the jewels were broken down and sold?"

"Well, I can't think of any sensible alternative," said Eadric. He stopped pacing and stood next to the desk, his eyes fixed on the open box as though it was a cobra readying itself to strike. "It's definitely the original crown, there's no doubt about that. And there appears to be a note in with it."

"What?" I got up and stepped over to the desk to join him in staring uncomfortably. If a stranger had walked into the room at that moment, Eadric and I would have looked like a pair of nervous brain surgeons, neither wanting to make the first delicate move. "I didn't see anything when I opened it at home. It was all a bit unexpected."

"I bet it was," said Eadric. "You should probably find out what it says."

"Do I have to?" I scrunched my face up.

"Yes," he said, "you do. Unless you're so used to people anonymously delivering globally important artefacts to your kitchen door that it's no longer interesting?"

"Oh shut up," I said irritably, peering at where the torn edge of a scrap of paper was clearly visible under the crown's lower edge. "How the fuck did I miss that?"

"Too busy feeling sorry for yourself whilst ignoring your true destiny?" asked Nik from the doorway. "Evening, Lil," he said, as he walked over to us. "What terrifying excitement have you got us into this time?"

"I haven't got anybody into anything," I said indignantly. "I—"

"Don't start," said Eadric wearily. "*Either* of you," he added, seeing us both opening our mouths to speak. "Read the note, Lilith," he went on. "Please." I huffed as I reached over and carefully caught the piece of paper with my fingertips. As I slid it out from underneath the metal, I was sure I could hear whispering in the distance. Bracing myself for I didn't know quite what, I turned the paper over and read the note scrawled on it. Then I handed it to Eadric without saying a word. He read it slowly, then turned it over to check the back. When he found nothing there, he turned it back over and read the message again, before handing it back to me. "Well," he said.

"Well."

"Well, what?" asked Nik. "Stop being so dramatic, for heaven's sake. We're not in Geneva now." I silently handed him the scrap of paper, which he read. Then he looked at me with wide eyes and gave it back. I looked down at the scrappy little note lying in my hand.

It's yours—if you want it.
W

I dropped with a heavy thump into a nearby armchair and centuries of dust bounced up in clouds around me. "This could do with a clean," I observed, trying to sound casual at the same time as attempting to ignore the bag on the table.

"That chair," said Eadric, "hasn't been cleaned for decades. Because it is incredibly fragile." As if mocking me, an ominous creak came from the back of the chair. "As well as valuable. No, don't get up," I'd pulled myself half upright and the right armrest made a cracking sound, "it's probably safer to stay where you are." He nodded at the bag. "What are you going to do with it?" he asked.

"Maybe I'll throw it in the Mersey," I said, grabbing the box lid from the corner of the room and dumping it into the bag without bothering to put everything back together. "Daisy could use a chew-toy." I was out of the room and heading downwards in the lift before either of them could think of a reply.

BEWARE GLASS
SLIPPERS

In the end, I shoved the crown in my wardrobe, just to get it out of the way. Then I decided it was probably a bit disrespectful to tuck something so historically important out of sight amongst my old shoes and jackets. After pulling it back out and staring at it blankly for a while, I compromised. The wooden box stayed in the wardrobe, but the crown itself now hung at a jaunty angle from the top corner of my mirror whilst I sat staring at it from the safety of my bed. Kitty wafted in at one point and gave me a sharp look, but said nothing. I finally dragged myself up off the bed when I heard the Liver Building clock chiming seven. Tying my hair up in front of the mirror, I was aware of the crown tugging at me. It had a magnetic warmth that I wouldn't have been able to explain if I tried, and I couldn't stop myself from putting a hand out to brush my fingers lightly over the empty stone casings around its base. "You've had a hard life," I said quietly, "haven't you?" Then I squealed, because it had given me a static shock.

"You okay, Lil?" asked Kitty, materialising in the doorway with a concerned expression on her face. She looked from me to the crown and back again.

"I'm fine," I said, brushing my hand on my t-shirt to get rid of the remains of the static. "Just didn't realise gold could give shocks, is all."

"It can't," said Kitty. When I looked around at her, she had her eyebrows raised in what I thought might be a disapproving fashion. "Gold is inert, pretty much."

"Oh," I said, giving the crown one last glance before I turned to get dressed. "I must've touched something else without realising."

"Must've," said Kitty blandly. "Anyway," she went on in a brighter tone, "I'm going to Shrewsbury in a little while. And I'll, erm," she blushed, "be staying overnight. If that's okay with you?"

"Ohhhh, you sneaky little madam!" I sat back down on the bed and grinned at her. "Planning a bit of quality time with Jonny, are we?"

"I am indeed," she said, unable to stop a grin creeping across her face. "He's going to give me a tour of all my old haunts."

"And this time you'll be able to haunt them for real," I said, snorting at my own joke.

Kitty rolled her eyes. "Honestly Lilith," she said, "I do sometimes wonder if you use humour to deflect your true feelings."

"A'right, Sigmund," I said, getting up off the bed, "I can do without an analysis session before I've even had breakfast."

"You don't eat breakfast," Kitty pointed out, watching from the doorway as I began my daily routine of throwing clothes everywhere in order to find the least grubby version of the same outfit I wear pretty much every day. T-shirt, mini skirt, leggings, sneakers—it's the perfect uniform and requires little-to-no thinking.

"I am *aware* of that," I said, shaking out a faded P.J. Harvey t-shirt I'd borrowed from Flis years earlier and never given back. It was ragged round the armholes, but would do for a day in Flora's. "No need to remind me of my shortcomings."

"If you had any major shortcomings," said Kitty, "I doubt that crown would be hanging in the corner of your bedroom like someone's niece left a bit of fancy-dress costume behind." We both contemplated the crown for a few long seconds. "Is it..." Kitty trailed off.

"Yes," I said, "it's glowing. God knows how." We both stared again at the old, dull metal, its faint halo clearly visible around the edges. "Or why." I dragged my gaze away and started rooting through my underwear drawer. "Anyway, shoo!" I said. "I need to get dressed and you do not need to witness my bare arse. Does Grimm know you're going away?"

"Oh," said Kitty, "he's so grumpy about it! I told him—'Grimmy', I said, 'Aunty Kit is allowed to see other people sometimes and you will be fine here with Lilith.' I'm not sure I convinced him," she shrugged, "but he shouldn't give you too much trouble."

"Glad to hear it," I said drily. "Does sir have a preference when it comes to his evening menu options?"

"Of course he does," said Kitty, my sarcasm clearly having flown right over her pretty blonde head. "At the moment, he likes the prawn terrine best. But we're nearly out of that, so if there's absolutely no other option, he'll have the mackerel confit."

"Glad to hear he's not picky," I said.

"I know," said Kitty, "he's such an easy little pusscat to have around." With that, she wafted happily out of the door.

"Don't forget it's knitting club tonight," said Izzy, after we'd dealt with the early morning rush. Like most cafes, Flora's has a regular ebb and flow. We're kept busy for the first hour by people coming in for takeout coffee on their way to work. Then it dies off a bit, leaving us with a few regulars who work at their laptops whilst eating pastries. I've got used to handing out baby wipes to the messy eaters who get sticky bits on their keyboards, mostly because I used to be one of them. Back when I worked in an office, I was forever having to get the I.T. guy to come in and pull keys off my computer in order to pick out the crumbs that were stopping me typing in full sentences. These days I'm restricted to staring wistfully at other people eating, so I at least try to be sympathetically helpful. Our busiest period is always lunchtime, when workers pop in for another takeout and tourists sit in the windows and watch the world going by outside. Then it tails off to a steady trickle until we close, which isn't til after nine in the evening on knitting club nights.

"As if I'd dare forget," I said, as I cleaned the spouts on the coffee machine. "Mapp would be heartbroken if he ever found out he's not the uppermost thought in my mind at all times."

"He isn't?" asked Izzy in mock horror. "Then who is?"

I gave her a Look. "No one is in my mind," I said, mentally daring the city to even *think* about saying anything to the contrary. "Or on it. I don't think me and blokes are a good mix."

"Who said anything about blokes?" said Izzy. "No one's discriminating round here, love."

"You know what I mean," I sighed. "Any time something exciting happens on the romance front, it's immediately destroyed by the stupid paranormal shittery that seems to be the constant background to my life."

"Talking of paranormal shittery," said Izzy, "I don't suppose you know anything about the kerfuffle up at the India Buildings last night?"

So much had happened in the last twenty four hours that I'd all but forgotten about the vampires. "I've no idea what you're talking about," I said.

Izzy arched a frighteningly neat eyebrow at me. "Hmmm," she said. "It's just that a mate of Damon's is working security there at the moment and he messaged their group chat late last night with a story about people climbing all over the building. Apparently they were fighting on the balconies and all sorts."

"First I've heard of it," I shrugged.

"There's a Porsche sitting outside there with a clear footprint hammered into its roof," Izzy went on. "Smallish-sized Doc Martins, the mate reckons." She looked me up and down. "You wear DMs, don't you?"

I waggled a foot at her. "I generally stick with Converse," I said.

Izzy didn't look remotely convinced, but decided to change tactics. "Heard anything more from Liam?" she asked.

I sighed as I swirled dregs of milk round in the bottom of a small metal jug. They swished like a miniature sea; the storm sending tiny waves crashing up the steep sides. "He left a present on my doorstep last night," I said finally.

"Ooh," said Izzy, brightening up, "how romantic! Was it flowers? If he was unimaginative enough to give you flowers, then at least tell me they were really fancy ones and not chrysanths? No one likes an outdated king."

I looked up to where she was standing at the metal sink washing her hands, her eyes narrowed in anticipation of Liam having betrayed himself by being cheesy. *Oh well*, I thought, *here goes nothing*. "It was a crown," I said.

"What?" Izzy looked confused. "Like a tiara? Is he expecting to take you to a formal banquet or something?"

"Not a tiara," I said, smiling despite myself. "A crown. A royal one. Quite an important royal one, as it happens."

"Whoah," said Izzy, turning to look at me properly, "he wants you to be his *queen*?"

"Looks that way."

"That's definitely a step up from asking you to take his nan to church," she said, waggling her eyebrows for emphasis.

"I thought we'd agreed to never talk about that again?" Stephen Brigsworth had worked at the desk next to mine, back when I was still a minimum wage office drone. A couple of years older than me, he'd clearly seen himself as something of a Casanova and had made a show of what Mum would have described as 'wooing' me. It had started with me finding a box of Black Magic chocolates on top of my in-tray one Valentine's Day, complete with card tucked into a ribbon with *'Sweets for my sweet! Guess who? X'* written on it in careful calligraphy. It hadn't taken me long to guess, because Stephen was going red in the face about three feet away. And he had ink stains all over his fingers. He'd then done what I could only assume had supposed to have been a smooth manoeuvre up from his chair and into a casual sitting position on my desk. Unfortunately for Stephen, his chair had been oiled whilst he'd been out for lunch the previous day by Sylvia from accounts, because the squeaking wheels had been driving her mad. The chair shot out from underneath him as he twisted upwards and he crashed to the floor, his head hitting the sharp edge of my desk on the way down. The impact knocked him out cold, leaving me to put him in the recovery position and call an ambulance whilst everyone else in the office flapped around in a panic. As the only apparently sentient person in the vicinity, I'd been asked by the paramedics if I'd accompany Stephen on the short trip to the emergency department. In my mind's eye I could still see the dried drool down the side of his face from where his mouth had been hanging slackly open and I really wished my immortal memory would start dredging up nicer things occasionally. Surely I must have *some* memories that weren't either heartbreaking or mortifying? Stephen regained consciousness before we got to the hospital and had the presence of mind to ask me for a favour while I was still feeling sorry for him. Which is how I ended up escorting his ninety-three-year-old nan to a funeral at the Catholic cathedral after work that evening, because he'd promised to take her but was busy having his brain scanned.

"It took *months* to get the smell of incense out of my nose," I said. "Haven't I suffered enough?"

"You ended up going out with someone's nan on a first date and you think I'm not going to talk about it forever?" chortled Izzy.

"I did not go on a date with his nan! Oh, hi Sean." Out of the corner of my eye, I saw Izzy slowly sliding down the coffee machine, crying with silent laughter. "Ignore Iz," I said with a fixed smile on my face, "she likes to wind me up."

Sean grinned crookedly at me. "I did wonder what sort of unusual private life you must be leading," he said. "But then it's always the quiet ones, don't they say?"

"That's for sure," said Izzy, suddenly recovering and jumping to her feet to make his coffee. "And our Lil's quieter than most." She gave Sean a frankly alarming wink. "If you know what I mean."

"I'd certainly be interested in finding out," he said, holding his phone over the contactless pay-point next to the till. "We should have that coffee some time," he said to me, taking the cup from Izzy and lifting it in salute. "We can discuss strange landlords and dating grannies. Cheers Iz." He turned and headed over to the window table before I could think up a suitable response.

"Oh, for fuck's sake," I groaned, "just when I thought it couldn't get any more complicated."

"And you haven't even explained the crown thing yet," said Izzy. "Is it a valuable crown? Could you take it to Cash Converters?"

"If I tried to pawn that crown," I said, "I'd either be sectioned or locked in the Tower of London. Quite possibly both."

Izzy's eyes widened. "And Liam gave it to you?" she asked. "Did he get on one knee? Will you have glass slippers?"

"This isn't a bloody fairytale, Iz!" I pulled the mop out from down the side of the fridge and started cleaning the floor in the hope of soothing my mind. "Why do I have to keep telling people this? It's my stupid bloody real bloody life, and it is getting more complicated by the bloody sodding minute. Urgh!" A slight crunching noise beneath the mop informed me I'd cracked the grouting between the floor tiles.

"At least it isn't the tiles themselves this time," said Izzy soothingly, taking the mop from my hand and putting it back behind the fridge.

"I'm not going to be Liam's bloody accessory," I said firmly. Izzy raised an eyebrow but didn't speak. We've been friends long enough for her to know when to let me get things out of my head, even if they don't quite make sense. "It's the power he's after," I went on, looking at her, "not me. I mean, I think he does like me—"

"Yeah," said Izzy, "I think he does like you. Enough to bang your undead brains out, at least."

"—but he's definitely thinking of me as a potential accomplice for his own plans. Not an equal."

"Get you," said Izzy, tilting her head to gaze at me, "being all perceptive, like. Look, Lil," she said, turning to wipe down the counter and smile at a group of students who'd just come in and were loudly discussing what cakes they could share between them, "you had fun. He had ulterior motives. Shit happens, love—it doesn't matter, not really. Sell the silly crown, let Sean quiz you about pensioner romance," she ignored my scowl, "and forget Liam Whatsisname. He was a loser, anyway. What can I get you today, my lovelies?" She beamed at the students, leaving me standing there glaring at the stupid broken floor.

"Do you have a moment to talk about our Lord and Saviour Cthulhu?" asked Mapp, brandishing what looked like a tiny knitted octopus in my face. Tonight's meeting of the Renshaw Street Knitting Club was the busiest I'd ever seen. I'd given up on my own project—a terrible attempt at crocheting a sloth, which currently looked more like a bad-tempered tardigrade—in favour of keeping the tea and biscuits flowing. At least keeping busy gave me less time to stew on the endless list of stupid things going on in my life.

"I reckon he'd make more sense than most people I know," I said. Mapp wriggled himself up onto one of the high stools we keep by the counter. He was dressed in purple silk harem pants over silver hi-top sneakers, topped with a gold and orange kaftan. "Do you ever give yourself a migraine when you look in the mirror?" I asked him.

"Only from the intensity of my innate awesomeness," said Mapp with a grin. He put the knitted toy on the counter and leaned forward. "Did you hear what they found in the river?" he asked conspiratorially. I was saved from having to answer by the door opening behind him. To my astonishment, it was Rachel. She was peering nervously inside, as if unsure whether to enter. Perhaps I had to invite her in? I tried to remember whether I'd said anything that could have been construed as a formal invitation when I'd first brought her home. While I was still dithering, Alan popped up behind her and ushered her inside.

"Come on, girl," he said to her, "you'll be fine here."

Mapp swivelled round to look at the newcomers. "Hello, hello, hello," he said, swooping over towards them. Rachel shrank back against Alan, who was already reaching past her to shake Mapp's hand.

"Hey mate," said Alan, "boss setup you've got here."

"I didn't have you down as a connoisseur of the yarn arts," said Mapp, gesturing them towards the last empty seats, tucked right into the corner. I came out from behind the counter to pull the chairs out for them, unsure of whether Rachel would dare speak. She was clutching a tote bag to her bony chest, and I wondered what was inside. It turned out to be a half-finished blanket in varying shades of pastel green and yellow. "Can I look?" I asked. She blinked at me in surprise but handed it over, carefully passing me the crochet hook and wool that was still attached to the unfinished side. It was made up of granny squares—all basic stitches, but very neatly done. "It's lovely," I said truthfully, handing it back. Rachel smiled shyly, quiet pride visible on her face.

"My girl's a smart one, eh, Red?" said Alan, sliding past me into the chair next to Rachel. "Thought it was time she met other people, y'know? Stretch her clever mind a bit." Rachel elbowed him at that, equal parts flattered and embarrassed. I was more impressed by her newfound ability to function amidst humans. Maybe the rat blood had been a good idea after all. "I'm just here to speak for her," this was to the woman next to him, who'd been coming to the knitting club for weeks and was working on a narrow scarf that was currently at least eight feet long. She'd once confided in me she came for the socialising rather than the craft, so had decided on the simplest project she could think of in order to give her more time to chat. The two women next to her were also regulars, who walked down from Gambier Terrace every week in order to cross-stitch rude words in neat lettering onto small, rectangular frames. They'd brought a younger man with them tonight, who I thought was possibly a nephew.

"Oh dear," said the woman in a sympathetic voice. "Is she...you know?" She scrunched her face and gave a little shrug.

Alan looked at her for a second, his head tilted to one side. Then he started laughing—a wild, 'heeheeeeee' noise that sounded like a donkey had its leg stuck in a metal grate. "There's nothing *wrong* with her, love!" he said, when he'd stopped his weird braying. "She just doesn't like talking to people, is all."

"Oh no," said the woman, "I didn't mean anything by it!" The younger man was leaning in to listen, clearly prepared to wade in if he thought anyone was being discriminated against.

Alan patted her arm. "Don't you worry, girl," he said kindly, "it's all good. My Rachel here just has her...habits. Y'know?" The woman clearly did not know, but wasn't going to risk further embarrassment by admitting as much.

"Do I know you?" she said, looking at Alan properly for the first time. "You look familiar, somehow."

"Yeah," said Alan easily, "I get that a lot. No idea who I'm supposed to be, mind. Want a top up?" He nodded towards her empty mug, sitting on the table in front of them.

"Oh," she said, flustered. "Yes, I will. Thank you." Alan leaned over and poured her a cup of tea from the pot nearest to him, before adding milk from a little metal jug.

"Your friends are all *entirely* mad," said Izzy, coming up behind me. I turned to see her looking over at Alan with a grin on her face. "Brilliant, but utterly mad. Anyway," she turned to me, "I'm off." I could see Damon outside on the street waiting for her and gave him a wave through the steamed up window. "You okay to finish up here?"

"Course," I said. "It'll be a late one anyway, I think, looking at how busy it is."

"You knitters," said Izzy, "all about the crazy rock'n'roll lifestyle."

"You know how it is," I grinned at her. "Sex and yarn and rock and roll."

"Always," said Izzy, holding up a hand. I dutifully high-fived her. "Laters, taters," she said. "Don't do anything I wouldn't." She laughed at my raised eyebrows and headed out of the door. I watched as Damon picked her up and swung her round, grinning widely.

"Aah," said Mapp, suddenly beside me, "love's young dream. Soon to be love's middle-aged dream, of course. Followed by love's really old and falling apart at the—what?" He finally noticed my expression.

"Don't talk about Izzy getting old," I said, my chest tightening even as I said it. "I can't bear to think about it."

Mapp slid an arm across my shoulders and pulled me against him. "Lili," he said, "my darling girl. Izzy will live a human life, filled with human joy and sadness. If she's lucky, she will die peacefully at a very old age, surrounded by people who love her." He turned his head to look down at me. "She's got the better deal, I reckon."

I twisted my face up, trying not to show just how upset I was. "I think I'm struggling to accept things," I said quietly.

"No shit, Sherlock." Mapp gave me a wide grin, and I was pretty sure I spotted a gold tooth that hadn't been there the last time I'd looked. "But realising that is the biggest step, I reckon."

"There's nothing I can do to change any of it," I said, "and that's what I hate. Not having control over anything."

"Oh, but to the contrary," he said, "I think you have an awful lot of control, if you only learn to head in the right direction."

I wasn't in the mood for yet another lecture about facing my destiny, so changed the subject. "What did they find in the river, then?" I asked, already knowing the answer.

"Been dumping your rubbish in the poor old Mersey," he said, giving me a sideways wink. "Haven't you?"

"Don't you *dare* say anything," I hissed, pulling away in order to turn and glare at him. "I had no *choice*, Mapp! And I can't let Izzy be dragged into this, she puts up with enough already. If the police want to talk to me, I'll just have to pretend I've lost my—"

"Shhhh," he actually put a finger up to my lips and it's a mark of how much I love him that I didn't punch him in the face right then and there. "You're safe," he said. "There wasn't enough left for them to confirm a cause of death."

"So they haven't been able to identify the body?" I felt a bit guilty about feeling so relieved, but sometimes you just have to put yourself first.

"Oh, they've identified him, alrighty," said Mapp. "He was wearing an unusual gold ring—coppers put the details out on local news sites and his wife recognised the description. Amazing it was still on him, to be honest." He eyed me knowingly. "All his fingers had been bitten off at the second joint." Christ. Daisy was certainly efficient, I'd give her that. "Fish must be hungrier than usual. Anyway," his expression was utterly impassive, "the ring had been wedged down into the flesh around the time of his death," I felt nauseous now, "and got itself stuck onto the remains of the hand bones."

"His wife?" Okay, now I really did feel guilty.

"He was an accounts manager from down south," said Mapp. "Xander Byfleet, thirty-four years old." He really had been looking rough when I'd had the misfortune to meet him, then—I'd have sworn he was in his late forties, at least. "Moved up here five years ago after getting married—his wife was originally from Southport and wanted to be closer to her parents." I wondered what it was about accounts managers that made them so terminally weird. Maybe they just drop out of the womb as fully formed lecherous creeps. "They lived up in Fazakerly," Mapp went on, "but no kids." Phew. Accidentally offing a would-be sex offender was one thing, but killing someone's dad was another. And no, that logic doesn't make sense to me either, but it is what it is. "They separated three months before he's thought to have died, after the wife found out he'd been having an affair with a teenage friend of the family. Police traced the teenager, a nineteen-year-old student from the English department up on Abercromby Square. She said she'd never expected him to leave his wife, and was horrified when he turned up at her halls after being kicked him out. Apparently he'd assumed she'd be thrilled and would want him to move in. So you can imagine the drama when she told him it was just a fling, and he needed to find someone his own age. She kicked him out after one night, and it's presumed he slept in his car after that."

"How do you know all that?"

Mapp looked smug. "Got contacts in high places, innit," he said, tapping his head knowingly. "Nah," he gave me an impish grin, "Jenny over there couldn't wait to tell me about it." He nodded to where Jenny the paramedic was screwing her face up in apparent confusion at a complicated Fairisle pattern. "Apparently it's the most excitement she's had on the job so far. Anyway, the wife said she wouldn't have wished him dead, but neither would she have cared had she never heard from him again. She was so upfront about it that the officer interviewing her apparently told his guv'nor there was no way she wasn't telling the truth. If she'd have been the one to push him into the river she'd have found herself a cast-iron alibi, not declared herself relieved. As for the teenager, she clearly just wants to pretend the entire sorry saga never happened. And who can blame her?" He shrugged. "Yer off the hook, Lil." That didn't make me feel any better, for some reason. "Anyway," said Mapp, pushing himself upright, "I must tend to my flock. Doreen over there," he pointed to a woman in her seventies with a sharp pixie cut and amazing legs, "is doing her best to seduce me. Don't give me that disbelieving look," he narrowed his eyes at my cynical expression, "it's true. She thinks I need a sugar mama to help run the shop and keep me on the straight and narrow. Who knows," he said, stepping backwards away from me, "I might just take her up on it." With that, he turned and launched himself on Doreen with a flurry of shrieking compliments about the baby bonnet she was knitting. I shook my head in amusement then starting checking everyone had enough tea and biscuits. You can never have too much tea and biscuits at knitting club. Cthulhu's law.

GODS AND MONSTERS

In the end, it was almost ten o'clock by the time the knitting club finally dispersed. Mapp waved off his acolytes in a flurry of hugs and air kisses and promises to check in with a couple of people who were stuck with their projects. I refused his sweet offer of help to clear up on the—legitimate—basis that I'd be quicker left to get on with it in peace, and then finally I was alone in the cafe. With no one watching me, I could do everything at full speed and I had the place tidied up and the dishwasher filled and running within three minutes. And only two cups sacrificed to speed-induced breakage, which was a record. I locked up and looked around for Billy, but he was nowhere to be seen. He'd been missing a lot over the last couple of weeks, which made me nervous for reasons I couldn't quite figure out. Telling myself I wasn't his mother and he was a fully grown adult ghost who was well able to look after himself, I headed up the fire escape.

I was surprised to find the flat in darkness, then remembered Kitty was off on her jollies to Shrewsbury. When I turned on the kitchen light there was no sign of Grimm either, but that didn't mean anything. He often sloped off when Kitty wasn't around, as though implying she was the only reason he ever came into the flat anyway. I closed the living room curtains and switched on the little lamp that sat on the table next to the sofa to make it look a bit more homely. Then I went back into the kitchen and filled the kettle. As it boiled, I rooted around in the cupboards for the fruit tea bags and, having noticed the 'best before date' was from the previous year, sniffed them for freshness. After deciding it was surely impossible for tea to grow poisonous with age, I used one anyway. Taking my mug out onto the fire escape, I sat down cross-legged on the top platform and carefully put the mug down next to me. Leaning back against the wall, I closed my eyes and breathed.

Initially there was nothing more than petrol fumes and industry and the faint hum of a breeze through telephone wires. My senses were being drowned out by the memories that were still trying to crowd their way into my head. I let myself be carried along with it to begin with. It's always better to swim with the tide until you find a place to climb out, rather than waste energy fighting the current. So I watched it all flicker through my head as though I was sitting in front of an old-fashioned movie projector. There was my twelfth birthday, when Mum took me and Izzy pony trekking. At the end of the ride I'd got off Blackie the little Welsh pony to stares and hushed whispers and stains on the pale tan saddle that told me I'd started my periods. My first day working at the Bluecoat, when I spilled tea on a customer who shouted at me until my new boss kicked them out for being rude to her staff. Then back to the very first time Izzy spoke to me, when she started at my school in year four and was given the desk next to mine. I had a sudden, intense image of Grimm on the day I brought him home from the rescue centre as an angry ball of fur, with sharp eyes and even sharper claws. There didn't seem to be any logic to the order in which memories were coming back. Although of course I wouldn't know if any major ones were missing anyway, if I couldn't remember them. It wasn't all personal stuff —there were flashes of television reports from when Labour claimed a landslide victory back in 1997, along with Tony Blair's angry and defensive face as he tried to justify the invasion of Iraq and his popularity began to wane. A still photograph of the Toxteth riots popped up, surprising me because it happened before I'd even been born. I must have read about it at some point. Newspapers have always liked to knock this city off its perch whenever the opportunity arises. Then they accuse Liverpudlians of having a chip on their shoulders. I reckon anyone could be excused for being snarky if their home town was done over by the media on the reg. When my brother popped up in the next rambling thought—a vague memory of a family trip to a 'pick your own' strawberry farm, at which Cally had eaten so much he'd been sick in the car on the drive home—I cut it off sharply. I'd made my peace with my dead brother and wasn't about to go wriggling back down that miserable rabbit hole. Instead, I began sending the memories off down my imaginary mental river, each thought floating on a leaf that swirled around in the eddying current. Every time my mind tried to drop a new memory into my head I popped it on a leaf and sent it on its way, until all I was seeing in my mind's eye was a meanderingly peaceful river covered with leaves. I breathed again, just once, and the scent of frankincense filled my head. "Fuck off," I called out pleasantly, without opening my eyes. "Or I'll throw you off another building."

"I'd really rather you didn't," said a voice from below me. "I'll never get the stains out of that shirt." I gave in and opened my eyes.

"Hi," said Liam, emerging from the darkness of the car park. He was wearing a knitted cotton sweater and loose-fitting dark trousers over what looked distinctly like high-top sneakers. He looked *ordinary*. "Can we talk?"

"No, we bloody well cannot," I said, glaring down at him.

Don't trust him.

As if! I rolled mental eyes at the city. *I wouldn't trust that slimy scrote as far as I can throw him.*

Which is actually quite a long way.

Touché.

"You're cute when you're talking to yourself," said Liam. "Has anyone ever told you that?" Before I could come up with a suitably sarcastic retort, something moved in the darkness behind Liam. To my astonishment, Grimm strolled out of the shadows and rubbed himself against Liam's ankles, purring so loudly that I could hear him from my perch at the top of the fire escape. I stood up and leaned over the railing, glaring disbelievingly down at my idiot cat.

"Get up here, you traitorous little shit!" I yelled down at Grimm, who pretended he hadn't heard me and miaowed at Liam for attention. Actually fucking *miaowed*, the hypocritical little toad. Liam bent down to pick Grimm up as though it was the most natural thing in the world for one of history's most famous monarchs to be standing in a car park in Liverpool, playing oochie-coochie with a cat. If I still had a fully functioning internal system, I was pretty sure my head would have blown right off with the pressure of my fury. "GET IN THE HOUSE RIGHT THIS SECOND," I bellowed. Even Grimm can't ignore The Voice, not that it stops him trying. I could see the internal struggle going on in the cat's head, even from a distance. He glared up at me for a few long seconds, whilst Liam smugly continued to tickle him under his chin and tell him what a good boy he was. "NOW!" I hurled my mug at the pair of them, rage making me reckless. Liam ducked, and the mug hit the opposite wall with a loud crash. Grimm finally decided to bail, but Liam was still holding onto him. I watched claws raking down Liam's face as Grimm spat and hissed, writhing like an octopus escaping from a fishing net. With one last yowl, the cat sprang free and leaped onto the fire escape. He shot past me and into the house at such speed that I heard a muffled thud as he hit the side of the sofa. Liam stood below me, one hand up to his face where the deep red weals were already healing.

"It's lucky I'm up to date with my shots," he said mildly. "Now you've got it out of your system, perhaps we can finally talk about what we should do."

"I've got nothing to say to you, *William*."

"If it helps any," he said, "I'm far more Liam than William these days."

"Really?" I said. "Given up fighting and pillaging and taking over other people's territories?"

"Who says Liam doesn't do those things as well?" he said.

"So why would I want to talk to someone like that?"

"I understand how it feels," he said softly. "The unexpected power. People being attracted to you even as they're feeling threatened by you. The memories. Oh god, the memories. Red, I know what it's like to have a head filled to bursting with the knowledge of everyone and everything you've ever known or done. I *know*." He smiled faintly in the artificial light.

"You can remember everything?" I asked, curious despite myself. "Almost a thousand years of...everything?"

"Yes," said Liam, "I can. Tiring, isn't it?" From this angle, he looked weary, and older than I remembered. But then, I'd been quite distracted the last time we'd met. Mostly by his nakedness. I did my best to push the memories away and glared down at him.

"It's certainly something," I agreed. "But I'm still pretty sure you're not a good person for me to be talking to, no matter how much we've got in common."

Liam tilted his head and looked up at me. His expression was open and friendly, and his eyes crinkled up at the corners as he smiled. "It's like a modern-day Romeo and Juliet," he said, "with you up there on your balcony and us each belonging to opposing factions."

"Except I'm not stupid enough to fake my own death," I said. "And I strongly suspect you wouldn't take poison if I did."

"It would be a pointless exercise," Liam shrugged, "as the poison wouldn't kill me."

"Why the opposing factions?" I asked. "Why can't you all just kiss and makeup? Take some time to figure it all out between yourselves. Maybe go on Oprah."

"Because I'm the one true ruler of this nation," said Liam flatly, "and I intend to take it back. "

"Get on with you," I snorted. "What's your real plan?"

Liam frowned slightly. "That *is* my plan, Lilith," he said. "And I would like you to be part of it." I stared at him, waiting for the punchline. When it didn't come, I sat back slightly and gazed at him in silence for a while.

"Well," I said eventually, "that's a shame. Because I don't want to be part of your stupid plan. It's about time you went back to your own territory, Liam O'Connor," I said. "Go away, and don't come back. You can find some other woman to deceive and drag into your scheming. I'll go fetch the crown. You can find someone else to wear it."

"No." His voice was flat. "It's yours."

"Well, I don't want it."

"It doesn't work like that, Red," he said, looking up at me with a faint smile. "That's not how any of this works."

"We still have choices, Liam," I said. "We can all decide not to follow our prescribed destiny. Especially if that destiny is really fucking stupid."

"Can we?" he asked, and there was a wistful tone to his voice. "Can we really? I'm not so sure about that, Red. There's a reason I've been kept alive all these centuries. There has to be."

"Why?" I stood up and leaned over the top of the safety railing, looking down on him. "Why does there always have to be a reason? You might have grown up in an era of gods and monsters, but I live in a more enlightened age. In case you hadn't noticed."

"Because if there's no higher power," said Liam with a shrug, "what's the point of any of it? Of us?"

"I hate to break it to you," I said, "but I don't think there *is* a point. To any of it."

"Nor to us?" I shook my head. "Could we...discuss this inside?" he asked.

"Nope," I said, pushing myself back from the railing. "I'm going to finish meditating. I have a *lot* of thoughts to get rid of." With that I walked inside, locked the door firmly behind me and determinedly did not look out of the window to check if he was still there. I walked into the living room to find my phone glowing with a notification. I picked it up and opened the message, despite knowing it was almost certainly a mistake to do so. All it said was *'10am tomorrow?'* along with an address on the outskirts of town. Dropping onto the sofa with a weary sigh, I peered over to where Grimm was glaring at me from the armchair. "Since when were you so bloody judgmental?" I asked him. But the cat didn't reply.

However much I knew I probably shouldn't, I made myself presentable the next morning and managed to leave Harrington Street without anyone spotting me. I knew Flora's was busy enough to keep Izzy distracted because I'd spent too long staring out of the living room windows and seen people going in and out. And Billy's doorway was empty, so he was probably round the corner on Mathew Street, listening to more of Ifan's tall tales. That man really appreciates an audience. I'd given myself enough time to walk over to Aigburth at a human pace, but still managed to be early. Determined not to look eager, I loafed around on a quiet residential street until a quick peek around the corner told me my date had finally arrived. Pasting a bright and hopefully confident smile on my face, I sauntered casually up the street. "Hi," I said, sitting down at the small table that was set out on the narrow pavement.

"Hi yourself," said Ivo with a smile. "I've taken the liberty of ordering you an espresso. I hope that's okay?"

"Thanks." I settled back in my chair and looked around. "I haven't been over this way in years." Not that anything had changed very much, other than the shops and cafes looking like they'd all had a lick of paint. There were definitely more people wandering around, though. Three miles and endless worlds away from Liverpool city centre, Lark Lane is the kind of place that gets described as a 'hidden gem' in the Sunday supplements. You know an area has truly made it when the staff in its cafes automatically offer you oat milk for your coffee without being asked.

"I remember when all this was still just fields," said Ivo, and I knew he wasn't kidding. "Or rather, hunting lodges and woodland. Greenery as far as the eye could see. Mind you," he peered around himself, "it's still practically rural compared to the town centre."

"Are you staying here?" I asked.

"Nope. I'm in my usual rooms."

"I can't believe they still let you stay," I said. The last time Ivo had visited Liverpool, the top floor of the Hope Street Hotel had ended up out of commission for weeks.

"I paid the repair bill upfront," he smiled, "and added a bit extra to make up for the inconvenience."

"Life's always easier when you've got bottomless funds," I agreed.

"There has to be some advantages to living for centuries," shrugged Ivo. We both sat silently as a waitress came out with our drinks on a tray. She put them down on the table with instructions to 'Enjoy!' and twirled back off inside. "It's a bit aggressive," he said eventually, "isn't it?"

"What's aggressive?" I swirled my espresso in its tiny cup, watching the crema spiral against the white porcelain.

"All these instructions to enjoy things," he said. "Why should I 'have a nice day'," he did the bunny ears with his fingers for emphasis, "just because someone told me to?"

"We went on a school trip when I was six," I said, "and the teacher in charge told us very firmly that we *would* enjoy ourselves, as though it was a threat. Sarah Foxham cried on the bus on the way there, because she was so worried that she'd get into trouble if she didn't have the time of her tiny little life."

"What did Sarah Foxham look like?" asked Ivo, looking curious.

"She was a bit taller than me," I said, "with yellowy-blonde hair that I think was supposed to be cut into a bob, but always frizzed up by the end of the day. I suspect her mum straightened it each morning before she left for school. And she had sticky-out teeth—just the top two. Not badly enough to need braces, but it made her look a bit like a hamster. One of her fingers bent back further than the others, and her favourite outfit was a green Adidas t-shirt over red shorts. She said her shoes were uncomfortable, so she used to change into her P.E. pumps when she got to school each morning. They really stank by the end of the summer term. What?" Ivo was grinning at me over the top of his coffee cup.

"That memory of yours is getting impressive, Red," he said. "I do hope you manage to develop a coping system. Otherwise you're going to get overwhelmed with it all."

"I've already got one," I said. "It's called 'lock it in the fuck-it box and keep moving'."

"Do you think you'll team up with Liam?" he asked suddenly.

"What?" I said, startled by the change of topic. I wondered uneasily just how much Ivo knew. "What makes you think I'd do that?"

"Oh," said Ivo, "I don't know. Power, maybe? After all," he looked down into his coffee, then back up at me, "Liam's probably the closest you're ever going to get to a truly equal match."

"He's a king," I said, "and I run a coffeeshop. We're hardly equals."

Ivo raised an eyebrow but said nothing. "He's also a lying little shit," I went on. "So no, I won't be doing anything with him. Ever again."

Ivo gave me a speculative look. "Nothing at all?" he said, his eyes crinkling up slightly at the corners.

"Shut up," I said, grinning despite myself. For all his faults—and there are many, some of them more dangerous than others—I'd always enjoyed Ivo's company. About a decade older than me in real terms, he looked like an old-fashioned movie star in his sharp clothes and had the twinkling eyes to match. He was also an absolute shitheel and didn't bother hiding it. But he was also funny. And he could be sweet at times. For all I made light of it to Izzy, I really did have a soft spot for Ivo. Not that he could ever know that, because he was no better than Liam and would absolutely use any vulnerability on my part to his own advantage.

"So Red," he eyed me speculatively, "how's it going?"

"In what way?" I fiddled with a sugar sachet, which is one of my favoured avoidance techniques.

"Oh, you know," he said, "just in general. Getting used to the after-life, trying not to get murdered by vampires, that sort of thing."

"You heard about that as well, then," I sighed. "I swear I could fart and half this city would know about it within twenty minutes."

"Aah, such ladylike company," said Ivo. "I'm not sure I'd want to be in the same room as a revenant with wind," he went on, looking thoughtful. "One would have to consider the toxicity levels of waste gas emitted from an undead corpse."

"Yuck."

"You started it." Ivo grinned. "I've missed you, Red."

"Don't start."

"Start what?" he asked. "Just telling the truth. You're the most fun this country's seen in centuries. The dead bits of the country, anyway."

"Do you think Mab might be up here again?"

"I don't know," he said eventually. "She doesn't keep in touch."

"And that bothers you?"

"She's my daughter," he said. "I want to know she's safe. Even if she does hate me."

"If you care about her that much," I said, "then why did you keep her apart from her mother for more than a century?"

"It sounds so cruel when you put it like that," said Ivo, leaning back in his chair and gazing across at me. "It wasn't quite like that, of course."

"Then what was it like?" I said. "Because from where I'm sitting, it looks very much like you ruined both their lives. And that's what's at the root of everything awful either of them have ever done."

"I can understand why you might see it like that." He looked thoughtful. "But I didn't do it out of cruelty. The truth, Red, is that I had no choice in the matter. Both Maria and Mab's happiness had to be sacrificed for the greater good. They couldn't be allowed to know each other."

"Why?"

"Because they are—were—dangerous. Individually, each of them had powers not even I quite understand. Maria could do things Mab couldn't, and vice versa. Had they joined forces, I suspect this city would have been reduced to rubble long before the Nazis tried their best."

"You're not serious?"

Ivo nodded, a wry smile on his face. "I am," he said, "and in many ways you did the netherworld a favour by destroying half the puzzle. I do still miss Maria sometimes, you know," his eyes tightened briefly, "but we can't always get what we want."

"Sometimes," I said, "we just get what we need." He gave a little shake of his head and smiled. "Maria wasn't *that* strong, Ivo," I went on, "and I'd have fought Mab off in the catacombs if you hadn't helped her escape. I might even have killed her." He shrugged. "Have you considered that maybe they'd both have been nicer people if they'd been allowed to know each other?"

"Yes," he said, "I have. Endlessly. But all any of us can do is make decisions based on what we think is best at the time. And then we have to live with the consequences of those decisions." He leaned forward, his face earnest. "I don't know if I did the right thing, Red—but I know I did what was best at the time. For all of us."

"Do you remember what it was like to have a mother?"

I could almost see the mental shutters coming down behind his eyes. "Yes," he said finally, "I do. All these centuries later and I still remember my mother. My entire family are legends, Red. Not in the way the word is so often used in the modern world, you understand. My family were —and are—legendary. Tales are told of my father's heroics, as well as his occasional cruelty—to my mother, as well as our enemies. But my mother, too, had her faults. So I can't in all truthfulness say if one was a better person than the other."

"What do you remember about your mother?" I persisted.

"Her scent," Ivo smiled. "She smelled of damp moss and saltwater, and the dog roses that grew wild in the woods. And she had the most incredible eyes of the palest lavender-grey."

"Was she kind?" I asked.

"Mostly," he said. "Kindness meant different things back then, of course. She ensured we didn't go hungry and had a roof over our heads, even if that roof was sometimes nothing more than a deerskin tied between the trees. And she made sure we could fight. Perhaps that was her greatest kindness." His eyes were focused on the distant past now, rather than the sights and sounds of modern suburban Liverpool. "She taught us how to survive."

"She sounds..." I struggled for the right word, "...fascinating." Ivo's gaze returned to the present and focused on me again.

"William Morris once wrote a poem about my parents," he said. "It's amusingly sweet and not very truthful. But to inspire poetry a thousand years after one's death? I think that probably counts as legendary."

"Someone wrote a song about me once," I said. "It was terrible."

Ivo tilted his head. "Was your would-be swain not the musical type?" he asked.

"Oh, it's not that," I said, "he was actually quite good. Played guitar in bands and wrote all his own songs. Everyone loved him." I smiled. "Ifan reminds me of him sometimes," I said. "Although Ifan has been rather more successful over the years."

"So what was wrong with the song?"

I looked at Ivo. "It was all about what an awful person I was and how he needed to walk out on me and find someone better. I know," we both started laughing, "how awful is that? And people really liked that bloody song, so even though we sorted things out and stayed together for a while afterwards, he'd still have to play it at gigs. And I'd be standing there, the dutiful girlfriend. Smiling and singing along about how horrible I was."

"Oh Red," snorted Ivo, "you really are ridiculous sometimes."

"My life is absolute clown shoes," I agreed. "And now my afterlife is following the same pattern. Fun times, mate."

"It doesn't have to be this complicated," said Ivo.

"How do you figure that out?" I scuffed my sneakers on the pavement underneath the table. "Because all I do right now is get up and attempt to work in Flora's and stupid things *still* keep happening."

"You could accept your destiny," said Ivo quietly. "Then things would settle."

"But what *is* my destiny, Ivo?" I frowned at him. "Wearing an ancient crown and spending my days telling dead people what to do? That wasn't on my list of career options, to be honest."

"He's offered you the crown, then?" Bollocks. Me and my eternally big mouth.

"Oh," I said offhandedly, "you know what I mean. Metaphorical shit."

Ivo tilted his head and smiled at me—and it was the smile of a big cat who'd just spotted its prey drinking obliviously at a secluded water hole. "If you say so," he said. "But if the Bastard *were* to offer it to you at some point, what then? If the crown's meant for you then it won't allow itself to be taken by anyone else."

I suddenly remembered something Grandad used to say. '*What's for you won't go by you, Lil.*' "Then I'd refuse it," I said, trying not to think about the crown that was right this minute dangling off the mirror in my bedroom, "and it wouldn't have anyone at all."

"And what good do you think that would do?" Ivo's gazed levelly at me, curiosity written across his face.

"Well, it couldn't make anything worse than it already is," I said, "and it might stop things happening at all." He looked unconvinced. "I need *time*, Ivo! I haven't even been dead a year, and I've spent most of it fighting people and generally trying not to get killed for good. I still don't understand the politics behind it all and I still don't see why politics should be involved anyway. It's okay for you," I was on a roll now, months of angst churning up inside me, "because you've been doing this for centuries and you have shared history with others in this ridiculous world. I don't." I looked at him pleadingly. "I don't have anything except my human best friend, the ghost of my flaky aunt, a cat who clearly views me as a disappointment and a bunch of men who all seem to want me to attach myself to them for their own hidden motives. I am sick of you and Liam trying to be seductive when all you actually want is power, and I am sick of not being able to even walk home at night without being jumped by fucking vampires. It is all completely and utterly *stupid*." I trailed off. "So there."

We sat in silence for a while. "What are you going to do about Mab?" asked Ivo, eventually.

"Wait for her to try to kill me again," I shrugged. "Not much else I can do. Doesn't exactly make life easy though, knowing someone's lurking in the background, just waiting for the chance to lop off my head."

"Tell me about it," he said. "That's been about the sum of my life for several centuries now." We both stared at our coffee cups for a while. "Off course," he said eventually, "if Mab doesn't manage to kill you, then Elizabeth will have to. At some point."

I jerked my head up to stare at him. "You're going to have to repeat yourself," I said, "because I'm sure I just heard you say Elizabeth will try to kill me."

"That is exactly what I said."

"But Elizabeth is the one person who's actually declared her loyalty!" I was stunned. "Why on earth would she want to kill me?"

"She isn't lying about her loyalty to you," Ivo said, his face devoid of emotion, "but Middlesex will always be more important to her. And Middlesex will not accept being ruled by the north."

"I'm not *in* the north," I said crossly. "I'm in Liverpool. You're more north than me, for fuck's sake!"

"But I haven't been offered the crown of the entire country," said Ivo. "Have I?"

"Why does Lia—William get to just swan in and put everyone in a flap?" I asked. "There's all this talk about loyalties and who's with the north and who'll stand with the south and 'hey Lil, stick this rickety old crown on and pretend you know what you're doing', but if William hadn't shown his stupid face, none of it would be happening."

"True." Ivo nodded.

"So why can't we all just ignore him and carry on as normal?" I demanded. "Why are we all panicking about what happens next and who rules what? Send him back to Hereford like a naughty child and be done with."

"Said like a true leader," grinned Ivo. "Which is why the city needs you. Middlesex might be prepared to fight against subservience, but don't you think Liverpool would do the same? Some would argue this is the most important city in the land, Red. It funnelled industry and people into this country at a speed no other city could match, and it has the pride and the power that goes with that. It might be a youngster compared to the others, but it has a spirit that even London would struggle to suppress. And god knows, it's tried."

"So I'll just add 'try not to get killed by the entire city of London' to my to-do list, shall I?" Ivo shrugged. "I thought Elizabeth was my friend," I said sadly. "I thought she was one of the few people who didn't have an ulterior motive. I thought she *liked* me."

"She does like you," he said. "But that won't stop her fighting to keep her place at the top of the pecking order. Crown or no crown."

"So what you're saying is that I'm doomed either way," I said. "In which case, I might as well ignore the crown thing entirely. One less thing to worry about."

"Or you could accept it and start living up to your publicity," said Ivo. "I'm sorry to be the one to tell you this, Red, but people are going to want you out of the picture. Not all of them human people, either. The crown would at least give you some extra protection."

"How?"

"You and William as joint rulers are a far more intimidating proposition than him lurking in Herefordshire and you bouncing around Liverpool trying to pretend nothing's changed," he said. "Whether you like the man or not, he's your best chance of survival right now."

"Why are you encouraging me to take up with Liam?" I asked. "Whatever happened to your terrible chat-up lines and barely concealed attempts to get into my pants?"

"Oh," said Ivo, with a grin that made me think of fairytale wolves, "I would still happily jump into any of your undergarments. So long as you were in them with me."

"So why push me towards your enemy?"

"Because then," he said calmly, "you can double-cross him. And I'll be waiting to help you." I felt my face drop in shock. "Playtime's over, Red," said Ivo, getting up from the table and brushing non-existent crumbs off his immaculate suit. "It's time to join the grown-ups."

Sounds Like
Queening To Me

"There's a parcel for you on the table out back," said Izzy, when I got back to Flora's. Business was brisk, and she had Todd working with her. "Nik dropped it off earlier, said you'd know what it was." As I headed through to the staff kitchen, I realised I hadn't asked Ivo why he was in town in the first place. I'd have expected him to stay well away whilst Liam was around, if only to conceal his own nefarious plans. And there *would* be nefarious plans, I had no doubt about that. Expecting Ivo to stay quietly out of other people's business was like asking a great white shark to ignore injured swimmers. He might not intend to hurt anyone, but his killer instinct would always take over eventually. Sighing, I dumped my bag next to the sink and picked up the parcel. "Anything interesting?" asked Izzy, sticking her head through the door.

"Maps," I said, using a cake knife to break the seal on the package. "Thought I'd do a bit of detective work."

"And Nik's been out to buy you a deerstalker and a pipe?"

"Ha ha." I tipped a sheaf of photocopies out onto the table, then reached in to pull out the small paperback that had got jammed in the wrapping. "I'm trying to track down the rest of the tunnels."

156

"And you couldn't use the internet?" Izzy asked. "Or go to the library?"

"As far as I know," I started unfolding the sheets of paper, which were all at least A3 sized, "Nik *did* go to the library. There'd have been no point doing it at home," I went on, checking I hadn't left anything inside the wrapping, "because none of us have a printer big enough."

"Yeah," said Izzy, "I get that. But why couldn't you go to the library yourself? Is Nik your serf now, or something?"

I laughed. "Can you imagine Nik as anyone's serf?" I asked her.

She shook her head. "Not really," she conceded. "But neither is it like him to go running errands for people."

"Nik loves the library," I said. "All that history and pomp and whatever else it is he gets off on these days. He likes librarians because they Know Things, and in return they all adore him because he's clever and funny and *just* old-fashioned enough to make them think of *Bridgerton*. And if you must know," I sighed, "I don't entirely trust librarians. So it's easier to let Nik go up there and search for me."

Izzy's eyes crinkled up at the corners and I knew she was trying not to laugh. "Go on then," she said eventually, "tell me why you don't trust librarians."

"They know too much!" I said, shuddering slightly. "They're *creepy*."

"But you used to love the library!" Izzy was on the verge of bursting into laughter now. "What on earth happened?"

"I did like librarians," I said, "back when I was alive. But that was when I didn't know an entire parallel world lived alongside the human one. These days I'm suspicious of everyone, pretty much. And that includes librarians. They *know* things." Don't get me wrong, I still love libraries themselves. Whether they're lush acres of mahogany bookcases set in the lavish silence of a private library, or squashed inside a concrete new-build tucked into the corner of a housing estate, libraries are one of the best inventions humankind ever came up with. Centuries-worth of books and information and stories, all just waiting to be discovered. But having that level of access to all the information ever—properly researched information, rather than random corners of Google—has got to do something to the human brain. The one and only time I'd visited Central Library since I died, the bloke behind the counter looked me up and down and checked my card more carefully than was comfortable. It was as though he knew something wasn't quite right. Like I say—librarians make me nervous. Even the ones who like bananas.

"God, you're weird," snorted Izzy. "You're literally a dead woman walking and your boyfriend is a king who's been around for nearly a thousand years—"

"—Liam is *not* my boyfriend," I interrupted.

"Whatever," said Izzy. "You're dead. Most of your friends are dead. At least one of your friends is, quite literally, a bloody vampire. And here's you, scared of librarians. Oh, mate." She shook her head and disappeared back into the cafe. Sighing, I spread the papers out onto the table and weighed them down with the book, which turned out to be a thin but old biography of Joseph Williamson. I didn't think it would include anything I didn't already know, on account of the man himself being a friend of mine, but bless Nik for trying. The maps were more interesting. The biggest one was a beautifully drawn diagram of the original Liverpool to Manchester railway and its later extension from Edge Hill down into town. Nik had had the foresight to also get a large map of the Williamson tunnels. After a bit of digging around in the kitchen drawers, I found some loose paper clips and pinned the two sheets together, then held them up against the kitchen window. The printer paper was cheap and thin enough for me to make out both sets of drawings overlaid on each other. I could see where Stephenson's railway crossed through Joe's excavations. That would have been a fun conversation to witness—George S explaining to Joe just why he'd cut a route straight through the little man's pride and joy. Stephenson's men hadn't known the tunnel even existed until they broke through and— quite literally—fell into it. Legend has it the unexpected sight of people wandering around in the dark depths convinced them they'd unwittingly dug down into the underworld itself, and they ran away in panic.It was ironic to think that, had the same happened just a few decades later, they'd have been correct in their assumptions. The less excitable Stephenson was so impressed by the workmanship found in the unexpected tunnels that he employed some of Joe's men to help finish the route to Lime Street.

. . .

I was still pondering the maps when Izzy stuck her head back through the kitchen door. "I'm nipping down to the docks," she said. "Gonna say hi to Daisy. Want to come?"

I looked up reluctantly from my maps, which were turning out to be far more interesting than I'd expected. "Why are you visiting Daisy in the middle of the day? What if someone sees her?"

"Oh," said Izzy airily, "I visit her in the afternoon quite often." It was the first I'd heard of it. "So long as you walk up out of town a little way, no one really notices. And when they do, they generally assume she's just your regular human, practicing for a Channel swim or something." Daisy swimming the Channel would be a sight to behold. It would certainly be the fastest crossing ever. "I've got her a bag of scraps from the fishmonger," Izzy went on, "and they're going to stink out the fridge if I don't shift them quick. It's quieter now. Todd'll be fine on his own."

"Why," I asked, "have you got fish bits for Daisy? Is it her birthday or something?" It occurred to me that I didn't know if Daisy had even been born in anything approaching the usual way. Maybe she'd been spawned. I briefly had uncomfortable visions of her parents, deep in the Mersey, mum squeezing eggs out into the water and dad waiting to flap fishy sperm over them. Then I decided to never think about that ever again.

"Figured she deserved a reward," said Izzy. "You know," her voice dropped to a dramatic whisper, "as she sorted out that body for us."

Ugh. "Yeah," I said, getting to my feet, "I guess she does. Let me just put this lot away and I'll come with."

"Anything useful?" asked Izzy, nodding at the maps.

"Yeah," I said. "Maybe."

~

"You know people are starting to talk about the vampires?" asked Izzy as we walked to the river. Albert Dock was busy with tourists, so we were following the Strand down into Wapping, where it would be quieter.

"I've never been inside that pub," she said, as we walked past the Baltic Fleet, "which is surprising. Isn't it supposed to be built over tunnels?"

"This entire city is built over tunnels and nothingness," I said. "So it's probably not really such a surprise that it currently appears to be the centre of the known spooky universe. But yeah," we stopped to let a woman pass us with a toddler in a pushchair and pair of very lively twins of about five, "there are supposedly tunnels from the pub to the dock. And more tunnels leading to the old red light district up at Cornhill."

"Priorities," nodded Izzy. "I like it. So what are you going to do about the vampires?"

"I don't know," I said honestly. "I need to figure out why they're coming back first, I think."

"Well, don't leave it too long," said Izzy, as we waited to cross at Queen's Wharf. "I'd rather not risk being chomped, thank you very much."

"Joe's vampires wouldn't hurt anyone intentionally," I said, "but I these aren't the same. They're too human to have been eating rats. I think they really are feeding on people."

Izzy shuddered theatrically. "How are they doing that without anyone realising?" she asked. "It's not like corpses are turning up on the reg."

"Iz," I said, "you know as well as I do that pretty much every supposed fetish is acceptable these days, so long as it's all consensual. I think," the green man popped up and we headed across the road, "they're probably convincing humans it's just a kink."

"That doesn't sound very consensual to me," said Izzy, as we headed past the dock and down to the river path. "Not if their human partners don't know what they're letting themselves in for."

"And there's my problem," I said. "How am I supposed to persuade creatures of the night that they need to sate their undead bloodlust in an ethical manner?"

"Well, I guess that's something you're just going to have to figure out," said Izzy, "if you're going to be in charge and all."

"I keep telling you, I don't *want* to be in charge."

You don't have a choice anymore.

"And you can fuck right off."

160

"Excuse me?"

"Not you, Iz," I sighed.

"Right," she said, realisation dawning. "So you're not going to be in charge and you're not going to sort out the vampires, but you have the city in your head and *it* thinks you're its queen even if you don't agree with it. Am I right so far?"

"I'm not head of the city itself," I said. "I keep telling you that. It's more...I don't know," I trailed off as a group of very slow joggers came past us, "...just the spirit of the place. The undead bits."

"Sounds like queening to me," said Izzy. We walked silently along the river path for a while. "So, do you think it's all connected?" she asked eventually. "Literally, I mean. The tunnels and the vampires and all this sudden spooky shit that was never around before."

"It was always around," I said. "Just not visible."

"Same difference," she shrugged. "We can stop here," 'here' being in front of the statue of John Hulley, "Daisy likes this spot."

"Isn't it a bit overlooked?" I asked, turning to look at the row of townhouses behind us. "What if someone looks out of their window?"

"The only people living in those," Izzy said, jerking her head at the houses, "are incomers with more money than sense. I don't give a shit what they think."

"Fair enough." We sat by the railings, incomers ourselves, dangling our feet over the edge. The tide was on the turn, but the water was still high enough that I could feel occasional splashes up against the soles of my sneakers. Izzy dug around in her tote and pulled out a small parcel wrapped in what turned out to be several plastic bags.

"I'll smell for days, otherwise," she explained. "The fish stink gets into everything."

"That's what comes of having mermaids as friends," I said.

"Ooh," said Izzy, "I forgot to tell you! I met another of Daisy's lot the other day."

"I knew she couldn't be the only one," I said. "Did it look like her?"

"Not 'it'," said Izzy in a reproving tone, "*she*. And yes, she did. Slightly longer hair, maybe a bit older than Daisy? But just as pale and interesting."

"I wonder how many of them there are out there?" I watched as Izzy pulled a disposable glove out of her bag and put it on.

"Learned the hard way," she said, waggling blue latex fingers at me. "Takes ages to get the stink of fish guts out of my fingers." Stretching her head as far away from the bag as possible, she delicately pulled out a severed fish head and threw it. It dropped into the water with a plop, before bobbing back up and floating around sadly on the surface. "Wait a minute," said Izzy, "it won't take her long." Within a minute, I could see movement further out into the river. A ripple formed and started making its way towards us, building to a point as it picked up speed. There was a sudden splash and the fish head disappeared, only to reappear again a second later, gripped firmly between Daisy's teeth. She grinned and threw it up into the air, opening her mouth wide to catch it on its way back down. "Hey, baby," said Izzy with obvious affection, "want more treats?" Daisy bobbed around excitedly as Izzy tipped the rest of the bag into the water. And then, as if they'd heard us talking about them, another head popped up next to Daisy. "Oh," said Izzy, "you're new! This isn't the one I met the other day," she said, turning to me. Another splash made us both look towards where a third asrai had appeared behind the first two. "This is her. Oh my god, Lil," said Izzy, "what if there's an entire shoal of them out there?"

"If there is," I said, "then I pity any fisherman along this river. Because they've got some serious competition."

We left the Mersey mermaids to their carnivorous frolicking and made our way back to Flora's. Izzy went inside to finish the afternoon with Todd and, as there was no sign of Billy, I decided to take a wander round the corner to Mathew Street. As I'd half expected, I found my favourite ghost—don't ever tell Kitty I said that—sitting in the empty doorway opposite the Cavern pub, with Ifan busking next to him. Ifan's eyes were closed as he strummed his way through an acoustic version of 'It's A Shame About Ray,' whilst the usual gaggle of teenage girls stared adoringly at him from a few feet away. The pub must have been quiet, because for once the doorman was making no effort to move the girls on. Billy raised a hand in greeting as I approached.

"Hey," I said, crouching down next to him, "how's business today?"

"Made enough to see him through another day or so," said Billy approvingly. "He always does."

"Where's he staying?" I asked. Ifan finished the song and went straight into 'Zombie' by The Cranberries without opening his eyes. Ifan rarely opens his eyes when he's playing, he says it breaks his concentration.

"Ask no secrets, get told no lies," said Billy with a wink. "Nah, I don't know, Red. None of my business, now is it?"

"Guess not." I wriggled down onto the blanket next to him and we sat listening for a while.

"Figured out the rest of your life yet?" said Billy, eventually.

I leaned my head back against the wall and closed my eyes. "I'm going to do things my own way, Billy," I said. "Whatever anyone else thinks."

"Good for you," he said. "More people should make their own decisions, to my mind. Be far less aggression in the world."

"Do you think?" I opened my eyes and turned to look at him. "Cos there's a good part of me that's terrified I'm about to mess everything up big time."

"Red," Billy said kindly, "I'm not sure any of it could get messier than it already is." He bumped me companionably with his shoulder and I noticed how much less bony it felt. "You'll be grand."

It was two in the morning and I was sitting in the back room of Flora's, gazing blankly at the pile of notes that now sat alongside the maps Nik had brought from the library. I'd given up on my original plan of meditating the night away when Kitty had reappeared without warning towards midnight. She'd then insisted on giving me a minute-by-minute account of her visit to Shrewsbury, which mostly seemed to consist of sitting on park benches and gazing adoringly into Jonny's eyes. But she was happy and I like people being happy, so I listened patiently until she finally talked it all out of her system. She then switched on the television and settled in to watch old episodes of Block-busters with Grimm. I'd tried to join in with their enthusiasm for retro game shows, but after my 'can I have a P please, Bob' joke had fallen on flat ears for the second time, I'd given up and headed downstairs. I was idly drawing cat faces on the tracing paper I'd clipped to a map of Edge Hill, when I heard a tapping noise at the window. Sighing, I got up to unlock the back door. "What are you doing here?" I asked Ivo.

"Can I come in?" he asked. "Or am I only worthy of outdoor conversation these days?" I gestured him inside and he stepped past me into the kitchen.

"You might as well sit down," I said, "as you're here."

"You don't exactly sound thrilled to see me," said Ivo. He pulled out the only other chair and sat at the table. He nodded at the pile of paperwork. "Planning a trip?"

"Planning whose backside I need to kick first, more like," I said, sitting down opposite him. "Just need to figure out exactly who's hiding out where, then I can go bang some undead heads together."

"That's the spirit," said Ivo. "I won't keep you from you work. Just thought it would be polite to pop in to say goodbye."

"Where are you going?" I asked, unexpected panic rising in my throat. "You can't just disappear!"

"Oh," he smiled, "I won't disappear completely. No need to worry about that. But it wouldn't be...prudent to stay around my former friends right now. Not with William back on the scene."

"Why on earth not?" I was surprised at how upset I felt. Ivo's ridiculously manipulative charm had become such a background to my life that it was difficult to imagine being without him. I stared in confusion as Ivo put a hand across the table to hold mine. His pale blue eyes gazed so directly at me that I was a bit nervous he might be able to see right into my soul.

"I'll always be around for you, Red," he said, "if you need me. Or want me." He shrugged. "Either works for me. But William *will* try to kill me. And this time it would be permanent."

"But why?" I asked. "He destroyed your grave last time and it didn't stop you coming back, so why can't he just learn to live with you as a neighbour? You don't have to be friends, for heaven's sake! No one's expecting the two of you to host joint barbecues or go watch the footie together."

"Heaven forbid," said Ivo, a twinkle in his eye.

"So why *can't* you just ignore each other?" I persisted.

"If I see him," said Ivo calmly, "I will have to kill him. He desecrated my resting place and forced me back into this world for all eternity. I cannot forgive that, Red."

"So Lia—William has to kill you before you kill him? That's what it boils down to?" Ivo nodded. "That's pathetic," I said. "The pair of you are acting like toddlers fighting over toys, rather than the supposedly intelligent men you actually are. How utterly ridiculous."

Ivo gave me a wry smile. "I'd expect nothing less from you," he said. "But it changes nothing. Either Normandy dies, or I do. You can't have both of us, Red."

"Who says I want *either* of you?"

"Who indeed," Ivo shrugged. "I suppose I'm guilty of making assumptions—I really should have learned my lesson by now. You don't do anything by the book, do you?"

I narrowed my eyes at him. "Why should I?"

"Good question." Ivo pushed his chair back and stood up, brushing nonexistent dust off his immaculate grey wool coat. "Can I offer you one piece of advice?"

"So long as you don't expect me to actually take it," I said.

Ivo grinned properly at that. "That's my girl," he said, stepping round the table to kiss me briefly on top of my head. "I need you to promise me something, Red." He held my arms as I turned towards him, and looked me straight in the eye.

"Depends what it is," I said, without conviction.

Ivo laughed quietly. "It's just one thing," he said. "Whatever happens, and whoever ends up in control—whether that's you or Liam, or even Elizabeth," no mention of Eadric, which was interesting, "you must remember not to trust *anyone*. Do you understand me?"

I pulled a face at him. "Durrrrrr," I said in a mocking tone, "as if I hadn't thought of that already. Of course I don't trust Liam or Elizabeth, that goes without saying. You and Eadric are a bit different, though."

Ivo shook his head. "This is why I had to see you before I left," he said. "You don't understand. Of all the people around you, I'm the one you should trust least. Not Middlesex or Normandy or even Eadric bloody Silverton and what remains of Mercia. It's me who's the real threat."

"But why?" I asked as Ivo walked to the door. "I get on better with you than I do any of the others! Apart from maybe Mapp," I added, "but then he's not in charge of anywhere."

"Because I can see your true potential," said Ivo softly, one hand on the door. "I can see what you might turn into. Thing is, Red," he opened the door and stepped outside, turning to look back at me, "I'm the only one who realises just how dangerous you're going to be." By the time I'd managed to open my mouth to speak, he was gone.

I was still sitting at the table attempting to make sense of what had just happened when a muffled creak heralded Rachel's arrival through the door from the internal staircase. I looked up to see the vampire peeking round the doorway. "Come on in," I said, "it's clearly the night for it." Rachel shuffled in, looking nervously around her as if concerned that Van Helsing himself might be hiding in the stock cupboard. "It's fine," I said, "I'm on my own."

"Heard-noise," mumbled Rachel. "Checking-you-safe." I looked up at her in surprise. Our resident vampire hadn't shown interest in anyone when I'd brought her home from Anfield cemetery in the summer. I wasn't sure whether it was Alan's company or her new rodent diet that was causing her to suddenly become sociable, but decided not to look a gift horse in the fangs.

"Thank you," I said. "I mean it. I'm not sure who's on my side and who isn't, these days."

"Lilith-is-good-person," she said, then blushed.

"Do you think so?" I asked. Rachel nodded.

"All-say-so," she said. "But-danger."

"Do you mean I'm in danger?" I asked. She shook her head. "I'm the danger?" A small nod. "But you're still here," I said. "Why do you stay here if I'm dangerous, Rachel?"

She gnawed at her bony knuckles for a minute before speaking. "You-my-friend-maybe," she blurted. "Stay-with-you. Fight-with-you."

"I really hope it won't come to that," I said, wondering for the millionth time when exactly I'd been dropped into a real life fantasy movie. "But I appreciate the support."

Rachel gave me a tiny nervous smile, then she nodded at the table. "You-know-where," she said suddenly. "Good-Lilith."

I frowned at her in confusion. "The map?" I asked.

The vampire nodded enthusiastically. "There," she said, jabbing her finger at an area I'd marked on the tracing paper. "There-there-there." Her ragged nail caught the paper, tearing it slightly. I really hoped it hadn't gone through to the map underneath, or Nik was going to have some explaining to do up at the library. He'd made it very clear that maps didn't usually leave the premises and an exception had been made only because they trusted him. "Oops," said Rachel, pulling her hand back and hiding it under the table.

"Don't worry," I said, "it'll be fine. I'll just tape it together." And I'm going to give you a manicure the minute I can persuade you to let me at those talons, I thought to myself. I looked down at where she'd been indicating and saw the crossed lines of my earlier scribbles. "Hmmm," I said, gazing at the spiderweb of tunnel and rail lines visibly crossing each other through the tracing paper. "Hmmm."

THE DINOSAUR WAS AN
ACCIDENT, OKAY?

"**D**o you fancy coming with us?" Izzy was saying, and it took me a second to realise it was me she was speaking to.

"Come with you where?" I asked distractedly, pulling clean cups out of the dishwasher and placing them on the shelf next to the coffee machine. Todd had come down with flu, and I was helping with the afternoon rush. I was still thinking about tunnels and railway lines in-between sneaking regular peeks at Sean, who was at his usual table. He was currently packing his books into his bag and getting ready to leave.

"See," said Izzy in a mock-hurt tone, "I knew you weren't listening to me. Six pound fifty, love," she said, holding the payment machine out to the woman at the till. "Ta." She turned to face me as the woman manoeuvred her tray off the counter. "I *asked*," she said slowly, "if you would like to come up the radio tower with me and Damon this evening. His cousin's the security guard there. He's going to take us up after it's closed for the day, so we can have it to ourselves."

"Why do you want to go up the radio tower?" Also known as St John's Beacon, the Radio City tower on Houghton Street consists of a narrow concrete column with what looks like an enormous concrete space ship perched at the top. The column contains a lift, which takes tourists up to look at the views from the panoramic windows that go all around the top section. Long used as the base for various radio stations, the tower still has 'Radio City 96.7' emblazoned around the outside in huge neon lettering.

"A'right, spider girl," said Izzy. "No need to be dismissive, just because you can climb it on the outside whenever you please."

"No I can't," I said. "You made me promise not to do it again, remember?"

"That is because you are quite noticeable when you decide to start climbing local landmarks," said Izzy in a patient tone of voice, "and I am getting a tiny bit fed up of you racing in through the back window without warning because someone's called the cops again."

"Oh, come on," I said, "that's only happened twice."

"Three times," said Izzy. "You're forgetting the incident at the World Museum."

"I told you, I didn't mean to break that dinosaur. Anyway," having finished with the cups, I started pulling clean plates out of the machine and dried them with a cloth before stacking them on the side, "you didn't answer my question. Why *do* you want to go up the radio tower?"

"Damon's never been up there," she said, "and it's been years since I've done it. I dunno," she shrugged. "I just thought it might be fun to do something together. All three of us."

"That sounds very much like a potential third-wheel situation to me," I said. "I'm not sure I want to be alone in a small empty room with no one but you and Damon for company."

"Maybe I could tag along?" We both looked up as Sean spoke. He was holding his empty coffee cup, which he placed on the counter. "Erm," he blushed, "sorry. That was a bit rude of me. I don't want to intrude on your outing, it's just that I've somehow never been up the tower. Which is a bit rubbish, seeing as I've lived here all my life. Don't worry if it's not convenient, though." He trailed off and looked worriedly from me to Izzy and back again. "Sorry," he started again, "I—"

"I'd love you to come with us," I said, before I could stop myself. "That would be really nice." I was horribly aware of Izzy standing next to me with her mouth open in surprise. Fuck it. This was *my* afterlife. It was about time I learned how to live it properly. As I spoke, I felt...*something* uncoiling inside me. Something hidden and powerful. A feeling of quiet excitement began crawling slowly up my spine.

"Brilliant," said Sean, who clearly hadn't expected me to be so enthusiastic. "I'll, errr, well,"

"Give us a couple of hours," Izzy said, coming to his rescue, "to get things finished up here. Then we'll all walk up to the tower together. That cool?"

"That's very cool," said Sean, backing away towards the door. "Very cool indeed. See you in a bit." We both gave him a tiny wave, and he scooted out of the door as though he'd somehow embarrassed himself.

"You okay, Lil?" asked Izzy. When I turned to look at her, she had a concerned expression on her face.

"Absolutely fine," I said, grinning widely. "Why do you ask?"

"You've got a glint in your eye," she said. I peered at my distorted reflection in the metal surface of the coffee machine, but couldn't see anything out of the ordinary. "Metaphorically," she added.

I straightened up, a newfound confidence keeping the smile on my face. "I think," I said carefully, fighting the urge to spin with glee, "it's about time I faced the future."

"That's nice," said Izzy, not sounding remotely convinced. "If you could maybe do it with the minimum of public embarrassment, that would be great." She turned to serve a waiting customer, but thought of something else and spun back round. "And," she added, "try not to break the entire city. I'm quite fond of it."

"Oh," said Nik, as I stepped out of the elevator, "you're being civilised for once."

"Fuck off," I replied amiably, "I just couldn't be arsed to climb. Where's the boss?"

"In his office," he said, nodding to the half-open door in the corner, "talking to Elizabeth." I faltered for a second, remembering what Ivo had said about Elizabeth's loyalties always being with her territory, however much she professed to like me. "Go on in," said Nik. "I don't think they're discussing anything secret."

When I stepped through the door into Eadric's office, I was surprised to find him sitting at his desk, with Elizabeth clearly visible on the laptop screen in front of him. He turned and grinned when he heard me. "I'm slowly joining the modern world, Lilith," he said with a smile. Eadric can be heartbreakingly beautiful when he smiles. Sometimes I have to remind myself that it would be inappropriate to develop a crush on him.

"Better late than never," said Elizabeth, from the little screen. "Apparently we have your mother to thank for this development, Lilith."

"You what now?"

Eadric swivelled round in his chair and grinned at me. "The delightful Helen introduced me to the wonders of digital communications," he said. "I happened to see her and Nik setting up this clever connection so they could chat with each other, and asked for an explanation as to how it worked. Your mother was kind enough to give me a short lesson."

I boggled at the idea of Mum—my *mum*—teaching two ancient undead creatures how to use the internet. "Did she insist on calling you Vladislav?" I asked. "Shall I leave you to do your dark bidding on the internet?" Both Elizabeth and Eadric looked politely blank. "Never mind," I said, "that one's a niche reference, even by my standards. But you can't seriously be telling me that Nik and my mother chat to each other via Zoom?"

"Why is that so unlikely?" asked Nik, coming into the room behind me. "Your lack of faith in my technical abilities verges on offensive, Ms O'Reilly."

"Nik," I said patiently, "you don't even use the phone if you can help it. You said smartphones are—and I quote—'*an intrusion into the god-given privacy of the modern gentleman*,' and that you thought they had almost certainly been invented by Satan himself."

"Everyone's entitled to keep some level of mystique," said Nik with a shrug. "But I enjoy chatting to your mother. And this way we can actually see each other. That seems more natural to me than talking into a small glass rectangle and having nothing more than other person's voice to interact with."

"What do you do if my dad walks into the room?"

"Your father thinks I'm one of your mother's tutors," said Nik, grinning. "He gets quite involved sometimes. It's very sweet. Although it gets a bit awkward when he starts telling me what he thinks of the Romantic poets."

"I bet it does," I said, imagining Dad lecturing Nik on the joys of iambic pentameter.

"How are you feeling after your unpleasant experience the other night, Lilith?" asked Elizabeth from the computer screen. "I do hope they're looking after you up there."

I squashed down the thought that perhaps she was just trying to find out how protected I might be. I'd have to give her the benefit of the doubt, for now at least. "I'm more than capable of looking after myself," I said. "You know that."

Elizabeth smiled, her porcelain face as beautiful as ever. "I'd expect nothing less from you," she said. "What do you think we should do about Normandy?" It took me a second to realise she was talking about the man, rather than the territory.

"I'm not sure there's much any of us *can* do at the moment," I said, finally pulling myself together and attempting to look professional. "Although I'd quite like to kick him in the nuts again."

"Aah yes," said Elizabeth, "I did hear about that." *I bet you did*, I thought. *I bet most of the netherworld knows all about me and Liam and are right now assuming I'll roll over and play doggo for my new boyfriend, like a naïve little kid.*

"My private life is no one else's business," I said, "and I would appreciate it not being discussed behind my back."

I heard Eadric suck his teeth, but Elizabeth laughed. "Quite right," she said. "Although I think there's a few of us who would have taken great pleasure in witnessing the incident. However, putting personal grievances aside for a moment, I do think we need to discuss future plans."

"I'll speak to you properly soon," I said to Elizabeth, "and we'll discuss things. Give my love to Jude."

"I will," she said, the corners of her mouth twitching into a smile. "I'm looking forward to working with you, Lilith O'Reilly." With that, the screen went black.

Eadric swung his chair round to look at me, irritation evident on his face. "Don't you start," I said, before he could open his mouth. Nik leaned back against the wall with his arms folded, an amused look on his face as he waited for the show to start. "All this talk of future plans," I went on, "is absolute bollocks. Sitting round a table and discussing who gets what and carving up the land to suit yourselves? You'll have to excuse my language here, but fuck that shit absolutely fucking sideways. No," I held up a hand to stop Eadric speaking, "you will *listen* to me. All this bullshit about how I have no choice? I absolutely *do* have choices, Eadric Silverton." I gave him a sharp look. "And my choice right now is to do exactly what I please. I am sick of people telling me I have power and I should learn to use it. You," I jabbed a finger at him, "keep saying I'll just have to accept it one day. Accept what, precisely? Being told what to do for all eternity? What are you expecting me to do when I'm queen of fucking everything, Eadric? Live in semi-isolation like Elizabeth and Jude, in order to keep up appearances? Who the fuck even *knows* how a queen should behave? *You* might," I gestured at them both impatiently, "because you're fucking ancient and stuck in the traditions of the past. I was born in the twentieth century, not the twelfth. We do things differently these days. And," I gave them both a warning look, "we are going to be doing things differently from now on. Because my life is fucking *batshit* and I am sick of it. We are going to do things *my* way. Now," I said to Eadric, who looked as though he was torn between losing his temper and giving me a round of applause, "if you'll excuse me, I'm off to see a man about a vampire."

"Come out, come out, wherever you are!" I called into the darkness. The tunnel in front of me might have been foreboding, but it wasn't going to stop me kicking some undead ass. I'd gone back to the flat to collect what I needed, then headed up to Edge Hill. The Wapping tunnel was closed in 1972 and lies empty and abandoned to this day, its gaping maw now nothing more than a dark splodge on Google Earth. The amount of online space taken up by urban explorers wandering around inside it, however, is testament to its importance at the time of its construction. The first transport tunnel ever to be bored underneath a metropolis, it was designed by George Stephenson in the eighteen-twenties as an extension to the world's first inter-city train service, which ran between Manchester and Liverpool. The nationally feted opening day of this global first for industry was marred slightly when Stephenson's infamous Rocket ran over Liverpool's incumbent MP, William Huskisson. After taking several hours to die of his injuries, Huskisson had the honour of marking the first day of commercial train travel by becoming the world's first notable railway fatality.

And there was going to be some more fatalities on the ancient tracks if someone didn't come out and face the music soon. "I know you're in there," I shouted, carefully staying out in the open. I could feel my new power surging through my undead veins, but I wasn't yet sure just how strong I was, nor how many pissed-off vampires I might be able to handle. There was a faint rustling sound deep in the tunnel, and I thought I heard whispers on the breeze. I'd waited long enough. "COME OUT HERE RIGHT NOW, JOSEPH WILLIAMSON!" I yelled, The Voice at full bellow. There was silence for a few seconds, then I saw something moving in the shadows. "Hurry up," I called cheerily, in my normal voice, "I don't have all day." He didn't look very happy about it, but the little man finally shuffled out as far as the mouth of the tunnel, where he stood glaring at me like a petulant child.

"There's no need to shout, Lilith," he said reproachfully. "I'm not deaf."

"And I'm not stupid, Joe," I said. "So why have you been treating me as though I am?"

Joe shuffled on the spot, his little feet doing an awkward dance on the stony ground. I noticed he was dressed in his smartest suit. It was at least two centuries old and covered in dust, but the quality still showed through. "You wouldn't understand," he said. "No one understands."

"Try me." I could see movement behind Joe, just inside the tunnel where daylight couldn't reach. "How many friends have you got in there?" I asked him.

Silence for a moment, then a quiet, "Not many. A few."

"How many is 'a few', Joe?"

"Enough to make you all think again about telling us what to do," he suddenly burst out, his voice louder and angry now. "This is *our* space, Lilith. The Silvertons don't get to rule us and nor do you. Huh," he made a point of looking me up and down, "a mere chit of a girl, trying to tell us how best to do things? As if we haven't been perfectly fine down here for more than a century? How dare you, Lilith. How *dare* you."

I stared at him in astonishment. Gone was the strange little mole-man I'd considered a friend since I died. In his place stood an angry man in his best Sunday suit, his face rigid with indignant anger. "What have I done to you?" I asked.

"As if you don't know," he spat.

"Errrrm...nope," I shrugged, "I got nothing. You're going to have to explain all this in simple bullet points, Joe. And," I'd noticed more movement behind him, "you can tell your idiot vampires to leave me the fuck alone."

"That's exactly it," said Joe, "isn't it? You're standing there issuing instructions to me as though you own the place, and you really think I ought to do as I'm told. Well, I *won't*," he actually stamped his foot. "I won't, because I don't have to and you can't make me."

"For fuck's sake, Joe," I rolled my eyes so hard it was a wonder he couldn't hear them, "just tell me what you want! What *they*," I waved a hand towards the tunnel, "want. I don't want to start an undead civil war like, but I really could do without being jumped by stupid sodding vampires every time I dare turn my back. Whatever happened to live and let live?"

"You called them stupid," said Joe doggedly. "Just then! You called them stupid. Everyone thinks my children are stupid, but they're not. They're *people*, Lilith. People like me and you. They didn't choose to become what they are anymore than you did. But you get to swan around like lady muck while they're forced to hide in the darkness and feel embarrassed about themselves, and where's the fairness in that?"

"Hang on," I was struggling to keep up with this new take on the vampire legend. "You're telling me you're standing up for vampire rights? Like, what—a shop steward?"

"That's exactly it," said Joe, his voice deadly serious. "Vampires have rights, as much as anyone else."

"Oh my days." I started laughing, despite myself. "They've been going to all this effort to kill me—me, a woman who's dead already, if you hadn't noticed—and all they actually wanted was to be *unionised*? Fucking hell, Joe," I snorted, "they could have just left a note on my doorstep! Why the gang attacks?"

"They weren't supposed to be attacking you," he frowned. "They just get carried away sometimes. They were supposed to be bringing you down here for a little chat."

"Couldn't you have just asked me yourself? I was sitting down in your tunnels talking to you just a couple of days ago. Wouldn't it have been easier to ask me then?"

"Too risky," said Joe. "We knew you'd been consorting with Normandy and we didn't know who else he might have with him."

"Whoah," I said, "I'm going to need you to roll it back a bit there. You said you knew I was *consorting*? Firstly," I drew myself up to my full height (I'm only five foot six so it probably isn't that impressive, but it makes me feel better), "I do not *consort* with anyone, Joe Williamson. Not that it would be any of your business if I did."

"Anything that threatens us is our business, Lilith," said Joe.

"No one is threatening *any* of you," I said firmly. "What makes you think that?"

Joe shuffled again and turned to look back into the tunnel. A tall, dark-haired vampire walked out of the darkness to stand next to him. The newcomer had the prominent teeth and bony features of all vampires I've ever met (which adds up to a lot more than I ever *expected* to meet, I can tell you that for nothing), but there was an air of intelligence about him that was usually lacking. "Good afternoon, Lilith O'Reilly," said the vampire politely. "I am...pleased to make your acquaintance." The only other bloodsucker I'd met who could hold a conversation was Rachel, and even she relied on a basic form of sign language most of the time. This one was up there with Christopher Lee in the deep-voiced-and-looming stakes. "I...uh...apologise for any misunderstandings."

I squinted at him. "Are you sure you're a vampire?" I asked. "Because they usually just skitter around like bad tempered little cockroaches. And they mostly don't talk."

"Oh," he said slowly, "we can talk. It can take many years of practice after our human deaths, of course."

"Why?" I couldn't stop myself.

"Because we're designed for killing," he said, "not standing around making small talk."

"Well see now," I said, "that's where we're going to have to come to an arrangement, isn't it? Because I can't have you killing people on my turf. You shouldn't be killing people on *anyone*'s turf, of course," I added, "but definitely not mine."

"Who's to say it's yours?" asked the vampire politely. Movement in the shadows behind him suggested other, possibly less polite, vampires were lurking in the darkness.

I'd had enough. "I'm done with all this stupid bickering," I said. "And it's clear that every last resident of the afterlife is *entirely* ridiculous. I'm including you in that, Joseph Williamson, in case you were wondering." Joe shifted from one foot to the other, clearly unsure of where this was going. "Eadric was right. Worlds do need rulers. But they don't need the sort of rulers who want to keep things for themselves. Or the ones who betray each other just to collect more and more power until they go insane with it. What this world needs," I reached into the satchel that was slung over my shoulder, "is someone whose only requirement of her loyal subjects is that they STOP BEING ABSOLUTE FUCKING DICKHEADS." The metal was warm beneath my fingers and I felt such power creeping up into me that I almost bottled it. But what was the alternative? If I didn't take this enormous step into the unknown, I was doomed to an eternity of bickering immortal politicians and regular vampire ambushes. "You asked who says this is my territory," I said to the vampire, holding his gaze. I felt calm now, the small gold circlet sending its protection up into my body even before I'd taken it out of the bag. It needed me. And, I finally realised, I needed it in return. "This says it's mine," I said, smiling broadly at the vampire—and I placed the crown on my head.

I'd like to be able to say that the vampires immediately fell to their knees, awestruck by my power, but that would be a lie. What actually happened was that they all stood staring mutely at me, clearly unable to see what was going on inside my head. I, on the other hand, was undergoing some form of insanely fantastical transformation and the only reason I wasn't flailing and screaming in panic was that it was all so intense I couldn't even move. I could *feel* brand new neurons sparking into life inside my head, all racing round to make connections and growing, growing... Energy flashed from my fingers, a light spectrum far beyond the reach of the human eye. Suddenly, everything made sense. Thoughts rearranged themselves into orderly lines and snapped down into neat little boxes of memories, some of them from long before I was even born. I had visions of the city as it used to be, with houses muddled along the edge of a creek and naive little boats bobbing around in the Mersey. London spun through my mind like a speeded-up movie flashback—versions of the capital I'd never knowingly witnessed even in history books, its slums and shacks spreading along the banks of the Thames even as I watched. Elizabeth popped up briefly, her brilliant smile casting light down onto me as though giving me her blessing. Granny Ivy whooshed past like something out of a fairytale adaptation, but as real as the ground beneath my feet. Kitty danced behind my eyes and Jonny gazed on her with such adoration that my cold dead heart clenched with emotion. I saw Izzy behind the counter in Flora's, making coffee for Sean as her flowery dress sparkled with shards of light. And Grimm—beautiful, terrible Grimm—grown huge as a house and watching over me, always watching...Mum laughed with joy and Cally danced under an apple tree whilst Dad looked on, grinning at the astonishing wonder of it all. Liam was far away in the distance, trying to reach me but failing, as Ivo looked on, an unfathomable expression on his face. And Billy...Billy was alive and beautiful and laughing along with me, his infectious smile widening as he broke into a lilting song of ancient times, his voice crisp and clear on the wind that blew around us. Everyone was there—Ifan and Eadric and Nik, Maria and Martha, Rachel the vampire with Alan following behind like a devoted pilgrim.

Mapp swirled around in a cloud of tulle and Heggie's little eyes lit up in adoration. Everything and everyone and everywhere broke through my mind and it was *wonderful*.

I hit the ground with a force that shocked nonexistent breath out of me and lay there for a moment, revelling in it all. A voice on the periphery of hearing brought me back to my new reality. "Who," said Joseph Williamson, "are you? Who are you *really*?"

Finally, I knew. I got to my feet and bent to pick up the crown, which had fallen from my head. Tucking it back into the satchel as though I'd just picked it up at the shops, I looked at the little man with bright, clear eyes. The vampires were huddled behind him, as if for protection. "You know exactly who I am, Joe," I smiled. "I'm Lilith."

New Dawn Fades

My phone rang as I climbed out of the Wapping tunnel. Jumping up over the edge, I scared a cat who'd been sunbathing at the top and it disappeared in a cloud of terrified indignation. Flopping onto the grass, I rooted the phone out of my pocket. "Hey babe," said Izzy when I picked up, "don't forget we're doing the tower thing in twenty minutes." *Shit*. I wondered just how well I'd be able to cover up my newly upgraded personality. After all, it's not often you realise you're the walking, talking reincarnation of an ancient legend. Although people like Liam and Ivo actually *were* the original legends, so at least I wouldn't be the odd one out at parties.

"I haven't forgotten," I lied, "just had to see Joe about something."

"Awww," said Izzy, "how's he doing? Give him my love."

"Will do," I said, getting to my feet and starting the walk back down into town. I'd have to sort things out more formally with the vampires at some point, but it could wait. My skin was tingling all over and I was struggling not to break into a run. "I'm nearly home," I said, "just need to get changed."

"We're meeting at yours anyway," said Izzy, "so no rush."

"Is Sean coming to mine as well?" I wasn't sure how I felt about letting a famous crime writer into my home, with its scruffy decor and grumpy cat. Not to mention the resident ghost.

"He is," she chirped happily. "I arranged things with him after you left. Kitty says she'll stay out of the way, so no one asks awkward questions."

"Well that's something," I said, not remotely reassured. I turned onto Myrtle Street, which was annoyingly busy for a cold and dull autumn evening. A flash of something white in the distance made me pick up my pace. A woman with white-blonde hair had just come out of Cafe Nero at the junction with Catharine Street and was heading down into town. Something about the way she moved made me suspicious. "Look," I said to Izzy, "I just need to go check something out. I won't be long. Stick the kettle on or something."

"Lil," she said, "this is your chance to have a normal double date with a normal human being. Zero pressure, just fun."

"You try being an undead soul-sucker and then tell me about zero pressure," I said. I stepped into the road to pass a woman with a pushchair and narrowly avoiding knocking a cyclist off his bike. As he yelled and I flicked the requisite V-sign at his back, the woman with the white hair disappeared from view.

"Do not fuck this up for yourself, Lilith O'Reilly," said Izzy sternly.

"I'm always trying not to fuck things up for myself," I said, breaking into a loping run, "but things are clever and mostly do the fucking up by themselves. Zero effort on my part. Got to go, catch you in a bit." Shutting off Izzy's frustrated squawking, I wedged the phone into my waistband and jammed the satchel back onto my shoulder. The crown clanked heavily against my hip, with more weight than was natural for the amount of metal. When I got to St Luke's, I hesitated for a second. Bold Street was the less likely route for Mab to have taken, because it's always so busy. On the other hand, it's easier to hide in a crowd. As I was crossing the road, a white flash further down Renshaw Street informed me I'd chosen wrong. Heading after her and picking up speed as much as I dared, I almost missed Mapp coming out of his shop. He did a classic double take at me, which made me worry that the change might be more visible than I'd thought. Then he sensibly decided to prioritise the current issues.

"You've seen her then?" he asked, a purple silk scarf blowing up and around his face like a cloud as he spoke.

"Yup," I called as I zipped past, "I'm on it. Let Eadric know." Then I skidded to a halt and ran back. "Look after this for me," I said, pushing the satchel into his hands. Mapp peered inside and then looked back up at me, his big dark eyes wide with astonishment. "And for god's sake, keep it safe."

He stood upright and saluted."Aye aye, cap'n," he said, and without another word, turned to head back inside. The door closed decisively behind him, leaving nothing other than the faint smell of incense. I headed back down Renshaw Street, frantically looking for Mab. Finally I spotted her. She'd stopped and was looking around, as if unsure as to where to go next. I wondered if she was looking for me —and if so, was it to find me, or avoid me? Her pause gave me time to close the distance between us and I was less than twenty yards behind when she apparently came to a decision and headed left onto Ranelagh Street. I jogged down to the corner just in time to see her take an immediate right onto Great Charlotte Street. Bollocks. If she went into St John's shopping centre, I'd never find her. Sure enough, I spotted her distinct hair again as she walked in through the entrance. Bloody marvellous. As I headed up the steps after her, my phone rang.

"Where are you?" demanded Izzy. "We're going without you if you don't get back here in the next five minutes."

"You go on ahead," I said, walking in through the doors and looking round for Mab. "I'll catch you up."

"Lil," Izzy actually sounded tearful, "I just wanted us to do something normal together, y'know?" Her voice dropped. "Sean's here and he's putting a brave face on it, but he clearly thinks you just don't want to see him." Fucksake. I might as well give up and become a nun now; save myself the endless doomed attempts at having any form of love life.

"Of course I want to see him," I soothed. "And I want to do fun stuff with you as well. It's just, well—" Right then I saw a flash of white in the distance, which turned left as I watched. "Look, Iz," I said, jogging again, "things are very different these days. We both know that. But I can't help any of this any more than you can. I'm doing my best to cope with a situation I've never asked to be in. And right now, things are very complicated."

"I know you can't help it," said Izzy quietly, "but I can't help being sad, either."

"I know," I said, walking slowly through the shopping centre and keeping close to the walls to lessen the risk of Mab spotting me. "It'll sort itself out eventually."

"It had better," said Izzy, rallying slightly. "Because otherwise I'll have to start going out drinking with a vampire and a ghost. And even the Baltic isn't quite ready for that just yet. We'll go on ahead, then. But you catch up quick as you can, okay?"

"Okay," I said. "Promise."

"Hurry up, dead girl," she said, and cut the call. As I was jamming my phone back into my pocket, I spotted a blonde head disappearing behind a pillar not far ahead of me. Jogging as fast as I dared, I made it round the corner just in time to see Mab disappearing into JD Sports. I had a sinking feeling she might have realised I was on her tail and was hoping I wouldn't dare try anything inside a busy shop. Unfortunately, I didn't think I was going to have much of an option. Thankfully I managed to catch up with her just inside the entrance and grabbed her arm hard.

"Get outside now before anyone gets hurt," I hissed, dragging her backwards. The deep yell she let out confused me and I rocked back on my heels as the man I'd grabbed hold of whipped round to face me. He was tall and slight like Mab, but that was where any similarity ended. His blond hair was clearly a bleach job close up, and he was wearing more jewellery and eyeliner than Mab ever had.

"What the fuck?" he spluttered. "Are you insane?"

"Quite possibly," I said, already backing away. "Thought you were someone else." There was a loud crash that sounded as though it had come from the floor above us, followed by muffled yelling and screaming. "Really sorry!" I left him staring after me in shocked confusion and ran towards the escalator, getting to it just as an elderly man wobbled his way onto the bottom step ahead of me. He was dragging a shopping trolley behind him that completely blocked my way. Cursing the gods of indoor shopping centre design, I gave up trying to hide. I hopped onto the handrail and ran straight up it, shouting my apologies as people cowered away. "No time to explain!" I yelled as I jumped off at the top and turned to face the chaos. The noise was coming from the homeware store ahead of me, where the front window had been smashed by something or someone exiting through it at speed. People were milling around outside like confused cattle, and I heard someone on the phone to what was presumably the emergency services, telling them he'd seen a woman burst through the shop window before running off 'as if the devil were on her tail.' We discovered later that Heggie had been out on a shopping trip. He'd been given jade plant cuttings by the women from Gambier Terrace and needed plant pots. Mab had spotted him heading in her direction in the shopping centre and dodged into the shop to avoid him, only for him to walk in right behind her. She'd assumed he must be looking for her and—clearly unaware that he didn't actually have any dangerously paranormal powers at his disposal—decided to err on the side of caution by taking the fastest route back out of the shop. But those details only emerged later on. Right now, I didn't know what had happened and couldn't hang around to find out. My phone rang again. Seeing Izzy's name flash up, I decided I'd have to bite the bullet and tell her I wasn't going to make it to our double date after all. Gritting my teeth for the fallout, I picked up the call. "I know," I said, "I'm the shittest friend ever. I'm sorry, okay? Let's have a proper talk about it later." Izzy didn't say anything. "Iz," I wheedled, "come on, you know I can't help it." Still nothing. Maybe her signal had dropped out. I was just about to cut the call when I heard a crashing noise at the other end.

"Where is she?" demanded Mab, her voice clear as a bell down the line. I froze on the spot in horror. "Where's your precious little friend, Isobel?"

"Go fuck yourself." Izzy's voice wavered, but she spoke clearly. "Lil wasn't ever coming with us," she paused, "it was a trick." *Oh Izzy*, I thought, *you clever, clever girl*. "Bet you feel stupid now, huh?" There was a thudding sound and I heard a man's voice shout in panic. Sean. "If you hurt him," Izzy said, "Lilith will rip your stupid head right off your shoulders. Just like she did to your mother. A crash and a scream suggested Izzy had pushed things too far. Spinning on my heels, I headed back out of the shopping centre at full speed—which turned out to be so fast that I almost ploughed straight through the wall of the building opposite. I managed to skid to a halt with only a small chunk taken out of the stonework where my hand had hit it, and turned to head into the tower. It was already locked up for the evening and I had to shoulder the door open. I almost immediately fell over the body of a security guard and was forced to waste precious seconds checking for signs of life. Thankfully the woman was merely unconscious, although she had a cracking lump growing on her forehead. I turned her into the recovery position and made for the lift—which, to my horror, was out of order. I could hear noises above me, the sound travelling down the concrete walls. I ran back outside to the fire exit that concealed the emergency staircase, but it was fused shut. I'd seen that kind of bizarre welding before, when I first died and Nik had come over to Flora's to seal off the tunnel access from our cellar. Assuming I got out of the current drama in one piece, I was going to demand he show me how to do it. By the amount of crashing that was going on, it was clear that Mab was in a full rage at whoever else was trapped up there with her. I had no idea how many people might be in the building with Izzy and the others. There was nothing for it but to climb up the outside. Cursing under my breath, I headed back out onto the street and wedged the door shut behind me. I'd have to fix the Mab problem before I dared called an ambulance for the security guard, or risk more people getting injured. It wasn't properly dark yet and I thanked all the gods available that I'd just happened to wear all black that day. Tucking my hair down into my tshirt, I started scrambling upwards. I was a third of the way up when an almighty thud from the viewing platform above me made the entire tower shake. Just then, I heard a voice below me. "Muuuum," called a young girl, "there's a lady up there!" It was raining lightly now, and the concrete was slippery under my fingers. Wriggling upwards as fast as possible to avoid being spotted by anyone else, I lost my grip and nearly fell. Clinging tightly to the tower like a monkey up a tree, I forced myself to calm down and take it more slowly. I had indeed climbed the tower before—as Izzy clearly remembered only too well—but that had been early on a bright and sunny morning in the summer, when the stone was dry and I hadn't been in a rush. Another loud crash sent a shudder down the entire structure and very nearly knocked me off. I didn't want to be responsible for injuries caused by more than seventy kilos of undead woman landing on an unsuspecting member of the public, so I gritted my teeth and scampered the rest of the way as quickly as I could. When I reached the underneath of the viewing platform, I looked for the metal framework I knew lay around the edges of the plate glass windows above my head, and swung my arm out to catch hold. Using my own weight to propel myself, I swung out and up with as much force as I could muster.

I entered the viewing platform feet first through the window, in a move that would have made any stunt actor proud. But I didn't have time to feel pleased with myself, because right in front of me stood Mab. She had her back to me, with Izzy, Sean and Damon in front of her. They were pressed up against the partition wall that blocks the viewing platform halfway round, with Izzy in the middle of the two men. There was a visible crack in the outer glass to my right. Clearly Mab's temper hadn't settled any since the last time I saw her. I'd hoped to get the jump on her, but she immediately spun around to face me. "Hi Mab," I said cheerily, "how's it going?" Over her shoulder I could see Sean gaping at me with a 'wtf?' expressions on his face, whilst Damon appeared to be frozen in shock. Izzy, in contrast, was just shaking her head.

"Oh," Mab said, regarding me coolly, "you finally decided to join us."

"Yup." I could see Izzy trying the handle of the door behind them and just hoped it was unlocked. "So you can let my friends go."

"Ha," said Mab, "you really do think everyone is as soft as you, don't you?" I could still feel energy radiating from me and going by Sean's 'rabbit in headlights' expression, the others could too. But Mab didn't seem to have noticed anything was different. "No," she went on, "they stay here. Maybe I'll kill one of them. It's about time you know how much it hurts to lose people you love." Panic crawled across Izzy's face as she realised the door was locked. Shit.

"You think I don't know about losing people, Mab?" I said. "You brought my brother back to taunt me, remember? My baby brother, Mab. My *dead* baby brother. So yeah, I know all about losing people."

Her eyes didn't so much as flicker. "You won't notice one more then, will you?" she said, reaching an arm behind her and slowly raising it up. Nothing happened for a moment, then suddenly Izzy was thrown high into the air, hard enough that she hit the ceiling hard before crashing back down to the floor. Sean and Damon both yelled and launched themselves forwards, but Mab did something else with her hand and they froze when they stood. "STOP." My voice boomed in the cramped space.

Mab tilted her head slightly and gave a crooked smile. "Ohhh," she said, "aren't you the clever little thing?" She twisted her hand. Sean and Damon collapsed heavily to the floor, apparently unconscious. "Finally found your powers, have you?" Mab snarled. I said nothing, hoping Eadric would arrive to help me. Or Mapp. Even Nik would do in a pinch—I just needed backup. Since I'd accepted the crown, I was pretty sure I was capable of taking Mab down in a fight, but I couldn't risk it when my friends were trapped with me. Izzy had started making groaning noises on the floor, so at least I knew she was alive. Damon and Sean appeared to be asleep, each curled up on their side and facing away from me.

"Leave my friends alone, Mab," I said, my voice quiet and menacing. I felt ripples of energy running through my veins, and the power of eternity building in my chest. There was a faint humming noise on the cusp of hearing. I thought it was inside my head at first, but saw Mab's eyes twitch and realised she could hear it, too. Heat was building in my fingertips and I suddenly felt as though I might levitate with the sheer, animalistic fury that was taking me over. I gritted my teeth hard and concentrated on not losing it completely. Tempting as it was to pulverise Mab where she stood, we were at the top of a major landmark in the middle of a busy city. And whilst I could be reasonably sure of surviving a fall from this height, I couldn't say the same for the humans lying on the floor behind Mab.

"You will never rule over me, Lilith O'Reilly," said Mab. She moved faster than I could react, her hand twisting up and outwards. Before I could do anything about it, Izzy was lifted high into the air. Mab began laughing—an unnervingly hysterical noise that wasn't funny at all. I launched myself feet first and managed to kick her in the ribs, hard enough to feel at least one of them snap. Mab screamed in fury and, before I could do anything to stop her, launched Izzy at the window.

There was a crunching thud as she hit the glass and I screamed, a panicked gurgling noise that came from deep inside me. But to my astonishment, instead of flying through the window and falling to her death on the streets below, Izzy froze in mid-air.

"How *dare* you interfere in my business," said Liam O'Connor, pushing shards of broken glass aside and stepping through as casually as if he was walking in the front door of Flora's. He caught an arm round Izzy's waist as he did so and pulled her back inside with him. She collapsed onto the floor, gasping for breath. "You will stop this ridiculous behaviour right now."

"No." Mab looked nervous, but held her ground. "Why should I?"

"Because I told you to," said Liam. "And you will obey me."

"What if I don't want to obey you?" Her tone was belligerent, but I could sense her shifting her weight backwards slightly, as if debating whether to run for it.

"You will leave Lilith and her..." Liam gazed at my friends lying sprawled on the floor, "...*companions* alone. That is my final word."

"You promised me I could kill her!" yelled Mab. With a jolt, I realised she was talking about me. I raised my eyebrows at Liam, who shrugged.

"I hadn't met you at that point," he said to me. "So you needn't look so offended."

"*Why won't you let me kill her?*" Mab screeched. She was verging on hysterical now, bouncing from one foot to another and screwing her face up as if in real pain. "She killed my mother, William. My *mother*!"

"She was trying to protect her kingdom," said Liam. "Even if she didn't yet know it was hers to protect."

"That bitch," she gestured towards me, "is a murdering little cow and I want her dead. I get revenge and you get her territory." No wonder Liam had agreed to Mab's request. She'd clearly offered to help him take the city in return for being allowed to kill me. Presumably they'd considered themselves capable of taking on Eadric and the rest of the Scooby gang, so long as they got rid of me first.

"Charming," I said.

"I'm not going to war against anyone without good reason, Mab. Least of all Lilith."

"Then you're no better than her," spat Mab. She spun round to face me, one hand on her hip. I was expecting a lecture about how and why she hated me so much, but to my horror, Mab raised her arm and pointed a gun at me. Okay, so I'm no ballistics expert. Can't tell an AK47 from a Nerf gun, half the time. But the weapon Mab was holding was nondescript enough for me to suspect it was very much not a replica. Replicas are usually big and showy and look more dangerous than they actually are. Mab's pistol, on the other hand, was compact and subtle, and made of a dull metal that reeked of deadly concealment. Liam stepped forward and Mab swung the gun round to point at him. She stepped carefully backwards, closer to where my friends still lay on the floor behind her. Damon still appeared to be out cold, although I could at least see his chest moving enough to reassure me he was still breathing. Izzy and Sean were both conscious and watching everything from where they lay on the floor in frightened silence.

"Don't be ridiculous," said Liam. "You know you can't kill her with that." The look on Sean's face told me he didn't quite believe that and he began to slowly clamber to his feet behind Mab, despite my desperate attempts to warn him off with a sharp look and much eyebrow-waggling.

"Who said it was her I was going to kill?" asked Mab, and turned to shoot Sean straight in the heart.

Never Expect Gratitude From A Cat

I'd have seen Sean die right there in front of me, had Liam not demonstrated the reflexes of a striking rattlesnake. I actually saw the bullet leave the barrel of the gun and head straight for the centre of Sean's chest, even as Liam jumped forward to push him out of the way. All those months of wailing about the lack of superhuman eyesight and suddenly it installed itself just because I'd put an ancient crown on my head. It wasn't like in the movies, though—no overly dramatic slow-mo or whooshing noises. Instead, it was as if my brain was suddenly running fast enough to see and react to everything at the same speed as the bullet from Mab's gun. The metal glittered slightly as it exited the barrel, the noise reverberating around and down the tower. I heard distant screams from people on the ground and a yelp from Liam as the bullet hit him instead. He went down, landing heavily on top of Sean. Before I could decide who to go for first, Mab launched herself out of the broken window. A cry of terrified excitement rose up from the street below. Izzy scrambled across to Damon and managed to roll him over onto his side, all the while sobbing at him to wake up. Liam had rolled off Sean, but both men were still lying on the floor. Sean looked to be no more than winded, but Liam was groaning under his breath.

Billy sudden appeared, taking me by surprise. "Thought you might appreciate some backup, Red," he said. "Looks like I timed it right, aye."

"What happened to not being able to kill immortals?" I said to him, as we both bent down to where Liam lay and rolled him onto his back so we could see the damage.

"It won't kill him outright," said Billy, his voice quiet with panic, "but it'll surely do some major damage if we don't get that bullet out before his heart starts healing around it."

I stared at him in horror. "How the fuck are we supposed to do that?" I asked. "It's not like they keep emergency forceps up here." Sirens were getting closer, and I knew it was only a matter of minutes before the very human authorities arrived.

"Don't you have anything we could use to prise it out?" asked Billy. "Keys?"

"The keys to my flat are so rusty," I said, "I'd be worried bits of it might stay inside him and make it worse."

"Here," said a voice behind me. I turned to see Izzy holding out what looked distinctly like one of the butter knives we used in Flora's. "I sometimes have to force the lock on my front door," she said with an apologetic shrug, "so I took one to keep in my bag. Just in case."

I took the knife and looked down at Liam. "I think I'm going to hurt you now," I said, "so you have to promise not to punch me in the face."

His face screwed up into a smile that came out as a grimace. "You've hurt me already," he said. "What's one more time between friends?" Before I could talk myself out of it, I plunged the knife into the wound and immediately hit metal. Liam hissed as I wriggled the blade around inside his flesh. I was desperately trying to catch the edge of the bullet, but kept snagging the shattered edges of his ribs instead. Even as I watched, the flesh was tightening up around the bullet and shouting was coming from the bottom of the lift shaft. It was now or never. Pushing the knife blade as far down against the bullet as I could manage, I levered it backwards against the healing rib bone and pressed as hard as I dared. Suddenly there was a horrible sucking noise and the bullet popped out of Liam's chest as he groaned with relief.

"Get him to Eadric," I said to Billy, gesturing at Liam. "He'll be okay," I mentally crossed every finger I had, "but you need to get him out of here right now."

"What about Izzy?" said Billy, even as the lift clunked back into life

"I'm okay," she said weakly. "Just get yourselves out before the cops arrive. I'll make something up."

Billy bent down to pick up Liam and slung him over his shoulder as though he was a toddler who'd fallen asleep in the car on the way home from a day trip. "Make sure you get her, Red," he said—and both men disappeared into thin air. I turned to look out through the broken glass and could just see Mab's pale hair darting across the rooftops towards Church Street. As I turned back for one last check on Izzy, Sean lifted his head and looked at me.

"You know you're going to have to let me base a story on you," he managed.

I grinned at him. "It'll be a long book," I said—and jumped.

I pushed off hard with my feet in the hope of having enough impulsion to clear the street below and land on the rooftops opposite. It worked almost too well, and I nearly overshot the building entirely. I'd have fallen down the gap into Houghton Lane, had I not managed to hook an arm around an access ladder on the roof and swing back onto my feet. I had no idea where Mab might be headed, but thought she'd either go underground, or just run as fast as she could along the main road out of town. And if she managed to do that, I'd be doomed to having to watch my back until the next time she resurfaced. Because she would—Mab wasn't going to leave me in peace any time soon. The strange thing was that she'd probably missed the opportunity to kill me outright at least three times so far. I wasn't soft enough to think she might finally be developing some affection for me, but I did think it maybe showed her lack of experience. She kept flailing around dramatically, but rarely managed to follow her plans through. But I'd have time enough to think about it after I'd caught her. A muffled shout in the darkness ahead of me made me look across to the giant Marks & Spencer store that marked the start of Church Street. Mab was caught in the netting the store had installed in a failed attempt to keep pigeons off the roof. The arrival of the fire brigade at the base of the Beacon spurred me into making the leap. As I landed on the rear of the building where it was free of net, I heard the distant drone of a police helicopter. Hopefully I'd be able to get Mab down before any searchlights arrived. I raced across the complicated jungle of air-conditioning pipes and metal boxes filled with god-knows-what and scrambled up onto the roof proper. Mab was about twenty feet in front of me, kicking frantically at something. I stood quietly for a moment, debating the best way to grab her. Suddenly her head shot up and she looked directly at me. "I know you're there, you bitch," she yelled. "Running round like you own the place, you fucking murderous cow." I started picking my way across the edge of the building behind her line of sight, hoping to get her from behind. The netting came right across here, and appeared to be made of some kind of reinforced metal—presumably department stores are targeted by *really* determined pigeons. Tightroping along the ledge, I was within six feet of Mab when, with a scream of absolute fury, she managed to kick the metal box off her leg. Suddenly, the building below us turned into a fireworks display. I could hear muffled banging and feel thudding through the stonework under my feet as the store's electrical circuits all blew at once. Security alarms started to go off on the adjoining buildings, closely followed by those on the stores opposite. "Shit," hissed Mab. "Shit, shit *shit*."

"Get off the building," I yelled at her over the cacophony below us. "We can talk about this!"

Mab got to her feet and spun round to face me. "As if I'd ever talk to *you*," she spat. I leaped forward to grab her, but she somehow twisted out of my grasp, throwing herself off the roof and across onto the next block. I saw her topple over the ledge and for a second thought she'd fallen to the ground, but then she reappeared, scrambling up onto the tiles and picking her way across at speed, like a cat on a mission. I suddenly thought of *The Cat*, a cartoon strip in the Bunty comic which was definitely way before I was born. Mum must have mentioned it at some point. Sighing wearily at just about everything in the entire stupid world, I set off after my own would-be assassin. Although I knew the buildings well at street level, I'd unsurprisingly never thought to check what was on their roofs. It would have been quite the architectural education, had I not been chasing someone who would very much like to kill me, to a soundtrack of the sirens and screaming that was now coming from street level.

It was only after I'd made the leap of my life across Whitechapel and onto what felt like the very fragile roof of the HSBC bank that I realised where Mab was heading. "Don't you fucking *dare*!" I yelled, as she bounced across the dormer roof of the old Lord Street Arcade. I sped up, my feet barely touching the tiles as I raced after her, dropping onto the flat roof of H&M. The chimney stack at the back of my flat was just across Dorans Lane. Mab launched herself at it just as I made a desperate lunge for her. I lost my footing and fell down into the lane, hitting the concrete with a brain-jarring thud. Racing round the front of the building so fast that I struggled to bank the corner onto Harrington Street, I was irrationally furious to find no sign of Billy out front. I'd been hoping he'd have got back from dropping Liam with Eadric and his absence was worrying. As I caught hold of the fire escape and swung myself round and up to the second floor platform, I heard a loud screeching noise above my head. Looking up, I saw Mab staggering backwards out of my kitchen door, Grimm attached firmly to her face. My beloved plants went flying in all directions as she staggered back-wards, swiping at the cat and screaming in pain. Grimm clung on, one paw kept carefully free to claw at her. Suddenly, Mab toppled backwards over the railing with Grimm still clinging onto her. Screaming in panic, I jumped from the fire escape and—in a feat of athleticism I would probably never manage again, however lengthy my eternal existence—caught the cat just as he finally let go. I rolled into a ball with Grimm wrapped in my arms and barrelled across the carpark, coming to rest against the back wall. My beloved cat rewarded this display of heroics with a swipe across my nose, before scrabbling free and haring back up the steps into the flat. Getting to my feet, I was just in time to see Mab disappearing round the corner in the direction of North John Street. "Fuck*sake*," I muttered to myself as I picked up pace yet again, "they could have filmed this for Batman and saved themselves some money." I could see Mab ahead of me down the lower stretch of Harrington Street. Powering across the main road, I was gaining on her by the time she got to Castle Street and turned right. I realised she was heading for

Water Street and the back entrance to James Street station. And if she got below ground, it was game over—I'd never find her. Comforting myself with the thought that she might get eaten by a stray vampire, I set off after her, only to have to skid to a halt as a pair of police officers turned into Castle Street from the Town Hall end and started walking towards us. Mab turned to run and saw me approaching. She literally stamped her foot in anger before turning and beginning to climb up the front of the Sainsburys mini supermarket. One of the policemen spotted her and yelled. Not being able to think of any other option, I too started climbing. Mab had the advantage of the supermarket being in an old building, complete with handy ledges and window arches. I found myself scrabbling up the front of the Liverpool Gin Distillery, whose premises are much less ornate. I managed to clamber across to the empty building next door, which was far more accessible—although I did accidentally kick the stone nose off one of the plaques under the arches—and somehow got onto the roof just after Mab. She was heading diagonally across the block, leaping the narrow drop to Lower Castle Street and on to the roof of the cocktail bar on the opposite corner. I only knew it was a cocktail bar because Izzy and I had once been refused entrance for not being smart enough to impress their door security, and we'd refused to ever go back on sheer principle.

I doubted even Mab would be able to make the leap over to the Corn Exchange, and was right—she dropped down onto the road and ran up Fenwick Street instead. Putting all my strength into it, I launched myself across Brunswick Street onto the apartment building on the other side, then jumped straight over Mab's head onto the top of the India Buildings. Mentally thanking the vampires for having given me a helpful lesson in the building's external layout, I raced round the inner roof and dropped down in front of the entrance to the station just as Mab came round the corner. Screaming in frustration, she ran off down Covent Garden, with me hot on her tail. As she got to where the proba-bly-not-a-Banksy-after-all' used to be, she spun to her left and began climbing at speed up the more functional back section of Mersey Chambers, somehow levering herself up via the sloped oriel windows. Running underneath her fleeing feet fast enough to be all but invisible, I chose the easier route of the old bank next door, with its arches and ornamentation. Thanking the gods of architecture that Liverpool hadn't sacrificed too many of its old buildings on the altar of slippery and hard to climb modern office blocks, I headed upwards.

She's waking up again.

Not Maria? That was all I needed.

No, said the city, **the mother.**

I didn't understand what it meant until I got onto the roof of Mersey Chambers. The Liver Birds were still on their domes, but they were *angry*. Both Bella and Bertie were glowing, and what looked like electrical pulses were pouring out of them, the glowing strands flowing and writhing upwards as I watched. Bella still had her back to us, but I could feel her fury in the air. Bertie was glaring straight at us from across the Strand. No—he was glaring at Mab. She was ahead of me, near the front edge of the building. I thought she was debating whether to jump off, but just then she turned to face me. "You do understand," she said, "that I *will* manage to kill you one day?" She tilted her head and smiled. My vision began to fade into white at the edges, as though the colour was draining out. I knew exactly what she was doing.

"You can't scare me with fake memories, Mab," I said. "Not anymore." Even as I spoke, the white disappeared and my vision returned. A strange, high-pitched noise was building below us and I tried my best to ignore it. Hopefully it was just the locals kicking off at all the drama.

Mab scowled. "I don't care who you are," she said, "or what this stupid city thinks you might be." She stepped backwards closer to the edge, careful not to lose her footing. The noise was getting louder now —perhaps the police had realised where we were and had rightly assumed we had something to do with the drama up at the Beacon. My money was on Mab doing a runner up towards Vauxhall and disappearing into the Wallasey tunnel. "You will pay for what you've done," she went on, "if it takes forever."

"Good-oh," I said. "At least I won't get bored." Mab narrowed her eyes at me. "Why don't we have a chat about it?" I went on, conversationally. If I could keep her talking, I might be able to catch her off guard and rugby tackle her. It would to be really quick, though. I began bouncing slightly on the balls of my feet in readiness. "I'll call your dad and he can come fetch you."

"Go fuck yourself," said Mab flatly—and I pounced. I was fast, but not fast enough. With a final yell of fury, Mab turned and leapt off the front of the building—straight into the rising flames of a very angry phoenix.

Coming Out Of The Creepy Closet

Just as when Maria had trapped it in the cavern under Mathew Street, the mother bird was spitting with fury and determined to take it out on someone. Not everyone knows about the third, older Liver Bird on the roof of Mersey Chambers, but those who do, learn very quickly to be nice to it. She might be smaller than her offspring over the road, but she has a temper exponentially larger than the rest of Liverpool put together. And, clearly having been disturbed by paranormal weirdness one too many times over the past few months, she was not taking any prisoners.

Mab screamed as the bird barrelled towards her, its talons front and centre. It was like watching a gigantic eagle torpedoing down onto its prey—if the eagle weighed a quarter of a ton and was made entirely of fire. It grabbed Mab in its claws and lifted her off her feet, before landing in front of me, using her as a landing mat. "For *fuck's* sake!" screeched Mab. "Call this thing off before it kills me!" The mother bird's heavy, and she's got seriously impressive talons. As she shifted her weight on Mab's back, I could see her feet pressing heavily down into fragile human flesh. Mab might have stretched the definition of what it means to be human, but I figured that being asphyxiated by a metal bird probably wouldn't be a pleasant way to go.

"Why would I do that?" I asked. "You just told me yourself that you plan to kill *me*, Mab. I reckon I'd be better off letting her have her fun. One less thing for me to worry about."

"William won't forgive you," she spat. "He'll get his revenge."

"Have you forgotten you just *shot* him?" I asked. She really was absolutely certifiable. "I don't think he'll give a shit what happens to you, in all honesty."

"It won't have hurt him," she said, but she sounded fractionally less confident. "He can survive anything."

"Well," I said, "I asked Billy to drop him off at the Liver Building the best part of an hour ago, and Billy hasn't got back home yet." Mab grunted as the bird wriggled happily on her back. "Billy doesn't like being away from home, Mab. Which makes me think there's a major problem going on back at Tracy Island, don't you think?"

"Good!" Mab shouted suddenly. "I hope he dies! He told me I could kill you and he went back on his promise. He's a liar. You're *all* liars." I could hear the crack in her voice. "Let me go," she begged, clearly fighting back tears. "I'll stay in Liverpool and, I don't know, work for Eadric or something. Not for *you*," her voice was filled with venom, "but maybe him."

"We don't need you here, Mab," I said. "You're untrustworthy."

"Let...me...*go!!*" she howled again.

"You can get off her," I said to the bird. "She's not going anywhere." The bird scowled at me and wriggled around, using its wings for basic sign language explain just how stupid she thought I was. It then started making exaggerated pecking gestures at Mab's head. Presumably she was hoping for permission to snap Mab's head off with her sharp, metallic beak.

"I can't let you," I said quietly. "It's not her fault she's like this."

"No, it fucking isn't," hissed Mab, her face pressed hard against the roof tiles. "Let me go and I'll make up for it. Somehow."

"I told you," I said, shaking my head at the bird, who currently had her beak wide open over the back of Mab's head and was apparently debating whether she could fit it all inside with one gulp. "You can't be trusted."

"Let me up and I'll go away. Ireland, maybe. Find some family."

"You could get in touch with your father?" I suggested. "Build a few bridges, sort of thing."

"Maybe," said Mab. We both knew she was lying.

Coming to a decision, I nodded to the bird. "Let her go." The bird shook her head and bounced on Mab's back, making her splutter. Behind them I could see Bella and Bertie winding up to a full tantrum, their lights now spinning frantically in the night sky above the Liver Building. If I didn't do something quickly, they were going to fully kick off and then the police really *would* have something to think about. "LET HER GO." The bird's beak snapped shut and for a second, she glowered at me. Then she hopped backwards off Mab, giving her a sharp kick in the ribs as she did so. With one last scowl at the pair of us, the bird dropped back down to her perch below the roofline. There was a long, silent moment and then Mab slowly began to clamber to her feet.

"Do you know what your problem is, Lilith?" said Mab, when she'd finally pulled herself upright.

"Come on then," I said, wearily. "Your mother liked to lecture people, as well. I guess you're just following family tradition."

Mab's face tightened briefly, then she smiled widely at me. "Your problem is that you're too quick to trust people." With that, she flung herself backwards off the roof.

"For fuck's *actual* sake!" I yelled at Mab's retreating back, as she skittered across the roof of St Nicholas's church, before dropping down onto the Strand. The mother bird reared back up again and swung round to look at me. "I know," I said, "I'm an idiot." The bird flapped her wings angrily at me. "No," I said, sitting down on the roof of the building, "I'm not going after her. Let her run. She'll come back eventually, she always does." And until then, I thought, I'll be constantly looking over my shoulder. Which didn't sound like a fun way to live. But it had been a long night, and I wanted to find out how Izzy and the others were. And Liam. He might be a lying, deceitful scumbag, but at least he refused to let Mab kill me. That had to be worth something, right? I could see Mab racing across George Parade below us, her blonde hair clearly visible in the gloom. For a second I thought she might aim for the Liver Building and debated whether I should head over in order to help Eadric, but then I realised she was heading for the water. It wasn't an entirely stupid decision on Mab'spart. When you've got supernatural strength, swimming the Mersey is definitely quicker than negotiating the tunnels and their CCTV cameras. What she'd forgotten to take into account was the local wildlife. As she dived off the end of the terminal for the Isle of Man ferry, I thought I spotted something flashing silver out in the middle of the river. By the time Mab had surfaced and was front-crawling her way out into deeper water, the shapes were more clearly defined—three liquid arrows, heading directly towards the lone swimmer. When they hit their target, she disappeared under the water with barely a sound. "Aah well," I said to the bird, "at least I know Daisy won't be going hungry tonight."

Liam had already left by the time I got back to the Liver Building. Working on the assumption that there was enough chaos going on in the town centre for it to be unlikely anyone was watching the waterfront for signs of free-climbing redheads, I clambered up and in through Eadric's office window. I found him sitting at his desk, waiting for me. "I need to know that Izzy and the others are going to be okay," I said, without waiting for him to speak, "and then we're going to have to decide what happens next. Where's Liam?" I looked around the room and felt panic rising when I could find no sign of my erstwhile friend-with-few-benefits. "He was impressive up there, I'll give him that."

"I've no doubt he was," said Eadric. "And he was already healing when he got here, thanks to your quick thinking. We decided it was better to remove him from the city as quickly as possible."

"We?"

"I was on the phone to Elizabeth when Billy arrived with William," said Eadric. "She suggested it would perhaps be better to get him out of the way as soon as possible, and I agreed. We had a driver pick him up from here and deliver him to Speke, where Elizabeth has arranged for a private plane to be waiting." I was pretty sure the ability to just charter a jet at a moment's notice was a sign of having too much money, but managed not to say it out loud.

"And you both did this without asking me first," I said. My voice was calm, but a cold rage was developing inside and it was like nothing I'd ever felt before. "Don't you *ever* make decisions like that without consulting me in the future, Eadric Silverton." I stepped forward without thinking and, to my amazement, Eadric actually pushed backwards in his seat away from me. "Liam is indebted to me," I said, "and he knows that. It's his fault Mab felt able to come back to Liverpool. He messed up, and we all saw it."

"He tried to save you," said Eadric.

"He did," I agreed. "And then I saved him back. He won't come after my territory."

"Not yet," said Eadric, "but he won't stay away for long."

"I'll deal with that when it happens."

"So what next?"

Even as Eadric spoke, Mapp appeared in the doorway, looking more flustered than I'd ever seen him. He was wide eyed and clutching my canvas satchel, holding it out as far away from him as possible. "Take this from me right now, Lilith O'Reilly," he said, thrusting it at me. "I want no part of it. And it clearly wants no part of me, either." He practically threw it at me and wiped his hands off on his pink satin pyjamas as though they'd touched something truly horrid.

"What's it done to you?" But I could feel the relief the crown felt at being back with me, even as I held it in its old and tatty bag. "It doesn't want to hurt you," I soothed, as Mapp paced the length of the office. "It missed me, is all."

"That....that *thing*," said Mapp, still pacing whilst jabbing a finger in the direction of the bag, "is a liability. My entire shop is in disarray. In *disarray*, I tell you!"

"Your shop has always been a delightful portrayal of disarray," said Nik, coming into the room. "How can a silly old crown make it any worse?"

A faint wave of irritation came off the crown. I shook the bag slightly. *Behave*, I murmured in my head. *He means well. He's our friend.* The crown didn't feel convinced, but it settled slightly. Somehow, these internal conversations didn't bother me anymore. They were as normal as speaking out loud to another human, just with far more paranormal weirdness attached. "This is my life now," I said to myself as much as anyone. "We face this together, or not at all."

"You'd better go explain that to the birds," said Nik. Even as he said it, I felt the rumbling through the roof. "Bella is definitely on the verge of throwing an almighty tantrum," Nik went on, "and Bertie has gone so silent and rigid that I'm honestly a bit worried he might be having a seizure."

Without thinking, I picked up a paperweight and threw it hard at the ceiling. It cracked the plaster and fell back onto the carpet with a heavy thud. Eadric's eyes tightened, but he didn't say anything. "YOU CAN PACK THAT IN RIGHT NOW," I yelled at the ceiling, "OR I WILL BE COMING UP THERE TO HAVE WORDS." The rumbling stopped. "What?" I looked round the room to see Mapp, Nik and Eadric all gaping at me in astonishment. "They're just being bratty because I stopped their mum killing Mab," I said. "They'll get over it."

"Why on earth did you let Mab go?" asked Mapp. "You know she'll just keep coming back."

"Aah," I said, turning to look out through the old windows towards the dark waters of the Mersey. "About that..."

Izzy, Damon and Sean had all been taken away in an ambulance, after being brought down from the tower by the fire brigade. The attending police officers had included Jenny from knitting club, who'd been quick-thinking enough to update Mapp. They all had unspecified minor injuries, but were expected to be okay. "Jenny was a bit confused as to where you might have got to, though," Mapp had told me, once he'd settled enough to curl up in an armchair and sip on the medicinal brandy Nik had given him. "Apparently Isobel struggled to convince her not to send out an alert declaring you a missing person."

So now I was walking into the brand new emergency department just off Prescot Street and trying to ignore the headache-inducing smell of fresh paint, which was working its way up my nose despite me deter-minedly not breathing. With the help of a nurse who was friendlier than expected given the stress she appeared to be under, I eventually located

Izzy in a side bay that had its curtains pulled back to reveal her sitting up on the bed with a blanket wrapped round her knees and her left arm in a sling. "Fractured collarbone," she said, as I walked in. "And they think I might have a hairline skull fracture, so I'm waiting on an x-ray." I felt the tears welling up as I pulled a chair out to sit next to her. "Don't be starting that," she said sternly, "you'll only dehydrate." I sniffed and tried to smile. "That was scary, Lil," Izzy said. "Really scary."

"I'm sorry," I said. "I'm so, so sorry."

Izzy reached across with her good arm and patted my leg. "Ow," she said, pulling her arm back, "moving hurts. Look," she wriggled a bit in order to look at me better, "it wasn't your doing, it was Mab's. You and Liam saved the day."

"It's Liam's fault Mab was here in the first place," I said. "Although we've got Daisy to thank for getting rid of her permanently."

Izzy's eyes bugged out. "No?"

"Yep," I grinned. "The three fish-women of the apocalypse ate well tonight." Izzy made gagging noises at that. "How's Damon?" I asked.

"Sleeping it off a few beds down," said Izzy. "And Sean's next door," she nodded her head sideways, "probably already making notes."

"Too right," came a familiar voice over the partition wall. "I need to write all this down before I forget." I was up and round the corner to Sean's cubicle before he'd even finished speaking. The man himself sat grinning at me, a biro poised above a scrap of paper on his knee.

"Had to borrow the pen from a nurse," he said, waggling it at me. "And this," he flapped the paper, "is from my medical notes."

"You can't write about this," I hissed. "You'll get me killed! It's nerve-wracking enough coming into a hospital as it is, with all those doctors who'd just love to slice my brain up and put it through their scanners."

"Shhhh," Sean soothed, "I write fiction, remember?"

I leaned against the wall, and it rocked gently. "Oi," said Izzy from the other side, "enough of this city's been damaged tonight without you adding to it."

"Sean," I said, pushing myself up from the wall and making an effort not to touch anything else, "you saw what I really am. You *saw* it. I can't let you tell anyone else!"

"What are you going to do," he said, "off me with your undead powers?"

"Of course not!" I sat down on the edge of his bed. "It's just, well—"

"No one realises that the forces of paranormal darkness are live and kicking and living in Liverpool?"

"That's about it," I said. "And it needs to stay that way."

"And it will," said Sean. "Because—like I said—I write *fiction*. I'll start a new series and people will just assume I've gone down the urban fantasy route. No one in their right mind is going to consider the possibility that it might all be true."

"But it's my life you're using," I pointed out.

"Then I'll share the royalties with you," he shrugged. "Anyway, you owe me one." I raised an eyebrow at him. "We," he nodded in Izzy's direction, "nearly got killed because of your secret life, Lil. Maybe we'll be safer now we know what to expect. Although the possibility of having to wear Kevlar on a date is a new one on me, I'll admit that much." He grinned at me. "Assuming you want to go on a date at some point, that is?"

"Of course she does," said Izzy from behind the partition. "I'll kick her if she doesn't."

"For fuck's sake!" I stood up. "What is *wrong* with you all?" I glared at Sean and leaned round the wall to give Izzy a hard stare as well, just for good measure. Then I gave up and just stood in front of the partition, so I could glare at both of them at the same time. "Too many people know already," I said. "No one else, you hear? No one. And that includes Damon, Iz. I'm sorry, but I really do need to keep a lid on this. For all our sakes."

"Oh," said Izzy airily, "Damon's known for ages. Says it doesn't matter to him, he likes you anyway."

"What the *fuck*?" I looked at her in astonishment. "What happened to keeping my secrets? Ride or die, and all that?"

"You needn't start with that," she said, completely unbothered. "Damon figured it out for himself. Probably after he met Kitty for the first time and she disappeared through a wall." She shrugged. "Completely forgot it was there, apparently."

"Oh. My. God." I looked from Izzy to Sean and back again. They both grinned at me, although Izzy's was more of a wince. "You are all *entirely* insane."

"Oh," said Izzy suddenly, "I've got something for you! Pass my bag up, Lil." Still shaking my head in despair at the way this evening had turned out, I bent to retrieve Izzy's handbag from underneath the bed and put it on her lap. I then had to hold it still so she could open the catch with one hand. After rooting round inside it for a few seconds, she pulled something out with a squeak of triumph. "Thought you might like a souvenir," she said, dropping it into my hand. And then as an afterthought, "and also that it was probably better if the police didn't find it." I looked down at the bullet that lay in my palm. Smaller and heavier than I'd expected, the misshapen lump of metal had a scrape down one side, presumably from where I'd dug at it with the knife. "Didn't find the gun though," she shrugged apologetically. "Miss psycho knickers must have taken it with her."

"I'm not sure Mab's got anything anymore," I said. Just then, an orderly arrived with a wheelchair and informed us it was time for Iz to go get her head checked out. "Better make sure there's something in there," I joked, to cover my worry.

"I'll be okay," Izzy reassured me. "But next time, we need to know in advance when something dramatic's likely to happen." I helped her off the bed and into the chair. "That way," she said as the orderly turned the chair round to wheel her away, "I can make doubly sure I'm carrying my trusty butter knife."

"Perhaps you could ask Mapp to help?" suggested Eadric the next day. I was back up in the tower of the Liver Building, explaining to the Silvertons that several more humans now knew about the netherworld, but they weren't to worry about it. Nik didn't seem to care, but Eadric was taking more convincing. "He could just wipe their memories. And he's more accurate than you."

The bloody cheek. "No," I said, my voice firm. "We're not hiding anymore, Eadric," I said, "not from those who already know. People who believe in us have always believed. And those who don't, never will. Not even when they witness someone leaping from a high tower and landing like a cat. Mass hallucination is a thing, Eadric—even if it's literally in people's heads. We're coming out of the shadows and we're bringing everyone with us. Vampires, mermaids—hell, there's probably werewolves wandering Sefton Park at night and we just don't know about them yet."

"There hasn't been a werewolf sighting in Sefton since nineteen-seventy-six," said Eadric faintly. "I think they moved over to Toxteth."

"Then we go talk to them and explain what's happening," I said. "And the people of Toxteth will learn to accept that the full moon might occasionally bring very large dogs along for the ride."

"You sound very sure of yourself."

"That's because I am." Even as I said it, I realised it was true. Whatever had happened when I put the crown on for the first time, it had changed me. I wasn't entirely sure whether it would turn out to be a good or bad thing, but one thing I knew was that it was irreversible.

"It's your city," said Eadric. "I shall look forward to seeing what you decide to do with it."

"No," I said, my voice firm. "This is no one's city. It belongs to itself and always has done. I'm just a custodian. Of the weirder bits."

That's most of it, then.

Shut up. Just because we're working together now doesn't give you the right to be rude.

Truthful though.

"Gonna tell me why you were on the phone to Elizabeth in the first place?" I narrowed my eyes at Eadric. "Because all this communication is a very new development. What happened to staying out of each other's business?"

"Aah," said Eadric, "that was before you arrived. These days," he smiled at me, "everyone seems to want to get involved. You're proving very popular."

"Especially amongst the vampires," said Nik, coming into the office and flopping dramatically down onto a leather armchair. "One stopped me earlier and asked if I could get him an introduction to ol' Buffy, here."

"I don't know why," I said. "They made it pretty clear that they don't even *like* me."

"Aah, but that's where you're wrong," said Nik, steepling his fingers across his chest and gazing up at me with a thoughtful expression on his face. "They seem to be under the impression you're their saviour, somehow? There is apparently talk of you allowing them human rights. Imagine that."

"All I've done," I said, "is promise them they can unionise." Nik made a spluttering noise, but Eadric's face bore a mask of blank calmness. I was pretty sure he was screaming underneath. "Equal rights for all, remember? Even dead people. And people who eat people. Although I'll have to talk to them about the eating thing...anyway," I smiled brightly, "it'll be fine."

"What about the mermaids?" asked Eadric faintly. "Do they get concessions at the fish and chip vans on a Friday?"

"Don't be ridiculous," I said. "Mermaids don't like batter. Look, Eadric," Eadric looked, "you're the one who was so determined I'd end up in charge. And now I *am* in charge and I don't want to be, but I'm doing it anyway. So the least you can do in return is to try to look a bit less like you're sucking a bloody lemon. And you," I turned to Nik, "are to make sure my mother does well in her studies. Okay?"

"She won't need much help from me," said Nik. "But obviously one will be as supportive a tutor as is humanly possible. I've suggested she base her thesis on the dangers of judging poets by their private lives rather than their literary output."

"Shame the only poet she knows caused more gossip than rave reviews then, isn't it?" I said. Funnily enough, he couldn't think of anything to say to that.

I Can See
Clearly Now

ONE WEEK LATER

I felt invisible movement as the ghost sat down next to me. "Hey," I said to the empty air.

"Hey yourself," said Billy. I turned to find him looking at me. "You okay up here, Red?"

"It's all good," I said. "Bertie's nice company when you have a lot of thinking to do." The bird shuffled above my head in acknowledgement.

"You know there's a vampire on your roof?"

"Yup. My personal guard." When I'd declared my intention to continue living on Harrington Street, the only people more horrified than Eadric were the vampires. The flat wasn't 'appropriate for someone of my status', according to Aiden, the well-spoken vamp I'd met at the Wapping tunnel. To my utter surprise, he'd come into town to check on me after hearing about the drama up at the Beacon. When I told him I was absolutely staying put whatever he said, he'd actually gone down to the Liver Building and climbed up to Eadric's offices, in order to demand he talk some sense into me. Eadric had, in return, informed Aiden that he'd once again offered me the Albert Dock apartment, I'd once again turned it down and it wasn't his fault I was a bloodyminded idiot who was overly attached to her human friends. Nik had texted me a heads up as to what was going on and I'd stalked down to the waterfront in a fury in order to give them a lengthy lecture about the perils of both snobbery and patriarchy. Once I'd got it all off my chest and the pair of undead and overprotective meatheads had realised I really wasn't going to budge, I'd gone back home for a quiet evening in front of old episodes of *Bake Off*. I'd just started getting invested in the outcome of a small Welsh woman's over-sized and perilously wobbly lemon meringue, when I was disturbed by a noise from the fire escape. Cursing the fact that I only ever seemed to get interrupted in the early hours of the morning when I really *should* be left in peace, I pulled the door open sharply and scared a junior vampire who was settling down to roost on my front doorstep. "It's easier to just let them crack on with it," I shrugged. "Whatever makes them happy, and all that. Although I've persuaded them to hang out on the roof rather than the doorstep, because otherwise I keep tripping over them. They do shifts." I leaned back against Bertie's leg and turned my head to grin at Billy. "Pretty goth, huh?"

"Aren't you worried they might hurt the cat?" he asked.

"One of them tried," I said. "The first night. Grimm was coming back in from his evening prowl and the vampire on guard duty thought they'd have themselves a little late night snacky-snack." I snorted at the memory.

"What happened?"

"They learned that cats have very sharp claws," I said, grinning at him. "And that they're not afraid to use those claws to pull a vampire's skin right off its ratty little face. It was all I could do to persuade Grimm to drop it and get back inside the house. I'm pretty sure he was planning to stash it away to share with Rachel."

"Would Rachel really eat another vampire?" he asked. "Wouldn't that make her a cannibal?"

"Billy," I said, "we were all human, once upon a time. Well," I gave it some thought, "most of us were. So I reckon vampires are cannibals by default. And Rachel wouldn't have eaten it anyway, I don't think. She's happy enough with the rats that Grimm and Alan help her deal with."

"Everyone seems to be settling down finally," said Billy. "At least, as much as they ever could." He gazed out over the city. "Do you think things will be quieter now?"

"You sound almost disappointed," I said, smiling at him. "Afraid you'll get bored?"

"Nah." He grinned back at me. "It'd just be nice to not have to worry about you all the time."

"Don't worry about me, Billy," I said. "Worry about those who'd dare try to hurt this city while I'm in charge."

"There speaks a confident woman," Billy said approvingly. "I like it."

"Good," I said. "Because this is just the start of the adventure. Let's see where it takes us."

That's our girl, said the city. Suddenly it wasn't just an annoying voice in my head—now, it was part of me. It was me and I was it, as though it had absorbed something of me into its very being.

You wanted me, I replied silently, *and now you've got me. Let's just hope it doesn't work out badly for both of us.*

We'll figure it out together, the city promised. And for once, I believed it.

THE END

~

Turn the page for a sneak peek at what's to come in
CITY OF GHOSTS
Netherweird Chronicles, Book Four

CITY OF GHOSTS

"**Y**ou get your idiot ratty backside out of here right this second or I will come over there and move you myself!" I shouted across the crowded bar. Either the vampire I was shouting at didn't hear me, or he was too busy wowing the assembled throng with his undeniably impressive rendition of Miley Cyrus's *Wrecking Ball*. The pub was jammed with punters, all of whom seemed to be thoroughly enjoying the spectacle of a bloke dressed all in black singing as though his life depended on it. They weren't to know, of course, that the vocalist in question was a three-hundred-year-old vampire and the sunglasses he was wearing indoors were to hide his weird black eyes. Although I strongly suspected he was the type who'd have worn them as an affectation anyway, even if he hadn't been a member of Liverpool's very own Club Dead.

Coopers Town House is tucked away on Cases Street in the entrance to the Clayton Square shopping centre, and you could be forgiven for walking straight past without noticing it—if it's closed. If it's open, however, you'll be able to hear the noise from the other side of Ranelagh Street. "Leave him alone, you mardy cow," said a woman sitting at the table beside me. I turned to give her a Sharp Look, but she grinned back. "Come on, love," she said, "he's the best singer we get in here." She nodded towards the corner where my current least-favourite bloodsucker was finishing his performance with a dramatic sprawl across a table. "Let us enjoy it for a bit, aye?" I caught the vampire's eye just as the karaoke machine launched into *Wuthering Heights*, and was so fascinated as to whether he'd actually be able to manage the top notes that I forgot to drag his stupid carcass out of the pub before he started singing again. Sighing, I dropped down onto the bench seat next to the woman. "He's a regular," the woman confided, at such loud volume and so close to my ear that it was lucky I was already dead and immune to the dangers of hearing loss. "All the girls fancy him." The 'girls' appeared to have an average age of about fifty and were all several sheets to the wind, despite it being four o'clock on a Wednesday afternoon. I sat with my arms folded across my chest to show I was definitely still pissed off with him and that he'd better shift his ass the second he'd finished his Kate Bush impression. In return, the vampire upped his arm-ography— yeah, so I watch Strictly Come Dancing, what of it—and swung around happily as the crowd hollered along with him.

"You've beaten me to it, I see," said a voice in my ear.

I turned to the vampire who'd sat down next to me. "Again," I said. "You're going to have to keep better control of your minions if you don't want to be found out, Aiden."

"Aah," said Aiden, "can we not let him have his fun? He's spent decades in those cold, damp tunnels. It's good for him to get out in the open air a bit." I squinted at the head of the local vampire society to check whether he was being serious. "They need to integrate, Lilith. Not hide away. Was it not yourself who said we were going to be more open about our existence?"

"By which I meant that those of us who belong to the nether-fuck-ing-weird might try to subtly join in with human life," I said. "What I did not suggest was bouncing straight out of the coffin and into one of the busiest bars in the city centre." The singing vampire was coming to the end of the song and glanced over to make sure I was watching. When he saw who I was with, his voice faltered and he dropped the arm he'd been flailing around in the air. Aiden made a polite gesture that I chose to interpret as 'do carry on, we'll discuss this later' and the junior vamp immediately stopped singing. Putting the microphone down on the table and waving apologetically at the disappointed women, he wriggled through the crowd like a thin black snake and was out of the door before anyone could stop him.

"Ohhhh," I snarked, "he does what *you* tell him. What happened to me being Queen Of All She Surveys?"

"Lilith," said Aiden kindly, "you ruin that for yourself by being far too reasonable and loathe to use violence. Whereas Stefan there knew very well that if he hadn't left when he did, I might possibly have ripped his head off when I got back to the tunnels."

"Would you, though?" I asked. "Would you really rip someone's head off just because they were doing a bit of karaoke when they shouldn't have been?"

"I might," said Aiden. "And I might not." He winked at me. I don't know if you've ever had a vampire wink at you, but it's quite unnerving. Even to me, and I'm a certified member of the undead underworld. Aiden is, however, one of the few vampires I've met who's aesthetically pleasing to look at, which at least softens the effect slightly. He's not exactly handsome—at least, not conventionally—but at least he doesn't resemble an elongated humanoid rat, like the rest of them. Although Rachel, the woman in the flat below mine, is also a vampire and she mostly just looks like an underfed goth, so clearly there are exceptions to the rule. "That's the trick, Lilith," Aiden went on. "They can't be sure whether or not I'd actually carry out any threats, and it's enough to keep them under control. Most of the time, anyway."

"How's work going on the tunnels?" I asked, changing the subject. Aiden's vampire coven lived in the old Wapping rail tunnel, up in Edge Hill. Joe Williamson had been hiding them there for a good while before I found out about it, and things were still frosty between us. Not least because I'd cut Joe out of the equation and begun dealing with Aiden directly, in the hope of simplifying the undead politics that take up so much of my time these days. It had been agreed that the vampires could stay in the tunnels and make some home improvements, on condition they a) didn't upset the locals; and b) promised not to eat any urban explorers. I'd had to explain live streaming to a very confused Aiden, who'd struggled to grasp the concept of the entire world potentially being able to witness him chowing down on someone via a video link.

He'd asked to look at my iPhone in order to satisfy his curiosity, and it still had visible teeth marks on the back of its case.

"Work goes well, thank you," he said politely. "But we need to talk about something else, Lilith. I fear there may be a problem developing in this paradise we call Liverpool." Oh, how fucking brilliant. Just as I was beginning to think herding vampires was the most troublesome part of my daily life, the madness was clearly about to kick off yet again. Cynical of me, I know. But when you've just been through the sort of year I have—involving death, murder and serious damage to several major city landmarks—you learn to expect the worst. I got up to leave, and Aiden stepped outside with me.

"Go on then," I said as we walked past the fruit and veg stall that still seemed to be doing brisk business, even on a January afternoon, "hit me with it. What kind of batshittery am I being landed with now?"

"You use very strange words at times, Lilith," said Aiden. "I'm sure I don't understand some of them at all."

"Making up inventive curse words is my hobby," I said. "Sometimes it's all that gets me through the day."

"I see," said Aiden in a serious tone of voice. "Well, I'm sure you know best how to deal with the stresses of a position as lofty as your own."

"Cut the crap, Aid," I said, "and just tell me what the fuck's going on. I've promised Izzy I'll go to the cinema with her tonight and I've still got paperwork to do." Turns out being dead doesn't mean avoiding admin. That discovery is one of my biggest disappointments so far, I don't mind telling you.

"Aah," said Aiden, "the moving pictures! Such a delight." I coughed loudly. "Yes, yes, of course you're busy. I shall make your leave in the briefest of moments. I just thought you'd wish to know that the police have apparently been alerted to the discovery of a dead body, just off Great Homer Street."

"Is that up Everton way?" I might have been living in this city for well over a decade, but like many people, I mostly just know the bits I, well, *know*. I rarely have cause to go much further than Leeds Street, so my awareness of the north end of town is sorely lacking.

"It is indeed," said Aiden. "And a very curious case it is, too. They found the unfortunate gentleman inside a large piece of metal piping. He had clearly been there for some time."

"And you think it has something to do with us?" I hadn't had to deal with a corpse for a while. I should have known the peace and quiet was too good to be true.

"Not directly, no," said Aiden. "It's believed he somehow made his own way into the tube and got stuck. Probably suffocated, poor chap."

"Well, that's all very sad and everything," I said, "but why are you telling me about it? Horrible things happen to people by accident all the time."

"Aah well," said the vampire. He came to a halt, and I turned to face him. "There's the thing, you see. We already know the details of what happened, because it was investigated a very long time ago."

"How could it have been investigated ages ago if he's only just been found?" I frowned at him. "You're talking in riddles."

"Lilith," said Aiden, "the body in the pipe was found in nineteen-forty-five, during clearances after a bomb raid. And it was eventually decided by the coroner that it had probably been in that pipe some sixty years or more, before being spotted by children playing in the rubble. This new discovery is actually a very old one."

"Nope," I said, "I got nothing. You're going to have to explain this again, but in shorter sentences."

Aiden gave me a small, sad smile. "Lilith," he said, "the time slips are back."

∼

COMING DECEMBER 2023

Sign up to my mailing list to be the first to hear about upcoming releases and other interesting stuff - and get a FREE short story from Netherweird! tinyurl.com/netherweirdstory

Author's Notes

As always, I've taken liberties with some of the real-world history, geography and architecture of the people and places that make up Netherweird. The only thing that is entirely true to life is the eternal brilliance of Liverpool itself.

Lilith had her facts right, though—William's corpse did indeed go 'pop' in a dramatically gruesome manner during his burial in 1087. The story about Ivo's tomb being desecrated by the Norman invaders is also true, although in reality it happened before Eadric had become a (very begrudging) member of William's army. The fictional version of Eadric wouldn't have been around at the time the Domesday Book was being collated (although the real one was), but that's the joy of writing fantasy —reality can be twisted to suit the storyline, rather than the other way around. And anyway, all of 'history' is made up of stories told by individuals with personal motives for interpreting things in different ways.

Oh, and Ivo's family really are legendary. Someone should probably make a television series about them.

~

None of my books would exist without background support from my own beloved cast of weirdos. Thanks go to:

Jayne Hadfield, for services to extreme beta reading (and for not being scared to tell me when things make no sense whatsoever); Toni Hibberd, beta reader and grade-A cheerleader; Sal Geere, who has never met a punctuation mark she couldn't correct in some way (and writes the best editing notes); Tilly Melia—nearing her twentieth year of answering my endless ridiculous questions, yet somehow still speaking to me; Li Zakovics, the only reason I still live in the 'shire; Winston Gomez, who somehow manages to keep me sane; my mother, who probably deserves a long-service medal; and my boys, Jaime and Oscar, for making the world a brighter place by their mere existence. Love youse.